Second Edition

D1323010

Legacy of Love

Dana-Sue Urso

TATE PUBLISHING
AND ENTERPRISES, LLC

Published by Tate Publishing & Enterprises, LLC
127 E. Trade Center Terrace | Mustang, Oklahoma 73064 USA
1.888.361.9473 | www.tatepublishing.com

Tate Publishing is committed to excellence in the publishing industry. The company reflects the philosophy established by the founders, based on Psalm 68:11,
"The Lord gave the word and great was the company of those who published it."

Published in the United States of America

ISBN: 978-1-63122-246-7
1. Fiction/Romance/Western
2. Fiction/Christian/Western
13.12.04

PROLOGUE
November 1865

"We, the members of the jury, on the sole count of second-degree murder, find the defendant **guilty**."

A hush had fallen over the crowd right before the verdict was read, but now a collective murmur resounded throughout the room. All eyes zeroed in on the man standing at the defendant's table, the one wearing the chains. They couldn't see much as his back was to them, but they saw the slight slumping of the shoulders just before he deliberately straightened up, head held high. If they could have seen his face, they would have seen one full of conflicting emotions: anger, disbelief, bitterness, but most of all, regret and sorrow which were reflected in his eyes. If anyone had bothered to look.

The second man at the defendant's table, the one in the bolo tie and starched white shirt whispered something into the defendant's ear to which he responded by emphatically shaking his head. Then the judge spoke.

"Under normal circumstances, the sentence for murder is death by hanging," he intoned in a nasally voice. "However, due to the fact that the victim's own father, a fellow judge, spoke up on the defendant's behalf and asked for leniency, I have amended the sentence to the following."

Picking up a legal-looking piece of paper, the judge read grimly:

" 'The defendant shall spend the rest of his natural life in the Missouri State Penitentiary, working out his years at hard labor or some other capacity to benefit his fellow inmates as

5

the warden deems fit. The possibility of parole is negated by the fact that the sentence is reduced.'"

The judge picked up his gavel, looked at the defendant, and finished by saying, "The defendant is remanded over to the sheriff until the County Marshal escorts him to the penitentiary in Jefferson City." He brought the gavel down with a loud bang. "This court is dismissed."

Rumblings and mumblings began anew as the crowd stood up and began exiting the courtroom. The lawyer spent a moment talking earnestly to his client, presumably trying to convince him not to give up hope. But hope was something the defendant had run out of a long time ago, long before he ever rode into this inauspicious town that was so like all the others.

Although he had been somewhat grateful his lawyer had actually believed in him, the convicted man had known from the minute he'd been arrested that he would never be free again. The lawyer was young, fresh out of school, and full of ideals. He also was no match for the shark of a prosecutor the bustling town of Glendale employed for just such a case as his -- as the jury's verdict proved. They had taken all of 15 minutes to decide his guilt.

Shuffling along the boardwalk back to the jailhouse, feet encased in shackles, he could feel the stares of the townspeople. They had had no problem believing he had killed Scott Waverly and many had spent the last few days sitting in the courthouse for his trial.

Sheriff Ramsey grabbed onto his arm a bit too tightly as they went through the jailhouse door, roughly pulling him into the room. As they neared the doorway leading to the cells, the sheriff "accidentally" tangled his foot with the prisoner's

Legacy of Love

chained feet causing the bound man to trip. The sheriff
laughed, then shoved him into the cell door. The prisoner
caught his balance and stood upright, perfectly still, not
looking at the sheriff as the lawman removed his chains. He
then started to walk into his cell with as much dignity as he
could, which was precious little, prepared to be pushed from
behind. He wasn't disappointed. As he fell against the bunk,
the door clanged shut with an ominous finality.

"I'll be glad when yur gone," the sheriff told him nastily.
"Yur kind we can do without. It's too bad the judge and jury
went soft on ya."

His prisoner stretched out on the bunk and closed his
eyes, not rising to the bait, and was immensely grateful when
the lawman clomped back to the front room. The longer he lay
there, thinking about the next 40 or 50 years in prison, the
more his anxiety grew. His heart beat so hard and fast, he
thought it might rip its way right out of his chest; his hands
started to sweat, and he could feel his limbs begin to tremble.
He fought it back with an iron will that had helped him
survive situations no man should ever have had to endure.
The last thing he needed was to make a fool of himself in front
of the sheriff and this town. But as the bleakness and
emptiness of his life lay out before him, a life no longer his
own, a life of darkness with no warmth or peace, he felt very
alone. And very afraid.

CHAPTER 1
September 1868

Riverton, Colorado, was average in size, but still boasted the same saloons, general stores, hotel, blacksmith, and various other shops that seemed to be required in all western towns.

Riverton also had a train depot which ran along a small river south of town. That along with the throng of people walking in and out of the stores and along the boardwalks and streets meant that it probably prospered more than most. Surprising, really, considering the War Between the States ended just three years ago.

Jaxon Dumont led his horse, Blackjack, through the town, heading for the saloon to see if they rented rooms. His remaining money wouldn't last long so he had to be careful how he spent it; rooming at the saloon would be cheaper than at the hotel. He didn't look forward to spending anymore nights on the trail, at least for awhile. Hopefully, not before spring, if he was lucky. *Real* lucky.

What he needed was a job over the winter, one that paid enough for him to live either in a hotel or boarding house. Preferably the latter. But if his luck was like it had been over the last few months -- OK over the last few *years* -- then the winter was going to be long and hard. As if the fates could hear his thoughts, a cold wind blew down the street, kicking up dirt and dust, chilling him. His duster wasn't made to withstand winter temperatures, and buying a warm coat was at the top of his list of priorities -- priorities that really didn't matter all that much to him. But he had no choice if he was going to keep on trying to survive from one day to the next.

He was just so tired! Not just the bone-deep exhaustion that came from a hard   day's work, but the soul-deep weariness that wore him down day by day. He'd thought being a free man would change things, but apparently he was wrong. He knew what lay at the root of his fatigue and depression: unending loneliness, rejection by loved ones, relentless memories, & nightmares that continued to haunt him -- but thinking about it only made him feel worse. So instead, he pushed himself on, riding from town to town, trying to find something, **anything**, to relieve the emptiness inside.

For now, he would have to make do with renting a room, which he did quickly, taking a minute to drop off his precious few belongings, and then went in search of a general store to buy some needed supplies. As he reached to open the door of *Sam's Mercantile*, it suddenly swung open, and a woman backed out, her arms loaded with packages. He automatically reached out to hold the door for her -- he hadn't completely forgotten his manners -- but he inadvertently pulled it a little too far, and she over-balanced. Her packages flew out of her arms, and she half-turned around grabbing onto the doorframe to stop herself from falling.

After quickly steadying her with a hand at her elbow, Jax immediately knelt down and began gathering up the packages. "I'm terribly sorry, Maam," he said in his deep, raspy voice.

The woman dropped to her knees beside him. "Oh, that's alright," she flapped her hand at him. "No harm done."

She smiled in his direction, but it froze in place as she glanced over at him. He wasn't looking directly at her, but she could see the hard planes of his face, the set of his jaw with its dark 5 o'clock shadow, and the grimness of his mouth. As he started to hand her some of the packages, she felt a shiver run through her at the coldness of his eyes. Dark smoky gray in color, those eyes were strangely compelling, had perhaps seen too much in what had to be a fairly short life as he looked to be only in his mid to late twenties. His clothes were too black, his hair too long, his countenance too grave.

Noticing her stare, he looked away. As they rose to their feet, he asked the location of her buggy so he could stow her packages in it. She opened her mouth to refuse his offer, but changed her mind and led the way a few feet down the boardwalk, allowing him to put the packages in her small wagon. Feeling embarrassed for having stared at him, she tried to think of something to say. He lightly pressed two fingers to his hat brim, murmuring 'good day.' She got a glimpse of his eyes once more, surprised to see sorrow and regret. Something indefinable stirred in her as he turned away and walked into the store.

A few hours later, Jax sat by himself in the back corner of the *Last Resort Saloon*, slowly nursing the one and only drink he allowed himself; the last thing he needed was to squander his money on liquor. The saloon girls kept eyeing him, but he refused to make eye contact with any of them; he wasn't about to repeat the same mistakes he had in the past.

He was thinking about his conversation with the store owner where he'd bought his supplies which included a warm coat and gloves; unfortunately, they plus some other necessities had taken a good chunk of his money. He *had* to find a job. Mr. Anderson told him of a few possible prospects for a drifter such as himself. There were several ranches that

Legacy of Love

were usually looking for a wrangler or cowhand. *Billing's Feed & Seed* was actively looking for someone to load and unload train deliveries, haul deliveries to the surrounding township, and general work in the store itself.

Jax knew his way around a ranch having grown up on one and had in fact worked on one this past summer before continuing his journey west. But he wasn't fired up about spending the winter out on the range. Normally, he wouldn't mind, had liked growing up on the Circle D. But as he'd grown into his teens, he'd yearned for something more, something different. And he'd gotten exactly that! He was a visual aid on NOT being careful what you wish for. Getting away from the daily grind of ranching was part of what made him decide to leave home when he did. That plus a few high-handed ideals that had ended up slapping him in the face. He tossed back his drink, trying to put those memories away somewhere. Far away.

Working at the feed store probably wouldn't pay as much as an experienced ranch-hand especially since it wasn't full-time, he thought to himself, but it sounded as if it might serve his purpose better. His purpose. *Ha!!* His only purpose these days was just to survive from one day to the next without going crazy. To that end, he had worked his way through Missouri, Kansas, and now Colorado, riding aimlessly from town to town, going from one dead-end job to another, looking for . . . . . something. A home? Contentment? A true purpose? A calling? He paused on that last thought. He *had* a calling; he just chose not to use it.

Uneasy that his thoughts were heading right back down memory lane,   he headed up to his room for some much needed sleep. He would talk to Mr. Billings in the morning.

Dana-Sue Urso

Mykaela Caldwell groaned and yawned at the same time. Daylight was just creeping in around the curtains as Grindel cock-a-doodle-doo'd his good morning to the world. Stretching, Mykaela cuddled back under the covers, claiming a few more precious minutes of warmth before heading into the day. But Grindel, as usual, wouldn't shut up. And he had a voice that could wake the dead. Facing the inevitable, she braved the briskness of the morning and climbed out of her cozy bed.

It wasn't even October yet, but the mornings were chilly. Shivering, she dressed quickly, then headed into the kitchen area to light the fire in the cook stove. Wrapping herself in her cloak, she next headed out to do the morning chores. She worked quickly, noting that the stalls really needed a thorough cleaning, one of the myriad of jobs that needed done around the small farm. She wasn't physically able to do some of them like fix the holes in the roof or hammer in stronger clotheslines. She also couldn't afford to pay anyone to do them so she lived with a leaky roof and wobbly clotheslines.

Up until last month, she'd had a little extra money, although not much. The second story of her house was a combination bedroom/sitting room with an outside door. She had been desperate for money last winter and had rented the room out, rent including two meals a day.

Her first tenants had been a married couple; he worked on one of the ranches, but they had only stayed a month. Apparently, the wife needed more excitement than a small cow town could provide. Her second tenant had been the sheriff; he was new to town and didn't want to live in the jailhouse. He stayed through the spring until his cabin was built on the other side of town. Her last tenant had been a writer who had wanted some peace and quiet so he could . . . well . . . write. He'd stayed through most of the summer, but left in August for New York where he said 'all the great artists live and worked.' Mykaela wasn't sure if writing was an art, but what did she know about stuff like that? She had rented out the rooms for a total of 7 months. The money she'd made had paid some long overdue bills, but now she was almost back to where she was last year at this time. Needing money and having none.

Finishing her chores, Mykaela headed back into the house.

"OK, you two, time to get up!" she called into her children's bedroom. Silence. She began to make up batter for biscuits. "Time to rise and shine. "Let's go!" A little louder this time. Nothing. "I'd better hear the pitter-patter of little feet or else someone is going to pay dearly. Maybe with a wet sponge in the face."

Instantly, she heard feet hit the wooden floors. Grinning, she continued to fix breakfast. Behind her, a loud yawn was followed by, " I'm still sleepy."

"Me too!" Mykaela smiled down at her daughter, hair tousled, eyes half closed. Giving her a quick hug, she said, "But it's a beautiful morning." The little girl shrugged one shoulder and yawned again.

"Go on and get dressed; breakfast'll be ready soon," As her daughter shuffled back to her room, a whirlwind bounded out.

"Mornin' Mama!"

"Good morning to you, too. You sure seem to have gotten up on the right side of the bed this morning!"

Dana-Sue Urso

"We get to go in the woods and collect leaves and rocks and stuff. Don't you r'member?" her son reprimanded her, hands on hips.

"I'm afraid I can't keep up with all you do, Ryan," his mother admitted ruefully. "But I'm sure you'll have fun."

"I know we will," he agreed. "Tommy said he was gonna get the most, but **I'm** gonna be the one who gets the most." He thumped his chest.

Mykaela smiled ruefully. Never let it be said that her son wouldn't rise to a challenge.

Ten minutes later, she was seated across from her children, giving thanks for the meal. In her heart, she was grateful for her son and daughter. They were her life and joy, the reason she got out of bed in the morning. Their life together was hard; it was difficult to make ends meet, and more often than not, they had to do without. But she worked hard to provide the best life she could for them. There wasn't anything she wouldn't do for them.

Rachel, bless her heart, was still half asleep. She held her spoon limply over her scrambled eggs; she obviously hadn't slept well. She'd gone to bed later than usual as the children had insisted they celebrate their mother's birthday by fixing dinner. That had been a disaster in the making, the clean-up had been worse. Still, Mykaela had appreciated their efforts and allowed them to stay up an hour later than usual, to spend more time together, playing charades. Rachel was paying the price, but Ryan was raring to go.

Rachel's head suddenly jerked up, eyes wide. "Mama, I furgot to gather the eggs."

"Don't worry, I did it for you." Mykaela looked at Ryan. "And before you say anything, I already filled the wood box."

14

Legacy of Love

"I wasn't gonna say anything," he assured her without looking up secretly glad that he got out of one of his chores, too.

A half hour later, the children were dressed and on their way to school. They lived about a half mile from the eastern edge of town, a small woods in between. They lived far enough away to be away from the hustle & bustle of town, but close enough that Mykaela felt fine about them walking to school which was on a tract of land midway through town behind the buildings that made up the south side of Main Street.

She owned 25 square acres that stretched out behind and around the house. The woods met the larger forest along the back end of her property and behind the town's northern side. A branch of the Missouri River flowed along the south side of town, a half mile from the town center. The train depot sat on the western side with a bridge over the river for the train. Wagons and horses could cross on a barge about 5 miles north.

She had moved to her husband's farm nine years ago, right after they were married. After his death two years ago, she stayed in Riverton basically because she had nowhere else to go. And she liked the town; it was quiet yet busy, the townspeople were pleasant, and she had two part-time jobs. She assisted the town seamstress, Miss Hanks, who'd lived there since the town was first built, was close to 60 by now. She was able to hire Mykaela several years ago to help out once a week to help her catch up. It wasn't enough to live on, though, so Mykaela also washed linens for the hotel/restaurant and the saloon. Her back porch held three large tubs with a pump; the sheets and blankets were heavy; hence the need for stronger clotheslines. The income from both jobs plus what she could harvest from her garden barely put enough food on the table, and she almost never had fresh meat. They had a daily supply of eggs and milk, though, which she always remembered to thank God for.

Last year, she had felt the pinch and had been forced to take in the boarders. She didn't like to do it especially since the only ones who ever seemed to need a room were men. But she interviewed them carefully and then turned it over to God; so far, everything had turned out fine.

Taxes were going to come due in a few short months so, as she cleared the table, she sent a prayer winging upwards for God to send her a trustworthy boarder who would stay through the winter.

CHAPTER 2

Mykaela spent the day washing, drying, and ironing sheets, towels, and tablecloths. She'd done a lot of it yesterday, but needed to get them delivered by the end of the day. As she passed *Billing's Feed and Seed* towards mid-day, she saw the man from *Sam's Mercantile*. He was loading large bags of grain onto one of the out-lying rancher's wagon. As he straightened up, he unerringly met her gaze. As their eyes locked, Mykaela again felt a shiver run through her; he was dressed just like he had been yesterday: dark jeans, black shirt. The only thing missing was his gun belt; he even had the classic dark persona of a gunslinger.

As she continued to watch him, fascinated for some reason, he raised an eyebrow at her, but didn't turn away like he had before. In fact, if she wasn't mistaken, that was a mocking smile on his face. Affronted, she was jerked back to her driving by a shout. Her large half Belgians, Maestro and Velvet, were about to walk up onto the boardwalk, sending several people scattering. Cheeks reddened with embarrassment, she gained better control and continued up the street, not daring to look at the stranger again.

Jax untied his handkerchief from around his neck and wiped sweat from his brow, watching the woman drive off. He couldn't understand why she kept staring at him; he wasn't full of false modesty, knew that women usually found him attractive. But that had been in the past and now no decent woman would want anything to do with him. He deliberately dressed in dark colors in an attempt to keep others at bay. And if he was any judge of character, this particular woman was way too good for him. But he was forced to admit, she sure was pretty. She was about 5'5" with hair the color of chestnuts, tied into a long braid thrown over one shoulder. She had a small heart shaped face with a cute pert nose; her dark brown eyes had seemed to look deep into his soul yesterday. That made him uncomfortable and for that reason alone, wanted nothing to do with her. Turning, he went back inside the store to finish up his work day.

An hour later, Mykaela had completed her deliveries and picked up her children from school; she liked to give them a ride home on delivery days. They climbed in the back of their small wagon, chattering like magpies. Ryan talked a mile a minute about his day in the woods; Rachel kept interrupting, and they began to argue. Mykaela let it go at first as they usually worked out disagreements between them, but this argument began to escalate to a point where she needed to intervene.

Nearing the edge of town, she turned in her seat to reprimand them when a deafening series of bangs went off, almost right on top of them, or so it seemed. Her normally calm, placid, obedient half-breed Belgians took great exception, making their displeasure known by lunging into a flat out run.

Because Mykaela hadn't been giving them her full attention, the reins were slack in her hands. Velvet's reins, the female horse on the right side, flew out of her hands before she could recapture them. She managed to hold onto Maestro's reins, but by the time she could catch Velvet's, the horse had already grabbed the bit and was not willing to give it back.

Legacy of Love

Not overly concerned yet, Mykaela decided to let them run for a few moments, hoping that as they neared their property, they would slow and turn into it. She told the kids to stay down and hold on. Unfortunately, the horses had their own agenda which seemed to include going for a nice, long run. The only problem with that was that about a mile ahead, the road took a *sharp* turn to the right, following the bend of the river ½ a mile away; if they hit that curve at their current speed, the axle would undoubtedly bust sending the wagon and all occupants careening into the trees that lined the road on their left.

Mykaela pulled back on the reins, but to no avail. She pulled harder and harder, causing Maestro to shake his head; if his sister wasn't slowing, neither was he. Knowing that she had to convince him to slow down so that Velvet would follow suit, Mykaela stood up, braced her feet, and pulled as hard as she could . . . . suddenly flying backwards as Maestro's reins broke. She had known that the reins were thinning, but she figured they'd last until Spring at least. She'd been wrong.

Both horses were completely free now. Velvet wasn't giving up her bit, and Mykaela didn't have the strength to force it out at this speed. They flew past her house and on down the road. Right towards the sharp turn. Her mouth went dry. If she had been by herself, she wouldn't have thought twice about jumping out, willing to risk a broken leg rather than a broken neck. *But what about the children?* What if they didn't jump hard enough and landed in the road under the wheels. Heart pounding, she knew they had no choice. Slamming into the trees was simply **not** an option. They had to jump, and they had to do it now.

Dana-Sue Urso

She grabbed her seat back and began to yell instructions to them, wanting to cry at the frightened looks on their faces. All of a sudden, a horse and rider came thundering up along the left side of the wagon. He was going too fast to see his face clearly under his hat, but Mykaela knew him from his clothes -- it was the man from the feed store. He ran alongside Maestro and readied himself to jump on the bigger horse's back. Mykaela gasped as he leaped across, her hand at her throat, the other hand hanging on for dear life. She let out a sigh of relief when he landed safely although he almost overshot his mark and only by sheer strength was able to right himself.

Clamping his legs hard around the horse for leverage, he held on tightly to Maestro's bridle, leaning slightly forward. He pulled back on the bit AND forced the gelding's head to turn to the right. It was clear he wanted the horse to angle more to the right which would force Velvet to the right, and they could edge their way over off the road onto the grassy field and avoid the curve rapidly approaching. Velvet fought him at first. The man then reached his right leg out and shoved her in the shoulder. This was the incentive she needed; she turned out onto the grass, taking Maestro and the wagon with her.

The ground was hard and bumpy. They were all jolted as the wagon bounced its way along for several yards before finally slowing down. Just before the horses stopped on the far side of the curve, the right rear axle cracked and broke, causing the wagon to list, throwing the kids down the end of the wagon box where they landed in a heap. Automatically throwing the brake on, Mykaela clambered down to the ground and ran to them. Rachel was crying, and Ryan was doing his best to hold back the tears.

"Are you hurt anywhere?" their mother asked anxiously, reaching over the side to check them over. "Let me see." She lifted Rachel out of the wagon bed.

"I was scared, Mama," admitted Rachel, wrapping her arms around Mykaela's neck. "The wagon was going too fast. I don't want to do that again."

"Don't worry, sweetheart; I don't want to either." Mykaela looked at Ryan. "Are you all right?"

"I-I think so," he said shakily. "I banged my knee . . ." he showed her a large bruise. ". . . but I'll be OK." He finished bravely, not wanting to seem like a sissy in front of the man who'd saved them. Unlike his little sister, he knew how badly they could have been injured. Or worse. A little shakily, he climbed down.

Jax was standing at Velvet's head, rubbing her nose and murmuring to her, calming her as she breathed noisily, sides heaving; her brother was just as winded. When Jax noticed the boy glancing his way, he walked towards them.

"Is everyone all right?" he asked, glancing at the kids before zeroing in on Mykaela who nodded.

"I think so." She swallowed hard. "I don't know how to thank you. You risked your life for us -- there just aren't words . . . ." She felt tears prick her eyes. The man held up his hand.

"It's OK." He responded more sharply than he intended. He flicked a glance at the broken wheel. "I'm sorry about your wheel. I thought it prudent to get them off the road as soon as possible, what with the curve and all."

Dana-Sue Urso

"Oh, yes, absolutely," Mykaela vehemently agreed. "It's certainly not your fault. Better a broken wheel than . . ." she stopped herself as she remembered her children were listening to every word. She swallowed hard again. "Do you know what happened? The loud noise?"

"I'm not sure, but it sounded like firecrackers. A lot of them."

"Jimmy Thomas has some firecrackers," offered up Ryan. "He said his Pa got them from Denver."

Mykaels frowned. "I will be speaking with his father as soon as I can."

Taking a deep breath, she introduced herself and her children.

Their rescuer then followed suit. "I'm . . . Jaxon Dumont." He hesitated slightly as if he was afraid she would recognize his name. But his hesitation had nothing to do with that. In fact, it was her name that was familiar. He had been intending to see her about renting a room, although he hadn't known she was the same woman from the store until she'd introduced herself. After seeing her horses take off after the loud bangs, he'd followed, hoping she'd be able to control them; it wasn't as if they were race horses -- they were 1000 pound Belgians, for heaven's sake. But when the reins snapped, a gut-wrenching fear had come over him as he envisioned the three of them battered against the trees. It didn't matter that they were strangers and meant nothing to him; old habits died hard, so he tore off after them, relying on his swift thoroughbred to catch them.

"I'm very pleased to meet you, Mr. Dumont," she smiled at him, and Jax felt as if the sun had just peaked out over the mountains. Blinking to clear his obviously befuddled mind, he looked around to see if his horse was near.

Legacy of Love

"He's over there," the boy pointed across the road.

Good old Blackjack, ever faithful. He was chomping on what little grass there was, not looking any worse after his hard ride. "Can I go get him?"

"Ryan! You know better than to approach an unfamiliar animal," His mother admonished him.

"But Ma, just look at'im," Ryan cried enthusiastically. 'He's a real beaut!"

"Your son has an eye for fine horseflesh," Jax remarked, lips curving slightly upward.

"He loves horses," she smiled again, this time at the boy.

"He always asks for a horse for Cwistmas," Rachel spoke up for the first time, still held by her mother. "But Santa can't fit a horse in his sleigh."

"Or much of anything else," Ryan echoed bitterly, scuffing his shoe into the dirt.

"Ryan," Mykaela's voice was gentle, but firm and full of meaning.

Ryan was contrite. "I'm sorry, Mama. I just hope that I'll be able to have a great horse some day." He looked over at the horse in the field. "Like Mr. Dumont's."

"His name is Blackjack. Why don't you walk over with me to get him?" invited Jax. "If your mother says it's OK." They both looked at her expectantly, Ryan's eyes shining. She had no choice but to nod. She and Rachel watched them, Ryan talking a mile a minute as usual. Mr. Dumont tilted his head every now and then as if he was really listening. Mykaela was impressed. She didn't know many men who would take time out to indulge a little boy he didn't even know.

Dana-Sue Urso

Putting Rachel down and holding her hand, Mykaela went to her horses to check on them. They were sweating, but their breathing was almost back to normal. They were their calm, placid selves, turning their big brown eyes to her as if to say, hey, what's all the fuss about.

Absently stroking them, Mykaela continued to watch Ryan and Mr. Dumont. He was far enough away that she could appreciate him without calling attention to herself. He was about 6 feet tall with a lean frame. His shoulders were strong -- had to be to lift the feed bags she'd seen earlier. He was very good-looking with an angular face that held strength of character; his nose was slightly crooked as if it had been broken, his mouth full; there was a small scar on his right cheek. He had unusually long lashes, nice and thick, but they didn't look in any way effeminate. In fact, they framed his incredible eyes perfectly. But there was a hardness there, as if life had proven to be more than he'd bargained for, and he was trying to come to terms with it. He had his gun on, she noticed, wearing it comfortably. Although he worked as a laborer, she wondered if he really was a gunslinger.

Those eyes were carefully guarded, she noticed, as if he didn't want the world to see who he really was, and she didn't know if that was a good thing or a bad thing. His clothes were dusty and worn, his boots old. His hair was thick and raven-wing black, slightly wavy and needed trimmed. His 5 o'clock shadow gave him a mysterious almost ominous look, and Mykaela felt slightly uneasy in his presence. Then felt guilty for feeling that way especially after he had just saved their lives.

Legacy of Love

Jax untied Velvet and Maestro from their traces and helped Mykaela lead them back down the road to her barn. Her house stood 50 yards from the road, the barn to its right. He immediately summed up her situation: the barn doors were wobbly and off-track, holes marked the walls here and there, the chicken coop fencing was sagging, several clotheslines were leaning over, too close to the ground, the small front porch had a large hole to the right of the door, and the roof had shingles missing. He knew from Mr. Billings that she was a widow with two children to support. She definitely needed help around here, and that could work to his advantage.

As they stopped at the barn, Jax said, "Mrs. Caldwell, I was actually on my way to see you this afternoon."

"Oh, well then why don't you stay for supper," she generously offered, manners overcoming her nervousness. "It's the least I can do." She felt a little unsure, but wanted to do something to show her thanks.

"I'd. . .like that, thank you," he hesitated slightly, not wanting her to feel obligated, but he really needed to talk to her. "I'll be happy to stable the horses for you."

"That's not necessary, Mr. Dumont."

"It's no problem," he looked at Ryan. "Maybe your son could help me brush down Blackjack."

"Oh, boy," Ryan raced for the doors to open them, his eyes shining with excitement.

"Just be careful, Ryan. And don't forget Maestro and Velvet," Mykaela reminded him before leading Rachel into the house.

Supper was simple, but filling. She had left a pot of vegetable soup simmering on the stove most of the afternoon, and it was chock full of tomatoes, carrots, potatoes, celery, and green beans -- all gathered from her garden. They rarely had meat; she didn't know how to hunt and couldn't afford to buy beef from the local ranchers. All eight of her hens were laying, but she occasionally sacrificed one of them as long as Grindel and his brood kept producing chicks to keep the numbers up. She usually made do with vegetables and the occasional stew meat along with seasonings to cook tasteful meals. And of course there was always flour and cornmeal for bread. She also tried to make simple desserts for the children's sakes.

She was slightly embarrassed at the humble meal, but Mr. Dumont seemed to enjoy it. In fact, when she offered a second bowl, he readily accepted along with two more pieces of cornbread.

Jax was amazed at how tasty the plain meal was. Or maybe it was the fact that it was a home-cooked meal, something he hadn't had in a very long time. But whatever the reason, he thoroughly enjoyed it and told her as much. He was a little surprised to see her cheeks turn red, as if honest praise embarrassed her.

Ryan kept up a steady refrain throughout the meal, asking him where he was from, how good of a shot he was with his gun, how long he had Blackjack, how long he'd been traveling. Mykaela reined him in after awhile much to Jax's relief. It wasn't that he minded answering questions, but some of them were best left unanswered, and he didn't want to hurt the little fella's feelings. So he gave brief sketchy replies that satisfied the boy; Mykaela on the other hand wondered about the things he wasn't saying.

She had made a cherry cobbler for dessert and had no way of knowing that it was Jax's favorite dessert above all else; his mother had always made it for him on his birthday, when he was sick, or when she just wanted him to know he was special. Thinking about her made his chest hurt so much he didn't think he could get a single bite down. But not wanting to hurt his hostess' feelings -- especially after Ryan's comment that she "made the bestest cobbler in the whole state" -- he made the attempt.

Mykaela watched him toying with his dessert, thinking that maybe he just didn't like cobbler. But after eating a few bites, he looked up at her and said sincerely, "This is truly the best cherry cobbler I've ever had."

But Mykaela saw a haunted look in his eyes and wondered at it. It was as if he was remembering something painful, and that made her heart go out to him. He masked his emotions quickly by getting up and starting to clear the table which jolted Mykaela out of her reverie. "Oh, you don't have to do that." She stood and went to the coffee pot. "Please, sit down and have another cup. You haven't yet told me why you wanted to see me."

Sitting back down, he palmed the coffee cup and said casually, "I'd like to rent a room for the winter."

"I see." Of all the things he could have said, Mykaela would not have guessed this was one of them. But then, why not, she asked herself. He was new to town and needed a place to live. He just didn't seem like the kind of man who would be satisfied living on a small farm outside of town; she would have thought he'd be more comfortable in a room over the saloon. But then again, she didn't know anything about him. Well, OK, he was courageous and patient with little boys and appreciative of her cooking, but was that enough to allow a perfect stranger into her home?

Dana-Sue Urso

You let Abraham Mays live here, her conscience reminded her, *and the sheriff*. Yes, but Mr. Mays was a 50 something year old man who only had interest in his books. And as for the sheriff, she actually felt safe and protected with him upstairs. Jaxon Dumont was most definitely NOT 50 and had a dangerous aura about him. What if he was an outlaw? On the other hand, his speech proved he was educated, he had the manners of a gentleman, and he had risked his life for them.

Before she could formulate any kind of response, Jax went on. "I . . noticed that your farm needs a little work, some fixing up. I don't know what you require in the way of rent, but I don't get paid much working at the feed store. I was kind of hoping we could work something out."

"Work something out?" she repeated, a questioning look in her eyes. He nodded.

"Yeah, um, I could fix the place up for you, even take over some of the more difficult chores like mucking out the stalls, the outhouse, that kind of thing. And in return, maybe pay a smaller rent." He felt almost guilty with his suggestion.

Mykaela bit her lip, thinking. His offer was extremely tempting. In fact the first chore that had leapt to mind was chopping her winter supply of wood. She worked on it a little every day, but made very little headway as she just didn't have the strength to wield the ax for very long. Also, she needed a fresh supply of logs to cut because what she had on hand, once chopped, would only last until the end of October, if that. She had planned on spending some of her money on hiring someone to cut down some trees in the woods along the back end of her property. Mr. Dumont's offer may just be the answer to her many prayers.

Legacy of Love

She looked at him, saw him watching her. He appeared relaxed, simply waiting for an answer, but was that hope she saw in his eyes? The room was darkening, and she couldn't see him clearly. He appeared calm and almost insouciant, but she had the distinct impression that he was very attuned to her response. Which he, in fact, was. His life had gone sour for so long that when things started to go his way, he didn't trust that it would last. But yesterday, he had been hired to work through the winter. So easy, yet he had worried for so long. And now, another simple answer to his second pressing need, but she took so long to respond, he began to doubt his luck would last. Until she spoke.

"I do need help around here," she admitted. She named a very reasonable rent, one that would enable him to actually have a little bit of money left over at the end of the month for his necessities. They worked out an agreement where he would take over some of the daily chores, including the wood chopping, and she would provide him with meals and the stabling of his horse; he would buy the feed for all the horses (Mr. Billings had told him he could have feed at a discount). It was a win-win situation for both of them.

After supper, Jax insisted on fixing her wagon wheel, overriding her protests; it was such a simple thing, and he truly was grateful for their agreement which meant stability for him. He took stock of the tools she had on hand to use for repairs, rolled out one of the two replacement wheels that were leaning against the wall, and got to work. It took him all of 30 minutes to smooth it down; he then rolled it out to the field, leading the 2 Belgians so they could pull the wagon back. After he sheltered the vehicle under the roofed open side of the bar, he stabled the horses and saddled Blackjack.

Dana-Sue Urso

His plan was to move in after work tomorrow, then make a dent in the needed winter supply of wood as his first chore. He walked his mount out of the barn, preparing to leave when he saw Mykaela cutting her son's hair; she looked at him and smiled mischievously. Lifting the shears up, she snipped them open and shut several times, calling out playfully, "Next!"

Jax automatically reached a hand up to brush his hair out of his face. He did need a haircut, but wasn't sure if he should allow her to do the honors. His uncertainty must have shown because she said, "Oh come on, you're not afraid of me and my lil 'ol scissors, now are you?" *Clack, clack.* He didn't know what to make of her teasing; he wasn't comfortable around people, at least not anymore, and wasn't sure how to respond. "Besides, I owe you for fixing my clotheslines," She reminded him.

"Yeah, go on," urged Ryan, standing up and brushing hair off his shirt. "She does a real good job." The boy's haircut wasn't so bad, Jax decided. And sat down in the chair, letting Ryan hold his horse's reins. The next thing he knew, he was in heaven. Mykaela was running her hands through his hair to finger-comb it and get a feel for its thickness. He closed his eyes in ecstasy as goose-bumps ran down his arms and spine. No one had touched him so tenderly in a long, long time. Her fingers worked magic over his scalp, soothing and gentle, sending waves of pure pleasure through his body.

He had never enjoyed a haircut more and would have gladly sat there while she clipped him bald. Instead, she snipped here and there, shaping and cutting, but assured him she wasn't taking off too much. As if he cared. When she was done, he couldn't help but feel disappointed. Looking in her hand mirror, he was actually pleased to see she'd done a decent job. Although a few errant locks fell across his forehead, he no longer had to brush it out of his face. She'd trimmed the back to just above his collar and overall, it did feel lighter and more comfortable.

Thanking her and receiving a "My pleasure" in return, Jax climbed onto Blackjack and headed to town, waving his goodbyes. He marveled at the contentment he was already starting to feel. He even allowed himself to feel a little snippet of hope that his life may have actually taken a turn for the better.

CHAPTER 3

Jax knew it had been too good to be true. He had just arrived at Mykaela's farm the next afternoon, secure in the knowledge that something was actually going smoothly in his life. Then his optimism was abruptly shattered. He was just about to knock on the front door when it suddenly opened, and a man wearing a badge stepped through. His eyes met Jax's . . and time slowed down for both of them. Jax heard a rushing sound in his ears as the other man pulled his gun, pointing it steadily at Jax's chest. Jax wasn't wearing his gun and idly wondered if he would have gone for it. The man before him was wearing a sheriff's badge, but when Jax last saw him, he had been a guard at the prison where he had been incarcerated. Although Jax's faith in the law was skewed, surely the man wouldn't just shoot him down without cause and in front of a witness; Mykaela had also stepped out of the house behind the sheriff and was staring at them in disbelief.

"Don't move, Dumont," the sheriff warned, his gun not wavering, ignoring her. "Put your hands behind your head."

"I'm surprised you remember my name," remarked Jax casually, complying with the sheriff's order. But he was anything, but relaxed. In fact, his stomach was churning, and his heart was heavy, but not from having a gun pointed at him. No, he knew that his imagined peaceful winter living as a boarder at the Caldwell's was just a dream, and all because he had been afraid to tell Mykaela the truth -- that he was an ex-convict, a free-of-all-charges ex, but none-the-less, he'd been in prison for two and a half interminable years.

Legacy of Love

"I always remember the name of a killer," Sheriff Hoskins told him grimly. Jax tried to ignore Mykaela's gasp; he could feel her horrified gaze although his eyes never wavered from the other man. "How did you escape?" The sheriff was asking, frowning in concentration. "I don't remember any wanted posters coming across my desk."

"That's because I'm not wanted," Jax informed him drily. "And I didn't escape. My release papers are in my satchel." He nodded toward his horse.

Not looking convinced, the sheriff asked Mykaela get them. Jax could only wonder what she must be thinking. Neither man spoke while she slowly walked to Blackjack and reached into his saddlebags.

Upon her return, Mykaela held a small stack of papers, the top one the official release document. The sheriff quickly scanned it, knowing it was the real deal as he had seen many of them in the past. That, plus having received no outstanding warrants on the man before him, forced him to reluctantly holster his gun.

"Can't understand why they let you go," he remarked with a shake of his head. "Technicality?"

"Nope," Jax lowered his arms and folded them across his chest, his stance not quite threatening, but definitely standing his ground. "I was cleared of all charges."

"Really?" snorted the sheriff in disbelief. "After all that time in prison, you were cleared, just like that." He snapped his fingers.

"Just like that," Jax didn't offer any explanations because he seriously doubted the sheriff would believe him. Mykaela on the other hand was a different story. He'd tell her the truth about himself . . . . if she asked.

Dana-Sue Urso

When Jax refused to say more, Sheriff Hoskins turned to Mykaela who was standing by the front door, looking bewildered. "If he's your new border, you might want to rethink it. I don't care what the release papers say, he's a convicted cold-blooded murderer who should have been hanged."

At his words, a shiver ran down her spine. She was watching Jax. His defensive posture and glowering expression did nothing to reassure her. He'd admitted he'd been in jail. And whoever heard of someone being cleared of murder charges almost 3 years after being convicted? More than likely, the sheriff was right; he had been released on a technical issue his lawyer had undoubtedly come up with.

"If you want, I can escort him off your property." The sheriff was saying, a gleam in his eyes. For some reason, that rankled.

"He saved my life, Sheriff," she promptly informed him. "And my children's lives. I owe him the courtesy of an explanation."

Jax could have kissed her. Maybe he'd misread her after all. But after the sheriff tried again to convince her to make him leave, he himself finally left; he had only dropped by to check on her and the kids, something he did from time to time. But as he rode off, he clearly warned Jax to watch his P's and Q's while in 'his town.'

Mykaela took a deep breath before turning to face him. Her eyes were wary, her hands gripping each other in agitation, her stance one of nervousness and determination.

Speaking softly and gently, he said, "Thanks for what you said to the sheriff."

Legacy of Love

She nodded. "I have one question," she told him in a firm voice.

"Go ahead."

"Were you really convicted of killing a man?" Her knuckles were white, her eyes wide and anxious. She was afraid of him, and that hit him like a blow to his mid-section. But he refused to lie to her.

Taking a deep breath, he simply said "Yes. And cleared of all charges." He reminded her, then waited for her to ask him for an explanation, but he was disappointed. Apparently, having been convicted was reason enough not to trust him. He could see the wariness and distrust deepen as doubts rose inside of her.

"You should have told me," she said accusingly.

"You're right, Mrs. Caldwell, I should have. But don't worry, I'll go." He headed for his horse.

"How did the sheriff know who you were?" she couldn't help asking.

"He was one of the guards at the penitentiary during my first year there." When no more questions were forthcoming, he leapt up into his saddle, wanting to say something, offer up an explanation, but his pride wouldn't let him. Unfortunately, the Dumont pride ran deep in his family, and in him more than most. If she didn't want to know the entire truth, if she wanted to make connections and come to conclusions that weren't entirely true, that was for her to decide. He wasn't going to beg for a chance to explain what really happened. His pride was just about all he had left ever since his family had deserted him . . . . *No reason to go there*, he told himself fiercely, watching as Mykaela rubbed her hand down Blackjack's muzzle.

Dana-Sue Urso

"I'm really sorry things didn't work out," she said sincerely, looking him in the eye. The wariness was still there, but at least the fear was gone. "If it wasn't for the children . . ." she broke off and shook her head. "I'm sorry." She didn't know what else to say.

And she did look regretful. *Amazing*, Jax thought. She was sorry that she didn't want a "convicted killer" around her kids. He didn't blame her in the least and told her so. With that, he swung his horse around and headed toward town.

Mykaela watched him ride off, knowing she should feel relieved, but actually felt bereft and alone, questioning if she'd done the right thing. He had looked so . . . resigned, almost disheartened, and yet not in the least bit surprised. She imagined that he may have had a hard time since his release; the document had been dated just under 6 months ago. He obviously lived hand-to-mouth and apparently had no family. Or friends. But what was she to do? She didn't even *know* him. And she really did have the kids to think about. Who in their right mind wanted a convict living with their children? *But he saved their lives.* Ye-es, but what did one have to do with the other? He murdered a man!! *Didn't he?*

Mykaela frowned in concentration as she headed back into the cabin. She tried to remember exactly what had been said when the sheriff had confronted Jax. Jax had said he'd been released because he'd been cleared, that it wasn't because of a technicality. But what else could it have been? The only other reason she could come up with was that his original conviction had been overturned which meant that he hadn't actually committed murder. But if that was the case, why hadn't he just said so? Shaking her head, Mykaela didn't know what to think. Feeling very confused, she got back to work cleaning the stove and tried to convince herself that she hadn't just made a huge mistake.

Jax had several questions to answer. One, should he stay in this town over the winter as he'd planned, or go? His pride dictated that he stay, but common sense said to go. Two, if he stayed, should he tell Mr. Billings the truth about himself? Three, where would he live?

He took off to the hills, towards the mountains, behind the forest, to let his horse run. And also to give him time to think. Sitting by a clear brook an hour later, Jax made the decision to talk to Mr. Billings. If the feed store owner didn't want him working for him, he'd leave, head for another town, and pray he didn't run into anyone who knew him. He lay back, not minding the cool breeze that blew across the water, and closed his eyes, thinking about how he'd gotten to this place in his life.

It really was amazing how chance encounters can change one's life forever. But that's exactly what happened to him that day in Glendale, Missouri. He had ridden into that cowtown, planning on earning some quick cash in a poker game. Hard drinking and catching the eye of a pretty saloon girl were also foremost in his mind. *Anything to stop the memories.*

He wasn't a gambler by trade, but he had a quick mind with a good memory; he was also very patient. This combination usually earned him a tidy sum during most games he played in. That night was no exception. By the time he'd drank his way through most of a bottle of Tequila, he had won a satisfactory amount. He had been flirting with a cute little red-head the whole night and was now ready for a different kind of action with her, something she was most agreeable to.

However, when he made known his intention to quit the game, one of the men took major exception. His name was Scott Waverly, the town big mouth; he was also a sore loser which was made worse by the fact that he'd lost the most money at the table. He began arguing with Jax who refused to rise to his bait. But when the other man called him a cheat, Jax's inevitable pride kicked in. A fight broke out. The other man was younger, taller, and heavier than Jax, but he didn't have the demons in his soul that Jax did. Jax humiliated the other man by beating him down quickly. Jax told him in no uncertain terms that if he ever bothered him again -- or called him a cheater -- he'd kill him. They were just big drunken words meant to humiliate and intimidate the other man, but those words came back to haunt him several hours later.

He and the saloon girl spent a few hours together, then Jax needed to move on. He had a goal in mind, a destination he was anxious to get to, so he never lingered very long in any one place. Daylight was just breaking over the town while Jax saddled his horse in the alley between the saloon and the stable. He was tired, but anxious to be on his way. The after-effects of the liquor made his movements more sluggish as well as feeling some soreness from his earlier fight.

He had just strapped on his gunbelt when his instincts kicked in, saving his life. Hearing a soft footfall seconds before a knife would have landed in his neck, Jax ducked and swung around. The momentum from his attacker slammed him into Jax and the horse. It was Scott Waverly and from the murderous gleam in his eyes, Jax knew this fight would be different. Scott had drunk a lot more than he had, and the smell of alcohol was strong on his breath; there would be no talking him out of this.

38

Legacy of Love

Jax was wearing his holster, but it was empty. He usually carried his gun when he was on the trail, but had packed it in his saddlebags after riding into town. Kicking the other man away from him, Jax tried to get to the flap of his saddlebag to reach in for the colt. But Scott was quick and jumped towards him again, knife held high. As Jax grappled with him, he wondered when other people would be up and about. Right now, it seemed as if he and Scott were the only ones in town. Even the groom from the livery stable was absent.

Jax managed to knock the knife out of his hand, sending it flying. Scott scrambled after it, while Jax reached in his bag for his gun. This fight was senseless, and it was time to end it. As he drew the gun out of the bag, he whirled around, just in time to see Scott diving at him yet again. Side-stepping in the knick of time, Jax tripped on a piece of wood and fell. Landing hard, Jax was able to twist his body so that he could bring his gun up to face Scott, cocking it in the hopes the sound would stop the other man's attack. He had no intention of killing him; in fact, deliberately taking another's life, even to save his own, was not something he was willing to do.

Scott again leapt for him. He either didn't see the gun or didn't care. He landed on top of Jax, knife held high. Jax blocked it with the arm not holding his gun, but the other man's weight pushed down on Jax's gun hand, causing him to accidentally depress the trigger. The bullet blasted right through Scott's chest -- he died instantly.

Jax was immediately filled with a deep sense of remorse and relentless guilt. Although Scott had provoked the attack, Jax felt some responsibility for what happened. He was confident that after the sheriff investigated, he would be set free without charges even being filed, but would always carry this endless guilt with him.

Unfortunately, fate stepped in to ruin his life yet again because Jax hadn't counted on three things: first, by the time the sheriff arrived, the knife had disappeared so there was no proof Scott had attacked him -- he didn't even boast a scratch which only proved he was agile and quick on his feet, but to others, it may look as though he deliberately killed the other man, that no fight had even ensued; second, there were no witnesses to this fight, but there were plenty of them to tell the judge and jury of how angry the newcomer had gotten over being accused of cheating, that he had almost beaten Scott to death (a major exaggeration), not to mention threatening him; and three, Scott was the son of the county's most prominent judge who took exception that his only son had been killed. No one seemed to remember that this son had been a bully, a trouble-maker, a coward, an embarrassment to his family.

Things went from bad to worse in a hurry. Jax had been assigned an attorney from Jefferson City, fresh out of law school. Figured. But the one thing in his favor was that this lawyer, Daniel Goodson, believed Jax's story. Jax always thought he was supposed to tell his clients that he believed them and didn't have much faith in the man's ability to win. But he had to admit, Daniel worked hard to get the jury to disbelieve what amounted to circumstantial evidence. And although the jury came back with a guilty verdict, they had recommended life in prison instead of hanging, thanks in large part to his inexperienced yet enthusiastic lawyer not to mention the unexpected testimony by Judge Waverley, something Jax hadn't understood at the time.

Legacy of Love

Jax fell asleep thinking about Scott Waverly, the remorse still strong within him, which triggered his recurring nightmare. He awakened in a cold sweat, shaking from head to foot. It took many long minutes before he had himself under control and could mount Blackjack to head back to town, brooding yet again about the fate God had dealt him.

CHAPTER 4

Mykaela spent the next week in a constant state of worry. She had no contenders to rent her room, and winter was fast approaching. She still needed her winter's supply of wood, but couldn't pay anyone to haul and chop it. The arrangement she'd had with Jaxon Dumont had been perfect, and she often wondered if she should have let him stay.

She saw him still working at the feed store, was curious where he slept. She'd be surprised to learn that he slept in a cot in the storage room at Billing's. That Mr. Billings was a fair-minded man and didn't let the fact that his best worker in years had been in prison. Things happened, and people moved on. 'Live and let live,' that was his motto.

One evening, Mykaela was sewing patches on Ryan's winter coat. It was actually too small for him, but right now, she just didn't have the money to buy him a new one. She had knitted him and Rachel new scarves, fluffy and warm, which helped keep the cold out. For now. But her son was also outgrowing his shoes and would definitely need new ones by Christmas if not before.

She laid her head back on the chair and closed her eyes. Like Jax, she allowed her thoughts to carry her back to the day when her life also changed dramatically.

She was 17, living with her father in a small town in Arkansas. Her mother had died during her birth, and her father had always laid the blame at her feet. To the point that he was mentally and emotionally abusive to her during her younger years: always finding fault, criticizing her at every turn, telling her she was no good. As the years passed, she tried to get her father to love her by doing well at school, by cooking and keeping their cabin nice, abiding by his rules without question. But nothing did any good and by the time she was a teenager, she dreamed of the day when she would be rescued from her intolerable life.

The summer she turned 17, finished with school, she tried to work up the courage to leave. But she had no skills beyond housekeeping and sewing; no one she knew of needed those services. She was afraid to strike out on her own with no money or resources, and she had no relatives. It had always been just her and her father. Those days, her father barely worked enough on their small farm to make any money, most of which he spent on liquor. She became adept at growing vegetables and raising chickens which kept them from starving, but just barely.

One day, she was coming out of the general store when she tripped and almost fell. Would have if a certain gentleman hadn't caught her. His name was Danny Caldwell, and he went out of his way to make her feel special. He was a visitor in the town, passing through on his way home to Riverton, Colorado. He'd told her that he lived by himself on his farm where he raised wheat, barley, and rye.

While waiting for the stagecoach to have repair work done on two of the wheels, Danny was forced to spend a few days in town. During that time, he literally swept her off her feet. She was so starved for affection that she'd fallen hard for him, convinced that he was the answer to her prayers. Danny courted her for a week, then asked her to marry him; she didn't hesitate. She left that town, and her father behind forever.

Dana-Sue Urso

But the grass was definitely not always greener on the other side. After the initial honeymoon period wore off, Danny began showing his true colors. Basically, he was lazy. And he didn't have the excuse of alcohol abuse as her father had. He just didn't like to work. So Mykaela once again found herself finding ways to make ends meet which included taking in the hotel laundry and working as a maid for awhile.

But when Ryan came along a year later, she had to quit one of her jobs; Rachel followed two years later. For the next four years, Mykaela found herself more and more disillusioned with her life and her husband. He always had some excuse as to why the crops weren't planted on time thus cutting down on what could be harvested, complained that his back hurt too much to pull in the harvest so justified hiring it out which ate into her earnings and household budget. There was always something. They fought more often than not, her love for him fading over time.

She was determined to make the best of her life for her children's sake. Plus divorce was against everything she believed in. She prayed daily that her husband would change, she attended church regularly which was balm to her wounded soul, and she doted on her son and daughter.

What made her the angriest of all was the fact that Danny didn't want anything to do with the children. He never held them when they were little (*that was a mother's job*), he rarely played with them, and he was impatient with Ryan who liked to follow Danny around the farm, wanting to help. By the time he was five, he was fascinated with horses and begged Danny to teach him everything he knew about them. Although Mykaela thought he was too young to ride, she was upset with Danny for how he brushed the little boy aside.

Legacy of Love

Ryan never gave up hope that his father would make time for him, but as time wore on, Mykaela could see the hurt in his eyes grow with each day that passed. Nothing she could say to Danny changed anything; he just didn't care.

And then one day two years ago, Danny was making his last haul of logs for their winter supply of firewood; thankfully, this was one of the few chores he did not neglect. He was late getting home which was unusual for him. Mykaela waited until almost dusk and when he still hadn't returned, she bundled up the kids, then 4 & 6, and walked to town (Danny had taken the horses and wagon). She informed the sheriff that her husband was missing, and he dutifully gathered a search party and headed for the area of forest she thought he'd be. They were back within two hours; Mr. Anderson from the general store drove her wagon up, Danny's body covered up in the back; he had been crushed when a tree he had been chopping fell on top of him.

Mykaela mourned for him, not as a loving wife for her love for him had long grown cold, but out of sadness that the man she had had such high hopes of a life with was gone forever.

That had been over two years ago, and Mykaela struggled more and more each year to make ends meet. There were times she despaired that things would ever get better although she never gave up praying about it. Each winter was harder than the last, even when Danny was alive, and this one was beginning worse than ever what with an incomplete supply of firewood.

Sighing heavily, Mykaela banked the fire and went to bed. Maybe tomorrow would bring the answers she so desperately sought.

Dana-Sue Urso

What tomorrow brought was a rabbit and two pheasants, skinned and plucked, laying side by side on her doorstep when she opened the door. Ever since Danny's death, someone from town would occasionally give her wild game, knowing she had no one to go hunting for her. But they usually made themselves known, and then they would haggle over how she would pay with the final agreement usually being some bit of sewing in exchange for the meat. But as she looked around, she saw there was no one in the vicinity. And the animals had been prepared which was a first.

Her mouth watered at the thought of those birds and how she would cook them. Rabbit wasn't her favorite, but the kids liked it. And all three of them loved deer and beef, the two types of meat they rarely had. Frowning in thought, she shut the door, wondering.

Jax watched from the edge of the woods. He had gone hunting for himself the day before; it was no great strain to include her and Mr. Billings in his bounty. Jax really only needed a small amount and besides, the widow could use the fresh meat, he was sure. And giving some to his employer was his way of thanking him for the job.

As he turned to head back to town, he tried to figure out a way he could chop some wood for her without her feeling obligated pay him. And then he had to wonder why he even cared. Because he hadn't cared about anything or anyone for so long? Was that the reason? Or was it that he felt sorry for the Caldwell's? He admired the pretty widow for how she took care of her children, working two jobs.

He'd been raised to treat others well, to help wherever he could, especially widows and orphans like the Good Book said. But he knew just by the little bit of time he'd spent with her, that the Widow Caldwell wouldn't take kindly to anyone doing something for nothing. So he spent a good part of the day trying to come up with a way to help her and allow her to keep her pride and dignity.

Yet, again, Fate stepped in when least expected.

Jax was counting inventory in the back room toward the end of that work day. Mr. Billings really was a fair-minded man; he let him sleep on a cot in the store room so he could save money, but this arrangement wouldn't last longer than another month because there was no fireplace or woodstove, nothing to warm it up. This part of the country got mighty cold during winter and seemed to be starting early; October had just rolled in, but the nights were dipping down into the lower 40's and upper 30's already. Jax would have no choice but to spend his hard-earned cash on a hotel room. It really was too bad things didn't work out with Mykaela Caldwell; that arrangement had been perfect for him.

Heavy footfalls sounded behind him. He turned and was dismayed to see the sheriff walk in. The lawman hadn't harassed him this past week, as Jax thought might happen, but he or his deputy had always been visible as Jax worked at the store and made deliveries; it was obvious they were keeping an eye on him.

Not bothering to hide his displeasure, Jax remained squatting in front of a tall stack of feedbags, frowning. "Let me guess: someone's been found dead, and I'm the only suspect." Sometimes he just couldn't keep his big mouth shut. But the sheriff didn't rise to the bait. Little did he know how prophetic those words would one day turn out to be.

Dana-Sue Urso

"Not exactly," was the lawman's cryptic reply. He eyed the younger man with a hint of uncertainty yet determination; Jax continued with his counting, trying to portray an air of indifference.

"Do you know who Mrs. Brooks is?" The sheriff suddenly asked.

Jax nodded. She was the young minister's wife. He'd met her a few days ago when he dropped off a bag of feed for their buggy horse. She had been friendly, sweet-natured, and over 8 months pregnant.

"Well, she fell a few hours ago, tripped on her back porch steps. The reverend found her on the ground, conscious, but in pain." He paused, waiting for Jax's reaction.

"I'm sorry to hear that. I'm sure Doctor Greene will be able to help her." Jax said, not liking the direction he was sure the conversation would head next; he continued pretending to count feed bags.

"Doc Greene is in Denver for a cousin's funeral and won't be back until day after tomorrow." He paused again.

Jax's heart skipped a beat. And then another. And another before speeding up to double-time. He slowly stood up to face the other man and said very carefully, "Surely he has someone who fills in for him whenever he's gone."

Sheriff Hoskins nodded. "Mrs. Davison. She's the wife of our funeral parlor director, but once worked as a nurse. This time, she's in over her head; Mrs. Brook's water's broken, and she's having contractions."

Jax swallowed hard. "I can't help her."

"Can't? Or won't?" the sheriff looked at him disapporvingly. Jax just shook his head, but Sheriff Hoskins was relentless. "Are you, or are you not, a doctor?"

48

Legacy of Love

Taking a deep breath, Jax replied, "I am, but it's been a very long time since I've helped anyone outside of the prison. And even longer since I've delivered a baby. Especially in this kind of difficult circumstance."

"Look, I'm no expert, but even I know that bleeding ain't normal this late in pregnancy," the sheriff remarked. "There is no one else. She'll likely die if you don't help her." She'll likely die anyway, Jax thought to himself, knowing full well that many women don't do well following this kind of accident, not to mention the unborn baby. His heart felt compassion for her, but still he hesitated. He couldn't help wondering, *what if something went wrong, which was likely, would he be blamed? Was there a chance that he could go to prison yet again, for not being able to save her?* That thought made him break out in a cold sweat.

Sheriff Haskin's voice broke into his troubling thoughts. "When I left her, her contractions were 5 minutes apart. And she was in a lot of pain."

The reason Jaxon had become a doctor was because he wanted to help people; hence his obsession to help the Widow Caldwell. But he'd decided months ago not to find work as a doctor; he'd lost the confidence in himself. But now, his instincts were kicking in, and he found old habits were definitely hard to break. Besides, he kept picturing Misty Brook's face in his mind's eye, her kind, gentle, non-judgmental face, and knew he had to help her.

Sighing heavily, he replied, "I'll come."

Satisfied, Sheriff Hoskins followed him as Jax found Mr. Billings to tell him he was leaving for the day, then followed the sheriff to the parsonage behind the church. Neither one of them spoke, but each found it ironic that after the sheriff made it clear just a week ago that he didn't like having Jax in his town, he was now relying on him to save a friend. For that's what the Brooks' were, good friends whom he enjoyed spending time with. The Brooks had been in Riverton for almost 18 months now and carved out a niche among its people. He was a calming influence, peaceful, knowledgeable, patient, and a good listener. His pretty wife was charming and sweet, kind to all, and a great support to her husband. They were well-liked by most of the town, even by those who didn't attend church regularly.

Upon reaching the small one-story house, the sheriff knocked and opened the front door. A couple of ladies whom Jax vaguely recognized by sight if not by name were bustling around the kitchen area, boiling water, folding towels. Their movements were frenzied as if they weren't really sure what to do. Their eyes widened as they saw him, questioning. The sheriff nodded to them, but effectively ignored them, and knocked on a door just off the kitchen. Mrs. Davison opened it and quickly came out, shutting the door.

"It doesn't look good, sheriff," her voice wavered. "She needs a doctor."

"And that's what she's going to get," he told her firmly, indicating Jax. "This is Doctor Dumont."

She didn't bother to hide the look of incredulity on her face. "I thought he worked at the feed store."

"I do," Jax decided he'd better establish some authority to save time and trouble later on. "But I'm also a trained doctor with a medical degree. Now why don't you tell me how Mrs. Brooks is doing. Is she still having contractions?"

"Y-yes, she is. Five minutes apart," Mrs. Davison responded to his commanding tone. "But she keeps bleeding with every contraction. She's getting weaker." Just then a loud moan sounded from behind the closed door followed by soft murmuring.

"Sheriff, do you think I could have some of Doctor Greene's medical supplies brought over?" Jax asked, mentally readying himself to go in the bedroom.

"Of course. He'd be glad to let you have whatever you need." Jax rattled off a list and sent the sheriff off. Then he asked Mrs. Davison to take him to the patient.

Upon entering the room, Jax first saw the reverend sitting beside a bed, holding tightly to his wife's hand. His mouth was white from strain as he gazed lovingly at her, his eyes moist with unshed tears. Mrs. Brooks was holding onto him just as tightly, pain etched in every facet of her face. Her other hand was rubbing at her protruding belly.

Jax took hold of that hand very gently and smiled down at her.

"Mrs. Brooks, Reverend Brooks, my name is Doctor Dumont," the look of relief on the reverend's face gave his confidence a boost.

Mrs. Brooks was distracted from her misery long enough to remark, "But didn't you just deliver our feed?"

"Yes, maam, I did," he confirmed with a grin & a wink aimed at making her more relaxed around him. "I'm a man of many talents."

Mrs. Davison leaned over. "The sheriff vouches for him, Misty, don't worry. You're in good hands." Misty relaxed a little, trust filling her eyes; Jax hoped it wasn't misplaced.

He examined her quickly, but thoroughly, becoming alarmed at what he discovered. About an inch of the baby's life-giving cord was protruding into the birth canal, AND he --

or she -- was breech. The good news was that the bleeding wasn't too severe, just a trickling with each contraction.

She had been in labor about 6 hours, ever since the fall which was when her water broke. Jax knew that she would never be able to deliver the baby normally unless it turned to the correct position, but there wasn't enough time for that to happen naturally since she was in active labor. In order to turn correctly, the baby would need help. However, Jax couldn't turn him without risking putting pressure on the cord and effectively ending the babe's life before it began. The paradox was that unless the baby delivered both he and his mother would die. As much as Jax hated to admit it, there was only one viable option, but even that carried enormous risks. The only positive was that surgery was his area of specialty.

He explained all of this to the reverend and his suffering wife as clearly and gently as he could. He told them their only chance was for Misty to undergo a Caesarean section. He hated to see the look of fear and panic come into the young mother's eyes, but he wanted to be truthful. He knew instinctively that was what they wanted. The reverend, Andrew, blinked rapidly, holding tight to his wife's hand. Jax didn't give them false hope, but encouraged them with the fact that she was young and healthy which increased her chances of surviving the ordeal.

The three of them sat together for a few minutes longer, Andrew asking questions, Jax answering truthfully, confidently. Misty struggled with each contraction, trying to bear the pain with dignity. Jax gave her a small dose of laudanum from Dr. Greene's supplies which helped her to relax even more; he didn't want her to fight the contractions, but he also didn't want her to push when the urge came.

Legacy of Love

The Brooks prayed for guidance, not minding Jax's presence in the least. He was humbled by their faith as they gave over Misty's care and their baby's into His hands and into **his** hands. Saying his own quick, but very heart-felt prayer (something he hadn't been able to do for a long time), Jax prepared to face one of his toughest surgeries.

Mykaela dropped off the children at school then headed to *The Fabric Shop* where she worked for Miss Hanks. As she entered the small store, she was surprised to see several women clustered around, talking excitedly. One of them broke away and came up to her; Tina Michael's son was good friends with Ryan.

"Did you hear the news?" the plump red-head asked excitedly. Without waiting for an answer, she went on. "Misty Brooks had her baby last night."

"Is she OK? The baby?" Mykaela was concerned; she knew the young woman still had a few weeks to go.

"Oh yes, they're both fine. But she had to have a Caesarian. And received a blood transfusion." The portly woman shuttered dramatically.

Mykaela frowned. "Oh dear. Poor Misty."

Tina hurried on with her news. "Doctor Dumont did it."

Mykaela blinked. "**Doctor** Dumont?" she echoed in disbelief. It couldn't be.

"Yeah, I'm sure you've seen him working at the feed store. He's new in town, tall, dark, good-looking." Tina's eyes took on a dreamy quality. "Who would have thought he was a doctor? I mean why in the world would he be working at a feed store? But anyway, he saved her life. And the baby's. Everyone's talking about it."

Dana-Sue Urso

Mykaela could believe it. The Brooks were well-liked and respected. The fact that a mysterious stranger with a secretive past played a critical role in saving her life and the baby's just added to the drama. She wondered what people would say if they found out he'd been in prison for murder. *I wonder if the person he killed was a patient?* She thought to herself. *Maybe, it was later proven that it was simply an accident. I mean, doctors are human, too, just like everyone else. They make mistakes, just like everyone else.* As Mykaela allowed these thoughts to form, they led to other more practical thoughts. Like she probably should have let Jax Dumont rent her room. But then she remembered how dangerous he looked, how far from a doctor he looked. Doc Green was a grandfatherly type with a bushy handle-bar moustache and protruding stomach who shuffled around town with his black bag, offering his services to the people with a soft smile. The doctor back in her home town was younger, but very staid-looking who always wore a bow tie, thin-rimmed glasses, and a pointed moustache. Jaxon Dumont, simply put, looked like an outlaw.

Mykaela wanted to go see Misty, but knew she would need plenty of rest and probably wouldn't want visitors yet. Instead, she was in on the planning by the Ladies' Auxiliary to take evening meals to the Brooks for the next few weeks. Her turn would be in six days; she hoped Misty would be up for a short visit by then.

The time until then passed slowly. Mykaela went into town several times, but never saw Jax. She heard through the grapevine that he was sticking close to the Brook's as Misty recovered. She knew that Misty's life had been in danger and that "the new Doc" was worried about her still. Doc Green came back and pronounced himself pleased and satisfied with Doctor Dumont's handling of the crisis. He, too, kept an eye on Misty while also getting to know the younger doctor.

The day before she was due to take a meal over, Mykaela overheard Doctor Green and Sheriff Hoskins talking at the post office. The doctor was praising Jax's skills, then wondering why he was in Riverton working as a laborer. Mykaela held her breath as she waited for the sheriff's reply; she was standing by the window where the men couldn't see her, pretending to read over some correspondence as she unashamedly listened.

The sheriff didn't betray Jax. In fact, as far as she knew, only she and the sheriff even knew about Jax's prison term. Maybe the deputy and Mr. Billings. She wondered why the sheriff hadn't blasted the news all over town after he confronted Jax that day at her farm as a way of getting him to leave town. But for whatever reason, he'd kept the news to himself and now Misty and her baby were alive and well, thanks to the efforts of an ex-convict-physician.

"I knew him a few years back, saw his skills as a doctor," the sheriff was telling Doc Green. "As for why he's here, I really don't know." He stopped then, almost as if afraid he'd said too much. A moment later, they came out and parted. Mykaela deliberately faced the sheriff.

"That was a very nice thing you just did," she told him.

The sheriff frowned. "I don't understand."

"You sounded sincere when you spoke about Jaxon Dumont's skill as a doctor."

"That's because I was," he confirmed. "He used to work in the prison's infirmary, patched up some pretty bad wounds, even treated the men during a cholera outbreak. The prison doctor used to tell me all the time how fortunate he felt at having such a fine physician to assist him." He shook his head. "It never made much sense to me that a man with that much dedication to preserving human life could just up and kill someone. But I believed that he had."

"Are you sure he did?" Mykaela surprised herself by asking. "I mean, he was released. Maybe someone else made a mistake."

Sheriff Hoskins looked off in the distance. "I just don't know. I mean, if I had never met the man before he came here, I would have believed he could be anything from a hired gun to an outlaw to a lazy drift-about. And easily believe he was a killer. But after seeing how he saved Misty and her baby . . ." he shook his head. "I don't know what to think. I guess I'll just keep watching and learning." He looked down at her. "I probably shouldn't tell you this, but I wired Glendale, the town where he was convicted, to see why he was released. I can't reconcile what I know from what my gut tells me."

"And what does your gut say?"

He took a deep breath. "That maybe looks and actions can be deceiving, that there are two sides to every story. That maybe, just maybe, innocent men do get convicted." With that thought, he tipped his hat to her and strode off towards the jail, leaving Mykaela with a lot to think about.

Mykaela drove her wagon up to the Brooks' door the next day, her heart heavy. They'd had a large deluge of icy, cold rain last night, much of it coming in through a couple of leaks in her roof. Even now, a frigid wind was blowing, her cape doing little to keep her warm. She needed a new coat or fur-lined wrap along with all the other items her family needed along with all the repairs needed at the farm, but what she needed the most was the money to pay for it all.

Determined not to be a sour-puss in front of the Brooks, she knocked on the door, holding a basket full of chunky vegetable soup with bits of beef (a wrapped package of beef had been waiting for her day before yesterday), sour-dough biscuits, and pickles. It wasn't much, but there was plenty of it.

A few minutes later, she was sitting at the kitchen table, talking to the reverend. She had said a quick hello to Misty who was still bed-ridden and dutifully admired the baby who was doing very well, considering his inauspicious start in a confusing world; Misty informed her proudly that his name was Christopher, Dr. Dumont's middle name. Neither doctor was in attendance at the moment. Reverend Brooks offered a cup of coffee before she headed back out into the cold. She refused at first, not wanting to bother him, but he had insisted. The hot drink filled her with a delicious warmth that seeped all the way to her toes.

They discussed the weather which had suddenly, though not surprisingly for this part of the country, turned bitter cold, a sure sign that winter was well on the way. He told her that Misty was very weak, but getting stronger every day; the ladies from the Ladies Auxiliary took turns coming in every morning and afternoon to help care for the baby which was a great blessing to him and his wife.

Then he asked her how she was doing.

"Oh, I'm fine," she responded too brightly.

"Glad to hear it," he said, looking at her intently. "How are the children?"

"They're fine, too," Even to her own ears, she sounded like a fraud, but they all really were fine. It's just that they could be better. Reverend Brooks didn't say anything, just kept watching her, a knowing look in his eyes. She had trouble meeting them, almost as though she had something to hide which she didn't. She just didn't want to trouble him with her problems after almost losing his son and wife. After a tense moment, she took a deep breath. "Can I ask you something?"

He nodded his head. "Of course."

"What if you knew something about someone that wasn't good, something from his past." She hesitated. "But when you met that person, he was totally different from what you would expect from what you knew about his past. Then you're put in a position to either trust that person . . . or not. How do you figure out the right thing to do?"

"You don't always," he replied, thoughtfully. "Sometimes, you have to rely on your instincts."

"But how do you trust that?"

"Well, if it were me, I'd turn it over to the Lord in prayer. Then I'd wait to see what He thinks."

"I have prayed. A lot," she told him. "And my instincts tell me to trust this person."

"But . . .,"

"But what if I'm wrong?"

"That's where you have to trust God."

Mykaela nodded, her expression still troubled. The reverend went on. "I do know that holding someone's past against them, especially if they've repented or paid for their mistakes, is not charitable." He reached across for her hand, urging her to look at him. "Perhaps if you talked to this person, you would find the answers you're seeking.   Mykaela gave him a little smile. "Somehow, I get the feeling you know exactly who and what I'm talking about."

He leaned back, casually picking up his cup and taking a sip, deliberately not saying anything. He didn't deny or confirm that he had been having some interesting conversations with a certain young doctor.

Ten minutes later as she was driving through town towards home, Mykaela thought about her conversation with Reverend Brooks. Although young, he had a wisdom beyond his years. He and his wife were known for their charity work and had occasionally insisted that she accept offerings of food or clothing. The reverend's understanding and compassion were soothing to her troubled soul, and what he said now made sense. Jaxon Dumont had more than proven himself trustworthy. What more did she want?

The feed store loomed closer. She wondered if he even still worked there. Maybe he had quit and decided to set up a practice. But their town couldn't really support two doctors. Her heart skipped a beat as she thought about the possibility that maybe he would leave in search of a town who did need a doctor. But wouldn't he have already done that? So many unanswered questions, that was the crux of her problem with him. *'Perhaps if you talked to this person, you would find the answers you're seeking.'* She went over the reverend's words. *Maybe he's right. I should have done that in the first place.* Determined to get to the bottom of things, she parked the wagon in front of the store and went in search of Doctor Dumont.

CHAPTER 5

Jax glanced out of the window to gauge the time. About 4:00 or so he figured. He would finish cleaning out the storeroom, then head over to the Brooks to check on Misty. So far, she was recovering as well as could be expected. She was understandably weak and tired, had lost more blood than he would have liked and had needed a blood transfusion which thank God, had gone well. With proper rest, nourishing food, and attentive care, she should make a full recovery.

As for the baby, he was healthy and strong. Unfortunately, Misty was too weak to nurse him, but a formula had been made that was working just fine; baby Christopher had a great appetite. Jax still felt a little embarrassed and unworthy that the little tyke was named for him. In fact, his guilt had weighed on him so much that he had felt compelled to tell the reverend -- during one of their many chats since the delivery -- that he had been in prison. He'd half expected to be thrown out, but Andrew Brooks had simply looked at him and said, "I thank God that you were released in time to come to Riverton at the exact time you did, or I would be a widower right now. And fatherless"

His complete belief and faith in him had nearly done him in. No one had believed in him in a long time, including his own family, and he had felt a sudden urge to weep. That had been 3 days ago, and Jax still couldn't quite get used to the fact that he was still more than welcome in the Brook's household, let alone allowed to continue to care for Misty.

He found that he looked forward to his evening visits. Misty was so sweet and trusting, always grateful for anything

Legacy of Love

he did for her, no matter how small. And he enjoyed talking to the reverend. They would sit for awhile each evening discussing everything from the war to how many territories were becoming states to how bad the winter was likely to be. They discussed religion and God and faith, something that had been lacking in Jax's life for quite some time. Andrew Brooks always knew the right thing to say, or so it seemed, and Jax found himself opening up to him about his lack of faith these past few years. He also believed that God had abandoned him.

The reverend was never judgmental, only encouraging, reminding Jax that God had never left him, but had carried him through the dark times. Jax used to believe, but something had changed during the war which led to a complete lack of faith that day in Glendale when the guilty verdict was read. But now, for the first time in several years, Jax felt the stirrings of faith once again. And maybe they had always been there; he'd never stopped sending up little prayers during times of need, although never really expecting an answer. Until recently.

Jax finished his chores and began locking up. Ever since Mr. Billings had found out he was a doctor, he had trusted Jax to lock up for him. Today was Friday, and the store closed at 4:30.

As he was pulling closed the big doors in the front, he saw Mykaela hurrying up the steps to the platform. As she stepped up on the dock, a gust of wind nearly pushed her back down the steps. She clutched her cloak around her, brushing errant strands of hair out of her face. Her nose and cheeks were slightly reddened, and she wasn't wearing mittens. Jax frowned at that. Surely she knew how important gloves were in these cold temperatures.

"Good afternoon, Mr. Dumont," she said, adding shyly, "Or should I say Dr. Dumont."

"How 'bout just Jax," he replied. "Come in out of this wind." He led the way to the office which was still warm from a small cook stove even though Jax had already banked the fire. Mykaela held her hands over the top, basking in the warmth.

"You really should wear mittens." He gently admonished her.

"I know," she agreed. "My old ones are too frayed. I'm knitting myself new ones." Taking a deep breath, she looked up at him, her courage almost leaving her as she met his hooded dark gray eyes. His hair was mussed, falling over his forehead, and he needed a shave. Dressed in the inevitable dark clothes, she found it very hard to believe he was a doctor. It wasn't the fact that Tina was right about his looks. And it wasn't that he wasn't smart enough; he had a natural intelligence that was easy to see.

But he had that aura about him, dark and dangerous. He was an enigma, full of secrets. Doctors were supposed to be happy and jolly; Jax was about as far from jolly as the devil himself. Some doctors were studious; Jax didn't look in the least bit scholarly. In fact, the thought of him sitting through a medical lecture on the human anatomy seemed ludicrous. Yet, he had saved Misty's life by performing surgery so he had to have had medical training. There were just so many inconsistencies.

She thought about the troubles she faced at home, all the needed repairs and chores, she thought about her children and their needs, she thought about what the reverend had said about trusting God and her instincts. And she suddenly knew

62

what she had to do.   Just like that, she was filled with certainty.

Looking Jax in the eye, she said, "I wanted to apologize for what happened that day the sheriff came by. I shouldn't have backed out of our agreement. I should have given you the benefit of the doubt, but instead I condemned you without so much as a by-your-leave. And I'm sorry for that, too." She paused to take a breath, then hurried on before he could say anything. "So, I was hoping you would forgive me and agree to rent my room under our original bargain." She stopped, so afraid he'd say no, her expression earnest. She desperately needed him if she was going to survive the coming winter.

Jax gave no indication of how he felt about what she'd said because he couldn't quite believe it. She was asking *him* for forgiveness when she'd done nothing wrong? Was it possible that yet another person believed in him? Unbelievable.

"Don't you want to know the circumstances behind my imprisonment first?"

"Not really," she assured him, shaking her head. "If and when you're ready to tell me, I'll listen."

She seemed so sincere, Jax found himself believing her. "I do need a place to stay for the winter; I've been living here at the store, but it's already getting too cold to stay here for much longer."

Mykaela was glad to hear that he wasn't moving on yet. And said so.

"I agree to our original terms. And thank you." He held out his hand and felt a tingle creep up his arm as she placed her smaller hand in his. Her fingers were calloused, a reminder of the hard life she led. They were also very cold.

He turned to look at her palm, frowning at the bumps and cracks that ran up to her fingers. She mistook his look as disgust and tried to pull her hand away, cheeks reddening.

"I'm sorry for the way my hand looks," she apologized, clearly embarrassed. But Jax wouldn't let go.

He covered her hand with both of his to warm it.

"Mykaela, you have the hands of a woman who works hard to take care of her family. I'm concerned about their condition. They bleed sometimes, don't they." It wasn't a question.

Startled, she said, "Yes, sometimes, but that's to be expected."

Jax ran his own calloused fingers along her fingers and palm, unknowingly sending chills up her arm. "I have calluses, too, but they don't bleed. You need to rub udder ointment on them every morning and night. That will stop the bleeding and keep the roughness down." He released her much to her relief. "I'll bring some when I move in. Is tonight OK?"

"Um, yes, of course, that would be fine," Mykaela felt befuddled, her skin prickling where he'd touched her. Resisting the urge to rub her hand down her skirt, she made to leave. He walked her to the door, making plans to arrive at the farm by suppertime, after he'd checked on Misty.

Mykaela drove away from town feeling as though a weight had been lifted. She was going to have help, from a doctor no less, and maybe she could worry just a little bit less about the immediate future.

Moving in to Mykaela's home went smoothly. Jax felt a huge relief to have somewhere pleasant to stay for the winter.

Legacy of Love

He didn't mind the perpetually cool loft area as the bed was next to the stovepipe where it came up through the floor on its way to the roof; that small area was fairly warm when he went to bed. And he didn't expect to spend a lot of time in the room other than for sleeping. He was also glad to be able to help the Caldwells with the chores and upkeep of the farm that just could not be done by a woman and two small children.

Jax spent most of his spare time away from the feed store during the remaining few weeks of October, hauling and chopping wood, fixing the two roof leaks, strengthening clotheslines, and a myriad of other tasks that had been neglected over the last couple of years. He also gradually took over some of the less glamorous chores like mucking out stalls and cleaning the outhouse. After just over two weeks, the small farm was looking much better.

Jax didn't want to intrude on the family. Mornings during the week weren't too difficult as he was up earlier than they were and used the outside door when he left his loft. He had plenty to do in the mornings and usually waited until the children were on their way to school before heading in for his own breakfast.

After work, he still had more than enough to occupy his time, but Mykaela always insisted that he join them for the evening meal. Sometimes he did, sometimes he wasn't able to. When he was with the children, they didn't talk much at first. At least not to him. Even Ryan, who had seemed to have an unending supply of questions when they first met, remained pretty quiet whenever he was with them.

In the evenings, Mykaela cleaned up the dishes and helped the kids with homework. She always invited him to stay, but he would find something that needed doing in the

65

barn or on the property. He didn't want Mykaela to regret her decision in having as her boarder and with him around, she would be reminded that he was, after all, still an ex-convict, doctor or no.

On weekends, he usually worked a half day on Saturday and spent the rest of the day hunting for fresh meat. The first time he brought home a rabbit, she knew with certainty who had been dropping off the meat on her doorstep. But she never said anything as she didn't want to embarrass him. If he'd wanted her to know, he would have told her. Now, of course, since he was living with them, hunting was just something he did naturally, without fuss. And she accepted his offerings without murmur.

Sundays were quiet days; for those first two weeks, he refused Mykaela's offers to attend church with them; he was still finding his way back to God and just couldn't quite bring himself to attend yet. Talking to the reverend was helping, though.

On his 3rd Sunday morning at the Caldwells, he came in from the morning chores with a fresh supply of milk and eggs; the children usually performed these tasks, but he had finished his chores early so he went ahead and did them. Mykaela was at the stove mixing something in a pan that smelled wonderful. Living here and eating her cooking was not exactly a hardship, Jax thought to himself although he still had only sat with them a handful of times. He still felt a little uncomfortable being around them, felt he didn't have the right. He wasn't sure if this feeling stemmed from the fact that he hadn't been around decent folk in a long time or if he felt tainted because of his history and didn't want any of it to rub off. But Mykaela never made him feel unwelcome, in fact went out of her way to ensure that he was comfortable. When he was with the family, he would often catch one of them staring at him, then quickly look away; he tried not to feel self-conscious although it was difficult sometimes.

As time passed, thought, they began to be more comfortable in his presence. In fact, this morning, the kids were unusually bright and cheerful, chattering incessantly about this and that. Mykaela was very patient and responded with her attention divided between them and her cooking. Reminded of his mother, he was overcome by melancholy, which distracted him enough that he missed a question directed at him.

With a quick shake of his head, he said, "Sorry, could you repeat that?"

"I was wondering if you'd like to ride into town with us this morning. For church."

He hadn't been to church since before he left home. At first it was because of no opportunity. For the last six months, however, it was because he felt completely unworthy to be in God's house when he held such bitterness inside. But now, he hesitated. His talks with Reverend Brooks were helping him to change his perspective of God. He was realizing that his anger towards God had begun to fade, that he no longer blamed Him for his misfortunes. He found he wanted to attend the service and so he accepted her offer.

The four of them caused a bit of a stir as they walked into the sanctuary, but most people smiled or nodded their good mornings. It really was a friendly town, so much different than Glendale, Jax thought.

After the services, Reverend Brooks made a point to talk to him, telling him how glad he was that Jax was there.

Dana-Sue Urso

"How're you settling in at the Caldwell place?"

"Pretty well actually," Jax answered. "Mykaela is a gracious landlady."

He accompanied the reverend to his home to check on Misty while Mykaela took the children on home for lunch; Jax planned on spending the rest of the day hunting as he hadn't caught anything the day before. Mykaela spent the afternoon ironing some clothes she had washed yesterday including some of Jax's. She smiled as she recalled how she had insisted that he allow her to wash his clothes; he had insisted right back that that wasn't part of the bargain. She had pointed out that the daily chores of milking and gathering eggs weren't either. They had gone back and forth with her the ultimate victor.

It was such a little thing, and she truly didn't mind in the least. With that thought, she headed upstairs with a small pile of clothing; he didn't have a large wardrobe, but then, neither did she. However, as she looked around the room, she realized just how sparse his belongings were. On a hook by the washstand hung a pair of jeans and the pair of dark pants he'd worn to church. Shaving paraphernalia clustered around the wash basin. On the dresser sat his saddlebags, a comb, a small container of tooth powder, and a bottle of some sort of liquid, presumably shampoo. In her hands, she held two shirts, a pair of socks (two more pairs were downstairs that she wanted to darn that evening), two handkerchiefs, a flannel over shirt, one pair of long-johns, and a vest. Almost everything was black, dark red, or or dark blue.

She debated whether to set the clothes on the neatly made bed (not her doing) or put them in the dresser. Curiosity got the better of her. She opened the small drawer on the top right; it was empty except for two handkerchiefs. She placed the others beside it and opened the drawer on the left. A small purse was nestled next to the leather satchel that she already knew contained his release papers. But lying on top was a photograph.

Quickly placing the rest of the clothes in the empty second drawer down, she picked up the picture. There was a crease down the middle as though it had been folded and tucked away. The surface was rough, scratchy, but the people in it could easily be seen. A man and woman who looked to be in their 30's sat side by side on a bench, a young girl about five or six years old sat between them; she had her arms entwined through the arms of her parents and was openly showing her teeth, the front two missing. The woman rested a hand on the girl's leg. Standing behind them, looking over the shoulder of the man, stood a teenage boy, maybe 14 or 15. He had one hand on his father's shoulder. To his left stood another boy a few years younger, his hand on his mother's shoulder.

Mykaela easily recognized the younger boy as Jax; there was no mistaking those eyes even though the picture was in black and white. The most unusual thing about the photo was that the subjects appeared so relaxed, almost smiling. In fact, Jax's eyes held a mischievous light that the photographer had managed to capture; the care-free look on his face was in such contrast to the world-weary look he usually wore that her heart ached for him.

Mykaela assumed the people were his family, a subject he was always reluctant to talk about. She let her imagination run wild as she replaced the photo and headed back downstairs. Maybe they had been killed in an Indian uprising.

Dana-Sue Urso

Or maybe they had died of some dreaded disease such as Typhoid. Or maybe there had been a fire. She didn't even stop to question why she believed the people in that picture were dead. She could tell by the expressions on their faces that this was a family who loved each other; they weren't posed in the usual stiff way, but were comfortable and at ease.

Jax had spoken briefly of his mother in relation to her cooking, and there had been a soft quality to his voice, a remembrance of something good. But then he had shut down, clearly not wanting to talk about anything so personal; he'd had a hurt look in his eyes which she now believed was caused by the loss of his family.

She knew what it was like to be alone without parents or siblings or even aunts and uncles. But she at least had her children who were a great comfort to her. Who did Jax have? Was there anybody who cared about him? She didn't even know if he had any friends. Her heart once again went out to him, and she was even more determined to get to the bottom of his secrets so that maybe she could help in some small way.

As the day wore on, Mykaela began to worry. Jax had been gone since early morning, and it was now dark. Her thoughts strayed to the day when her husband didn't come home, and she felt a cold fear run through her. She prayed fervently that this day would not be a repeat. Her prayers were answered a short time later. Jax came in, stamping his feet and clapping his hands, heading right for the fireplace where Mykaela had kept a full fire burning.

"Whew! It is cold!" Jax announced, pulling off his gloves and warming his hands. Mykaela noticed how red his ears were and decided that she would knit him a scarf. As soon as possible.

Legacy of Love

"Here's a cup of coffee," she handed him a mug which he accepted gratefully. He then told her that he had managed to bring in two rabbits and a deer.

"A deer?" she exclaimed excitedly. "Really?"

Jax nodded. "Yep! A young buck. He was standing by a pond, trying to break the ice with his hooves. He didn't even see me. I almost felt guilty bringing him down." He grinned. "Almost."

The transformation of his face took Mykaela's breath away. He looked years younger, his eyes alive and sparkling with good humor, the smile smoothing away the hardness of his features. But what caused her sudden awareness was how breathtakingly handsome he was at that moment. She had always considered him good-looking in a rough, cowboy kind of way. His face held strength and his dark features gave him a rakish air that was attractive. But his eyes were usually guarded, even cold and distant at times, and she couldn't remember ever seeing him grin.

Realizing she was staring, something she was dismayed to think she did a lot, she turned to the stove. Not one to hold back something she felt strongly about, she remarked casually, "Go ahead and sit down. I kept your supper warm. And you should smile more often."

Jax had been heading to the table and it took several seconds for her last words to hit his brain. He paused in the act of pulling out his chair. Grin wiped off his face, he uttered, "What?"

Mykaela didn't answer right away. She placed a hot plate in front of him heaped with rice, beans, and cornbread, topped his coffee cup, and busied herself once more at the stove.

"You should smile more often." She finally repeated.

"Really? Why?" He sounded annoyed, although with her back to him she couldn't be sure.

"Because it looks good on you," Holding a towel, she turned back to him and leaned against the counter, a soft smile on her own face. "You wouldn't scare so many people."

He frowned, his fork halfway to his mouth. "Who do I scare?"

"Oh, come on," she flicked the towel good-naturedly in his direction. "You wear dark clothes, have dark hair and eyes, and always look ready for a fight. Who DON"T you scare?"

She was teasing him, he was sure of it. OK, almost sure. He ate in silence for a few moments.

"I don't usually have a lot to smile about," he reluctantly admitted.

"So why the dark clothes?"

"I like the color black."

"I'm not so sure black is a color."

Jax decided that this was a strange conversation to be having with his landlady. Up until today, most of their exchanges had been about the upkeep of the property, some of the goings on in town, and updates on Misty and the baby. Mykaela had asked a leading question every now and then that was more personal in nature, but he'd always been able to redirect her.

He was confused and thrown off-guard by her statement about him smiling. He truly didn't have much to smile about because his life was a long sad story that he didn't want to burden anyone else with. Riding back to the farm after shooting the deer, he had felt a modicum of pride, the good kind, where a man could feel satisfied about accomplishing something. He had felt the same way when he knew for sure that Misty and Baby Christopher would be OK. But these were the first times in years that he actually felt good about himself. It almost made him giddy.

When he'd stepped into the house and saw Mykaela smiling at him, he had felt a rush of warmth and belonging surge through him. This had only served to raise the good feelings he'd had about providing meat for the family. And so he had smiled. But, he didn't feel at ease now. Not knowing what to say, he kept his head down and finished eating.

Mykaela settled down into her chair by the fireplace and picked up her sewing. When Jax was done eating, he wasn't sure what to do. Mykaela had taken care of the evening chores. The kids were in bed, but it was kind of early to go up to his own bed. Usually he found some chore to do in the barn, but it was so cold out, he didn't want to leave the coziness of the cabin. He needed to clean his rifle, but wasn't sure sitting with Mykaela for an hour was a good idea. She was in a strange mood tonight and some sixth sense warned him that she wasn't done with him.

Deciding that he needed to do something to keep himself occupied, he pulled a small bench close to the fire across from her and set to work; the familiarity of gun cleaning would relax him. The atmosphere was pleasant enough, Mykaela humming softly while she worked, asking an occasional question about his day of hunting. 15 minutes went by. Jax was almost finished with his self-appointed task when he picked up on something he hadn't noticed before. Mykaela was using one foot to gently rock her chair back and forth, but the other foot was tapping the floor in quick motion. He then saw that she was knitting, something she did most evenings, but tonight, she was knitting so fast, her hands were almost a blur. The click-clack of the needles sounded like the tapping of a telegraph. Glancing at her face, he saw her biting down on her bottom lip. She was nervous about something, he'd bet his last dollar.

He contemplated that as he rubbed oil into the barrel. Was it him? Was she scared to be around him? She hadn't seemed anxious when he'd gotten home, but this was one of the few nights that they actually spent an evening in each other's company. He'd been there last night, but the kids had been allowed to stay up later as it was not a school night, and they may have seemed a kind of buffer. And anyway, he'd spent a good portion of the time in his chilly room, reading over a medical journal Doc Adams had given him.

It depressed him to think she was nervous around him, but he wouldn't blame her if she was. He could reassure her until the cows came home that he would never harm her, but what did she really know about him? Just that he'd been in prison and was a doctor. He wasn't sure the latter always outweighed the former.

He was about to just get things out in the open when she beat him to the punch, but not in the way he expected.

"Jax, I wanted to talk to you about something," she began. "Well, actually, I wanted to ask you something . . .OK, I have something to tell you . . *and* ask you . . ." Her voice trailed off, and she refused to look at him. Jax began to feel a little nervous himself, and his mouth went dry as he waited for clarification.

Mykaela looked squarely at him, took a deep breath, and said, "I was putting your clothes away today and came-across-the-photo-graph-of-you-and-your-family."

CHAPTER 6

The last was said so fast that it took a few seconds for her words to actually make sense. Nodding once, aware of where this was headed, he said, "I see." He began to methodically put away his gun cleaning supplies, deliberately not looking at her. He was pretty sure she'd probably snooped a little, and he didn't really blame her. It was his fault for not putting the picture away, deep inside his satchel where he usually kept it; although he didn't know her very well, he suspected that she would have respected his privacy enough not to open his personal papers. He had awoken from one of his nightmares last night, heart pounding, limbs trembling, and had taken out the photo as he usually found some solace in looking at it.

"I suppose you're wondering about it," he remarked after a few moments.

"I was, am, but I truly don't want to pry," she told him. "I'm curious, I admit. But if you don't want to tell me about them, I'll understand. I know we don't know each other all that well, but you are a mystery." She smiled a little. "And I've always liked mysteries."

She was right, they didn't know each other, but he hadn't felt this content with his life since before the war. It just seemed natural for him to be here, now, with this family, helping them. They had taken him in even knowing what he was, but without the full story. Maybe he owed it to her to tell her the truth. But it was a long and not so pretty story, one that he'd never told anyone the entirety of. He had spoken of some details of his life here and there with Reverend Brooks, more as a way of cleansing his soul and trying to find his way back to God, but not because he necessarily wanted to share his life with someone.

As a physician, he knew the importance of not keeping things bottled up inside. The power of talking and opening up was incredible, but not so easy. Plus, one had to find the right person to open up to, one who wouldn't judge, one who would try to understand. His own family hadn't been able to do that. How could a stranger? But sometimes, a friend could listen and just be there. Like the reverend. Like this pretty woman before him. And she *was* pretty. The firelight cast golden highlights upon her hair, a few strands escaping from the braid hanging over one shoulder to fall into her face as she bent over her knitting. When she looked directly at him, her eyes reflected the fire's light, turning them a rich sparkling chocolate. Her pert nose sat above a cupid's mouth with soft red lips. Jax felt a rush of heat spread through him and immediately chastised himself. Picking up the fire poker, he moved the wood around, forcing himself not to look at her.

Mykaela thought he was angry with her. She felt remorse for looking at the picture and promptly apologized.

"It's OK, really," he assured her. "It's natural to be curious." He paused. "It's . . . difficult for me to talk about my past. But it's not all bad." He wanted her to know that his life was the way it was because of his own doing, not because of his family.

"That photo was taken about 17 years ago. I was 12, my brother Jerrod was 14, and our sister Jenna was 6." He told her how he had fought against having to wear a bow tie that he thought made him look ridiculous.

"But you're not wearing a tie in the photo," she pointed out.

76

Legacy of Love

Jax couldn't help the grin. "I know. I took it off seconds before the photographer took the picture. My mother had instructed us not to move a muscle, so I knew she wouldn't turn around to check on me. The reason my head is tilted is because I had just pulled it off, away from my neck. The photographer was too busy with his plates and lighting that he didn't even notice."

"I have a feeling your mother noticed when she saw the picture," Mykaela remarked dryly.

Jax snorted. "She was most definitely NOT happy. I thought it was a great picture so she let me have it when I went away to medical school." He broke off here, staring into the fire, his lightheartedness gone. Mykaela waited, knowing instinctively that his tale was going to turn more serious. After a few moments, Jax quickly told her that he'd grown up on a small cattle ranch east of Boulder. He and his brother were taught the ropes of cattle raising, but it was Jerrod who found his calling. Jax had other ideas about where his life was heading.

"My father had our lives all planned out," he explained. "Jerrod would take over the actual running of the ranch someday, and I would be his right-hand man. I actually loved the horses more than the cattle and figured I'd become a horse breeder -- let Jerrod have the cows. But my father is a proud man; it's an unfortunate trait among the Dumont males, I'm afraid. He wanted his sons to follow in the footsteps of the Dumont men, from my great-grandfather down. It was tradition, it was what was expected. I'm a lot like my father which meant that I liked to have my own way." Jax's tone grew rueful. "This led to many clashes of the wills between him and me. My mother used to say that when the Dumonts are on the warpath, watch out!" He got up to put the bench back and settled in the chair opposite Mykaela, gazing once again into the flames.

"When I was 14, my parents went on a summer trip to Chicago to visit old friends," he continued. "Neither Jerrod nor I wanted to go so my parents allowed us to stay home. Jerrod was 16 and stayed in the house with our foreman. But I got to stay with my best friend, Mick, who lived in town. His father was the town doctor. We spent that summer helping Doc O'Malley in his clinic. He let us watch some of his surgeries and treatments, go on housecalls. I became fascinated with the patients and what ailed them. Mick and I made a pact that we would both become great doctors and work side-by-side in Boulder some day." Jax reached out to throw a log onto the fire. "My mother was completely supportive although I suspect she thought I was just going through a phase at first. But my father, well, he was NOT pleased."

Mykaela interrupted. "But I would think that a parent would be proud to have a son as a doctor. I know I would."

"You have to understand that my father's pride would not let him veer from his goals for me. I was supposed to run part of his ranch and that was that. I continued to learn the cattle business, but my fascination with medicine didn't wane like he hoped it would. I stayed at home for a year after I graduated from school to please him, partly. But also to wait for Mick. He was a year behind me. We had both been accepted into medical school in Philadelphia and were to start the fall after he graduated." He paused to take a deep breath. "I didn't tell my parents I'd applied let alone been accepted until the day before I was to leave. Looking back on it now, I can see that it wasn't very responsible of me to have held back from them. My mother didn't know whether to be happy and proud or sad and upset. My father had no such struggle; he was furious. He even forbade me to go, swore that I would be cut off from the family. I knew it was an idle threat, at least I'd hoped it was." He paused here, leaning forward in the chair towards the fire, hands clasped. "My father and I had an unusual relationship. I truly believed he loved me and always wanted what was best for me. He was hard on us, Jerrod and I, but also very encouraging of our efforts. As long as we tried our best, it was OK to make mistakes. He was a patient teacher, fair-minded, and treated us with respect especially as we grew older. But he had trouble showing his emotions, wouldn't let go of his pride long enough to admit when he was wrong. I think that's one of the reasons he was so tenacious about my continuing on in the family business." He paused again, gathering his thoughts. "As hard on me and my brother as he was, he was the opposite when it came to my mother and sister. It was easy to see how much my parents adored each other. My mother had a way with him that was a sight to behold. Don't get me wrong; he wasn't wrapped around her little finger, and he was the definite head of the household, but she could get him to talk and open up when no one else ever could. He smiled more when she was around then at any other time. With Jenna, he allowed her to learn some ranching skills, but insisted she also learn the more womanly pursuits." He smiled to himself as he thought of his little sister. She was always such a tag-a-long, wanting to be where he was, do what he was doing. He led her into more than her fair share of trouble. She could be a little nosy-body and a brat, but he adored her.

Dana-Sue Urso

He shared some of these thoughts with Mykaela who responded with "I guess what you're telling me is that there's hope for Ryan and Rachel to become friends some day."

"Absolutely!" He wholeheartedly agreed. "Anyway, I ended up leaving with Mick, my father assuring me that he wasn't paying my college tuition. Which was fine. I had other means and planned on working. I won't bore you with the details of medical school, but Mick and I both graduated at the top of our class and returned home. We'd been home for vacations and holidays of course, but my father and I never talked about the course my life was taking ever again. I knew he was still displeased with me. By the time I graduated, we'd come to a sort of silent mutual understanding; he wouldn't nag me to become a rancher, and I would gladly work on the ranch whenever I was home. By the time we finished medical school, Mick and I had lofty goals, unfortunately. There was no way Boulder could support 2 doctors at that time, not full time anyway, and definitely not 3. Doc O'Malley semi-retired which allowed Mick to set up practice, and I was OK with that. In medical school, I found that I had a calling for surgery and accepted a three year internship at the hospital in Denver. My father didn't say much; I think he was finally accepting the fact that I could lead my own life. So, I spent the next three years honing my skills as a surgeon." He leaned back in the chair, feet stretched out, hands cradling his mug. He looked very relaxed, but Mykaela saw how tightly he held the cup, the lines forming across his brow as he thought about his next words.

He went on to explain how he had been keeping up with the progress of the Civil War which had broken out about the time he finished medical school. He sympathized with the

Legacy of Love

South, but firmly believed that the nation should stay united; he also had a deep conviction that slavery was morally wrong.

As he read more and more in the papers about the war's devastation, he became convinced that he could help. Working in a field hospital was the best way to sharpen his skills as a surgeon. That thought, once planted, grew and grew, until he followed his heart and joined the Union army, again without telling his parents first.

"It was my life to live and no one else's, or so I finally told my father after I'd enlisted. He was livid that I would willingly endanger myself for a 'fool's war.' How I wished at the time that just once, he would see my side of things and give me his support," Jax said with regret in his voice. "But I learned that you should be careful what you wish for."

After some initial training, he was assigned to a mobile field hospital in Pennsylvania. He told her of how he and the other doctor spent most of their time patching up soldiers' wounds from bullets, bayonets, and shrapnel from cannon fire. He glossed over the more gruesome details of amputating limbs and treating repugnant diseases such as lice infestations, dysentery, and foot rot.

"After a year of seeing how badly the human body can be maimed, I began to pray more earnestly for an end to all the suffering," Jax shook his head. "There were so many young men, *boys* . . . . ., all willing to fight for what they believed in. I just wanted it to be over." He stopped speaking for a moment, his eyes meeting hers. She gave him a gentle smile that caused his heart to speed up a little.

"What you did for those soldiers, well, it was wonderful. So selfless. I'm sure they must have been grateful," she said.

He shrugged. "Some were. Some weren't."

81

"How long did you stay in? Until the end?"

She was troubled to see a shadow cross his face. When he didn't say anything, she leaded towards him. "What is it Jax? Did something happen?"

He nodded, not looking at her. "Oh yes, something happened." Silence.

"It's perfectly alright if you don't want to talk about it," she told him quietly. "I'll understand and won't be offended."

More silence, a hard swallow, and then, "In May of 1864, we received word that the front line was moving north which meant that our troops were being defeated. Everyone grabbed what they could, saddled horses, packed up. Most of our patients were able to ride out. All, but one." A pregnant pause. "Evan had been belly shot. I spent a lot of time searching for and digging out that bullet. He survived, but he was way too weak to move, let alone ride a horse. The only option was a wagon, but even then, I doubted he would survive. I waited as long as I could; packed my own things, his things, padded down a wagon. The other doctor and the aides tried to convince me that we wouldn't make it, the wagon would be too slow." He looked at her with anger reflected in his eyes. "They wanted me to leave him behind." He shook his head in frustration. "I took an oath to care for the wounded, not leave them for the wolves." He told her how he'd never forget the look on Evan's face as the young soldier asked him if he would be left behind. When Jax told him there was no way he'd leave him, the boy had actually started crying. "I managed to get him on the wagon by myself; everyone else was gone."

Legacy of Love

He stopped when Mykaela gasped and retorted indignantly, "How callous of them. What kind of men were they?"

"The kind who didn't want to get caught by the Rebs. And I don't blame them. I drove as fast as I dared to, but he became more and more pale, his cries of pain got louder. But I didn't have a choice; we had to get out of there!" He rubbed a hand down his face, suddenly weary. Mykaela had a bad feeling.

"In the end, it didn't matter; the others were right after all. We'd only driven about an hour when we were suddenly surrounded by a company of Confederate soldiers. They knew right off by my clothing and insignia that I was a doctor. The captain in charge took my gun and knife, then ordered his men to stand down, not seeing me as much of a threat. He didn't seem overly aggressive so I figured he was a reasonable man. I explained how sick and injured Evan was and asked if I could still drive him in the wagon." Jax explained how the captain had climbed in the wagon bed and looked the boy over, verbalizing his agreement that the young boy was indeed very weak. "Then, he took my knife and slit the boy's throat."

Mykaela gasped in horror, so shocked she didn't know what to say. But Jax went on with a fierceness she'd not heard in his voice before.

"I reacted without thinking. I jumped him, knocking us both out of the wagon, then pummeled him as fast and hard as I could." Jax shook his head in remembered frustration. "At that moment, I didn't care that there were 20 Rebs standing around who would undoubtedly kill me for attacking their captain. All I knew was that a 19 year old boy was murdered for no reason at all; it wasn't like he was a threat to any of them." He took a deep breath. "The soldiers pulled me off and some cocked their rifles. But the captain stopped them. I never really knew why, but I at least had the satisfaction of knowing that I was the cause of his black eye, bloody lip, and lacerated cheek. Unfortunately, the captain, although not wanting me dead for some mysterious reason, took exception to my 'mussing' his clothes,' as he put it and ordered his men to make sure I never felt the urge to attack him again. I have to say, they did a good job."

Jax didn't go into detail of the brutal beating he'd received. He had been lucky that his only broken bones had been his nose and a few ribs, plus he'd lost a few back teeth. He had multiple cuts all over his face, and his abdomen hurt so badly for days afterward, he'd been concerned about internal bleeding. And he still didn't know how his spine hadn't been broken as they had ruthlessly kicked him over and over. As for his face, the two black eyes trumped the captain's one, and he had so many cuts inside and outside his mouth that he'd swallowed blood for hours.

Mykaela fully understood what Jaxon didn't say. He had been punished very thoroughly for his attack and lived to tell about it, thank you God. But she felt sick to her stomach at the atrocities inflicted and suspected that this was only the bare bones of what his life was like following his capture. And she was right although he spared her most of the details of his imprisonment.

By the time they delivered him to Andersonville Prison, deep in the heart of Georgia, most of his wounds had healed. He spent the following year in as close an approximation to Hell as one could ever imagine. That summer, the prison held twice the number of men it was built for which meant that many spent all of their time without any shelter. A creek ran through the middle of camp, but was so putrid and filthy that no one could safely drink from it although that didn't stop some of the men. Food was a commodity to be fought over. By the time the camp was liberated in the spring of 1865, over 30,000 men had died from malnutrition, wound putrefaction, pestilence, and disease.

Jax helped the sick and wounded as much as he was able, but with no medical supplies, there wasn't much he could do. He despaired of watching the men, many of them younger than him, die from lack of basic necessities, and he often questioned how man could treat each other so abominably. He had never felt so helpless in all of his life and couldn't help wondering why he had been spared. It was during this time that his faith in God began to waver.

When he and the survivors were finally freed at the end of the war, most of them were severely weak and sick. Jax himself lost over 50 pounds, starving, and suffering from dysentery. He, along with some other fellow officers, were taken by train to Pennsylvania where they received proper medical assistance. He spent a month in a little town called Fullerton with Union sympathizers, recovering and regaining his strength. He had become somewhat confused and disoriented during this time, thus hadn't been able to contact his family or his unit yet. By the time he was strong enough to get around, he did notify his unit that he was alive, but hesitated in telegraphing his family.

Mykaela looked puzzled. "But why? I'm sure they must have been so worried."

Jax nodded. "I know. I -- it's hard to explain, but I felt so alone, deep in my soul . . . and so unbelievably sullied by living at that prison, I didn't want to bring my *uncleanliness,* if you will, to their door. I told myself I needed to feel clean and whole again. Inside and out. Get my head right. If I contacted them, then I would be defiling them too." Jax shook his head. "I know it doesn't make any sense, but I was so lost back then, so full of hatred and anger, I needed time to heal. So, I worked some odd jobs for awhile, earned enough money to buy Blackjack, and finally decided to head west toward home."

Jax had had a restlessness in him -- different than what he'd felt back home before going to medical school -- always feeling edgy and tense. He headed towards Colorado and home, primarily living on the trail, always looking over his shoulder, not wanting much contact with others, stopping at the occasional town for supplies or to gamble for money. His nightmares started around this time, waking him violently, drenched in sweat and shaking from limb to limb. He developed insomnia, afraid to fall asleep, and found the only way he could actually make it through the night without a nightmare was to drink himself to sleep. Or find solace with a saloon-girl. This he kept to himself, an aspect of his life he wasn't very proud of, ashamed to share with Mykaela.

"Every time I rode into a new town, I promised myself I would send my family a telegram," Jax said. "But each time, I found a reason not to."

He shook his head in self-recrimination. "I was convinced that I would know when the time was right." He found he just couldn't talk about his family just yet. "It's late," he observed. "And I have an early morning. Thanks for listening, but why don't we call it a night?"

"Of course," Mykaela agreed. She stood while he bent down to bank the fire. Placing a warm hand on his shoulder,

Legacy of Love

she squeezed it gently. "Thank you for sharing with me, Jax. I appreciate your trust in me. You won't regret it, I promise." And she walked away into her room.

Jax stayed where he was for several minutes. He could still feel the impression of her hand. She said thanks that he trusted her, but trusting her wasn't very hard to do. She was a trust-worthy person, kind and generous. She had a warm, giving heart; just thinking about her caused his own heart to beat a little faster. He rammed the logs too hard, sending up a shower of sparks and ash. Coughing, he paid more attention to what he was doing, closed the grate, and slowly headed upstairs.

He had no right to have any kind of warm, fuzzy thoughts about his landlady. She could do so much better than him. He would be forever tainted by his past, forever scarred. Was it fair to her, to any decent woman, to bring his baggage with him into any decent relationship?

He quickly readied for bed, the room chilly, his thoughts whirling and centered on the woman downstairs. He could feel the warm bricks she had placed under his covers at the foot of the bed, something she did every evening. The bricks were just one more thing she did to make him comfortable in her home. She was truly considerate and thoughtful, and he would forever be grateful to her for taking him in. But that was as far as his thoughts would go, he told himself firmly, then promptly fell asleep thinking about her and surprisingly managed not to have any nightmares.

Mykaela lay in bed thinking about all Jax had told her . . . and not told her. That he had suffered more than anyone ever should was a given, but she knew there was a lot more to his story. And that his family played a part in it somehow. She wondered why she felt so compelled to get him to open up to her. But she knew deep down that it was important for him to do so. Whatever demons haunted him would not go away until he came face to face with them. That's when he could finally begin to heal. With that thought, she settled down to sleep.

CHAPTER 7

Jax was up and gone very early the following morning; he had a special delivery to make in a town two hours away by wagon. The day before, Mykaela had given him a scarf that she'd knitted for him. He drove off that morning, tucking the fluffy red & blue scarf into his jacket, marveling at her kindness and grateful that he'd ridden into this town just a month ago.

Since it was Thursday, Mykaela had a full day of laundering planned. Ryan and Rachel were overly excited because today was their last day before a four day holiday weekend from school.

Mykaela was forced to hang the washed linens in the kitchen to dry as the temperature had dropped below freezing. She noticed clouds way off in the distance over the mountains that heralded snow, probably arriving sometime during the night.

Mykaela made good time on her duties, finishing all the washing by mid-afternoon. She put potatoes on to boil, planning on a Shepherd's pie for dinner made with deer meat, thanks to Jax. She was feeling the towels for dryness when the cabin suddenly shuddered violently. Frowning, she opened the back door, catching a face full of swirling snow; it was blowing all around the porch, falling thick and fast from a gray sky. She stood there for a moment not quite believing what she was seeing. Those clouds had been miles away just a few hours ago; rarely did a storm move so quickly and only then if a blizzard was coming. Dread filled her as she continued to watch the snow, knowing in her gut that an early season blizzard had indeed arrived.

Hurrying back inside, she checked the clock. The kids weren't due to be released from school for another hour, but surely, Mr. Wood, their teacher, would have seen the storm coming and sent them home by now. But as she rushed to the front door, a relentless voice in the back of her mind reminded her that *she* hadn't noticed the coming snowfall, so maybe the teacher hadn't either. Standing on the small front porch, she peered anxiously toward town, not that she could see much of anything. Even without the restricted visibility from the snow, the forest blocked her view.

She stayed there for several minutes, praying that the kids would round the corner of the trees any second. But no one came into view. And as the seconds ticked by, the snow fell harder and faster, the wind kicking up a notch, blowing that snow in all directions, a sure blizzard sign.

She went back inside and gathered up some items: a lantern, a length of rope that Jax had unkinked last night, her wrap, and newly finished mittens. She was just pulling on her boots, when the back door slammed open. Jax came stamping in, grinning, and slapping his gloved hands together.

"Whew--ie!! That is some wind. I do believe our first blizzard is here," he struggled to close the door, fighting the wind. "I just beat the worst of it; it was touch and go there for awhile." His voice was light and cheery, exhilarated by his race with Mother Nature. "I tied a length of clothesline from the barn to the back door." Turning, he saw Mykaela . . .and frowned. "What's wrong?"

Mykaela didn't trust herself to speak. When she saw Jax, part of her was disappointed that he wasn't the children, another part was grateful that he was home safe and sound, and yet another part of her wanted nothing more than to throw herself into his arms and cry her heart out over fear for her children.

Jax looked around the room, a sense of foreboding filling him. "Where are the kids?"

Mykaela's anxiety-filled eyes spoke volumes as did the equipment she had in her hands. She slowly shook her head.

His voice was grim as he asked even though he knew the answer "They're not home yet." He turned it into a statement. His heart sank as she shook her head again, eyes bright with unshed tears.

"I'm on my way to look for them," she was able to tell him with a hitch in her voice, taking a step towards the door. But he blocked her.

"I'll go."

She shook her head. "No. They're my children, my responsibility. It's my job to …"

He interrupted her. "Mykaela, do you have any idea how hard it is to find your way in a storm like this? Do you?" He grabbed hold of her shoulders firmly. "I've been in more than my fair share of snowstorms. I know how to get around as safely as possible. You need to stay here, warming blankets and bricks, heating warm milk for them when I bring them back." He looked steadily into her soulful brown eyes. "I give you my word I *will* bring them home.

Mykaela wanted so much to trust in him, her relief that she wasn't alone so palpable that she suddenly felt weak in the knees. Nodding her head in agreement, she asked him what he needed besides the rope and lantern.

Dana-Sue Urso

"What you have is fine, but I'll need more rope which I'll get from the barn." He rewrapped his scarf, then buttoned up securely, tightened his gloves, and headed out the door. After getting another length of rope, he began to make his way toward town. He waved a hand to Mykaela standing in the doorway. He could barely see her even though he was only about 20 yards from her; the blizzard was coming on fast. Luckily, he could just make out the darker outline of the forest and headed straight for it, walking as quickly as he could. The wind was getting ever stronger, and the snow was not only starting to layer the ground, but much of it was whirling around which was obscuring his vision.

Mykaela watched Jax until she could no longer see him. As she pushed the door shut with great effort, she sent her most fervent prayer winging upward, begging God to guide them home safely.

Jax made it to the trees glad to be able to get out of the worst of the wind. He walked just inside the tree line, able to see fairly well even though the wind blew the snow into the woods. He made the turn at the corner and eventually passed the feed store, then the post office, next the bank. The Caldwell children didn't usually walk this way; they headed out over the open prairie from the school, angling toward town, then around the corner of the blacksmith shop which stood across the street from the post office, then to the edge of the forest. But he was afraid to walk into the open without landmarks until he had checked the school. Maybe the teacher had kept the students there for safety; that would have been the smart thing to do.

Legacy of Love

He kept walking toward the center of town until he reached Floyd's hardware. An alley directly across led to the field where the schoolhouse stood. He stood right in front of Floyd's, noted the 'closed' sign, and peered across the street. He couldn't see the alley. In fact, he strained hard just to make out the vague grayness of the shops he knew were there. He thought he saw an occasional flicker of light coming from his right, but he couldn't be sure. He was tempted to just begin walking, knowing that he would probably stumble into the boardwalk. But there was a slight chance the wind and snow would disorient him enough that he would end up walking right out of town and into the prairie where he would be lost without landmarks.

Instead, he uncoiled the rope, two of them that he had already tied securely together; one would have been long enough to breach the distance between the east and west sides of town. Tying one end securely to a hitching rail, he slowly and carefully played out the rope as he walked across the deserted street, holding the lantern out with in front of him. He wasn't sure if the light it shed helped his vision, but he felt better holding it.

After only a second or two, he was caught up in a whirlwind where it seemed as if he was the only person on Earth. Becoming disoriented, he felt a sense of panic hit him even though logically, he knew that he was safe as long as he had the rope. But still, a part of him felt very uneasy and confused. Determined none-the-less, he kept his head down and continued walking.

Suddenly, he ran into something that doubled him over a little. A hitching post. *Thank God.* Going to the end of it, he stepped up onto the boardwalk and saw that he was in front of the telegraph office; he was two shops away from the alley, the rope actually angled back the way he'd come from. He had been more disoriented than he'd thought. Blizzards had a way of making it seem as if you were walking in a straight line, but in reality, the wind and pure whiteness of the blowing snow pushed you in a totally different direction.

This close to the buildings he was able to see them. He headed for the alley, tying the rope to the pillar on the edge of the boardwalk in front of Miss Hanks' sewing shop. Peering down the alley, all he saw was a complete whiteout. It would be like walking into an unknown world, but at least he could keep the buildings next to him on either side. Until he reached their end.

Having no other choice, he grabbed hold of the rope and let it guide him back across the street, untied it, then followed it back; he would need it to reach the school house which stood alone, nestled in a grove of trees, but with no landmarks between it and the back of the town.

From the corner of his eye, he saw a faint flash of light which seemed to be coming from Sam's Mercantile on the other side of the alley. Thinking maybe he would find out some useful information, he followed the boardwalk to the door. Going inside, he was blinded for a moment by the lanterns.

"Hey, it's the young doctor," he heard a disembodied voice say.

"Everythin' alright, Doc?" This came from someone else.

A third voice, "Give him a minute, would ya? That whiteout is as bad as bein' buried alive." An apt description, Jax thought. When he could adequately see, he noted some of the old timers gathered around the cookstove in the middle of the store. Some were sitting, some were standing, all were staring at him. "Come warm yourself, young fella," invited a grizzled man whom Jax thought was named Rusty.

Doing just that, Jax told them, "Can't stay long. The Caldwell children didn't make it home. I thought maybe you all may have heard something . . ." his voice trailed off. The men looked at each other, all thinking the same thing but not wanting to voice it. "Do you know if any of the others made it home? I thought Mr. Wood may have kept them at school when he saw the storm coming."

Mr. Anderson was at the counter, looking at him solemnly. "My kids are home. From what they told me, Mr. Wood didn't notice the storm until it was practically on top of us. He's from the East, don't know a blizzard from a Spring shower. He dismissed the students, then headed home posthaste, taking the Jones' boys and Mary Tabler home first since they live so far out."

Jax knew that the kids he'd mentioned all lived several miles outside of town, on the eastern side like Mykaela, but further north. An icy cold gripped him as he thought about Ryan and Rachel caught in this maelstrom, lost and alone. If he didn't find them soon. The shopkeeper went on.

"The sheriff was here a bit ago. He told us that he was going around to make sure all the town kids are accounted for. He hasn't come back yet."

Jax nodded. "I'm headed for the school just in case."

"What'll you do if you don't find them there?" This from a long-bearded man Jax didn't know.

"I'll keep looking for them," He informed them grimly. He had no choice, but he could see by the looks the others were trying to hide that they thought he would have no luck, that the kids were doomed. "I could use some more rope." He said to Mr. Anderson who gladly obliged with two more lengths; he took a few minutes to tie them all together, a total length of approximately 200 feet. The good news was that that should be more than enough to reach the school. The bad news was that the more ropes tied together, the more chance that the knots would give out especially in a blizzard wind, but he had no choice.

With words of good luck and be careful ringing in his ears, Jax headed back out into the fierce wind. He made it to the end of the alley and faced a gut-wrenching, fear-inspiring sight. The blizzard had intensified in the 10 minutes he'd been at the store. The sound of the now-howling wind was almost deafening. The whiteness was so bright his eyes hurt to look straight at it. And the wind was determined to reach every part of him that it could, sending icy cold drafts up his pant legs and down his jacket.

After several minutes of trying to tie one end of the rope to the ring attached to the side of the sewing store, he yelled up to the heavens in frustration for some help. He ended up having to take off his gloves; it took only seconds to lose the feeling in his fingers, but that was all he needed to tie off the rope. He checked its security several times before he felt confident enough to brave the onslaught between him and the schoolhouse.

An eternity went by as he fought the wind. He tried to keep his thoughts positive, but it was hard when he felt like the storm was beating him down. As he plodded along, the thought came to him how easy it would be to just lie down and let the snow overtake him, that it probably wasn't such a hard way to go. He'd thought about death a lot over the last few years, never really succumbing to the easy way out. But if he was honest with himself, death would end his loneliness and emotional pain. But he knew that as long as Mykaela was counting on him, he wouldn't -- couldn't -- let her down, no matter what.

With renewed determination, he stumbled along until he felt the rope pull which meant that it had played out. Not a good sign. Squinting, Jax tried hard to see something, a darkness against the whiteness. There, he saw it, off to his left. But when he reached it, he almost ran into it: a tree. He'd gone too far to the left of the school; he was standing at the edge of the small grove that curved around the school in a semicircle. This at least gave him some bearing, and he turned to his right, the rope held tightly, walking in that direction to give it some slack.

Jacx suddenly tripped over something, landing hard, but thankfully not letting go of the rope. A bucket. As he got to his knees, his hand hit something solid. Splaying it out, he discovered with great relief the wall of the school. He'd finally reached it. Following it along and around to the front, he tied the rope to the hitching rail, his numb fingers fumbling with the knot. He prayed intensely as he opened the front door.

Blinking to clear his vision, Jax found himself in a small foyer where coats were hung. As he opened the inside door, he felt such a sense of relief that he sagged against the doorframe for a second. Ryan and Rachel were huddled around the stove at the front of the room although from what he could see, there was no fire in the grate. Also standing close to the stove were several other children, the oldest looking to be about 13 or 14, the youngest smaller than Rachel.

He unwound his scarf and took off his hat. "I sure am glad to see you." He told them all, but looking at Mykaela's children.

When she saw who it was, Rachel ran over to him. Stopping right in front of him, she looked up at him with huge tear-filled eyes so reminiscent of her mother. "Are you going to take us home?" she asked in a tremulous voice. Jax hunched down on his knees.

"That I am, Sweetling." He assured her, smiling. Unprepared, she almost knocked him back as she flung herself at him. Burying her face in his neck, she said, "I'm glad 'cuz my Mama is missing me, I'm sure."

Wanting to shed a tear himself, Jax patted her back soothingly and said, "She certainly is."

Ryan came to stand by him, a forlorn look on his face, his eyes full of distress. "We tried to get home, but it started snowing so hard, I could hardly see." He scuffed his foot against the floorboard. "I didn't know what to do."

Rachel pulled back and said earnestly, "Wyan was so bwave." Her R's became W's whenever she was stressed or frightened. "He brunged us wight back to school, but no one was he-ew. But then the othews came." She flapped her hand at the three children still standing by the stove.

"Ryan did the right thing coming back here," Jax told her. Ryan's eyes lit up at the compliment. "You were a lot safer here than out there." He nodded to the window.

"Sir?" A tentative voice said. The older boy looked at him uncertainly. "Will we have to stay here until someone comes for us? I think there's enough wood for a few days; I was just about to relight the stove."

Jax could tell the boy was scared of being left here with the others. He had picked up the other girl who was about five, and she had silent tears running down her cheeks. Another boy, probably about ten, watched him with a hopeful expression.

Jax stood up, feeling a warmth steal over him as Rachel slipped her hand into his.

"What's your name?" he asked the adolescent.

"Will Benson. This is my sister Molly."

"No, Will, you won't stay here." His heart clenched at the looks of profound relief on their faces. "I'll take you into town to Sam's. The sheriff is checking on all the kids and will get you home."

"We live out past the railroad station," the older boy told him. "But Kenny here lives beside the depot."

"Don't worry. You'll have a place to stay until the storm lets up. But I'd better write a note on the chalkboard in case any of your parents show up looking for you."

"My Dad's the engineer. He's away right now, probably stuck in this storm." Kenny informed him matter-of-factly. "My Mom might come, though."

Jax hoped not.

"Our Ma has rheumatism," Will put in. "She won't be able to look for us. And our Pa's in Denver until next week."

Jax still left a note and then gave them all a pep talk. If the blinding snow and gale-force winds had given him the willy's, he could only imagine what the children would be feeling once they were out in it. He briefly thought about just keeping everyone here until the storm abated. But there was no way to predict how long it could last; it could be days, and there wasn't any food. Making trips to town didn't seem plausible when it would be better to just take them all there in the first place. Besides, he didn't want their parents to worry any longer than necessary. If someone decided to go searching for them and ended up getting lost in this blizzard.

Quickly, Jax outlined some directions. Will would go first, carrying his sister piggy-back and holding Kenny's hand; with his other hand, he would hold onto the rope. Jax would untie the rope, then follow Will while carrying Rachel and holding Ryan's hand; Ryan would hold the lantern. He warned them that the wind was exceptionally strong and that their one and only priority was to hold onto each other and/or the rope. He then gave them an encouraging pep talk and got ready to head out into the onslaught.

Making sure they were all bundled up tight, Jax opened the door. He had them line up, holding the rope as instructed. They were all standing so close they were touching, but that would soon change. In fact, the brutality of the blizzard almost had Jax changing his mind about taking the children through it.

But in the end, his plan worked out well. They headed out, the girls holding on tight, faces buried. The little boys held tight to their partner's hand which was a challenge at times. They stumbled several times in the deep snow, the wind helping to knock them over. If not for the secure hold of Will and Jax, the younger boys would have been unable to hold on. Jax walked as close to Will as he could to keep him in sight as best he could, trying not to trip over him all while holding tightly to the end of the rope, its slack blowing all around them in the horrific wind.

Legacy of Love

Will had his head bent and hit the back wall of the Fabric Shop with a thud. Jax ran into him, but at least they'd made it. As per Jax's instructions, Will rounded the corner of the alley and headed up to the street, Kenny in tow. At the corner, again per previous instructions, Jax still held Ryan's hand who then held hands with Kenny who was still holding Will's hand. In this way, they didn't need a rope to reach across the width of the alley, which was now completely obscured from sight, to the other boardwalk. Moments later, they were safely ensconced in Sam's store where the old timers fussed over them like hens with their chicks.

Sheriff Hoskins came in soon after and was very relieved to see Kenny, the only townie who hadn't been accounted for. After warming up, the sheriff took him home. When he returned, he told Will and Molly that arrangements had been made for them to stay at the hotel next door; Mrs. Willis, the manager's wife, would look after them until it was safe to take them home. Unfortunately, there just wasn't anyway to let their mother know they were safe.

Jax had to leave the Caldwell children warming at the store, eating crackers and cheese, while he went to retrieve the ropes. He needed them to get back to the farm. The sheriff and Sam had tried to convince him to keep the kids in town, stay at the hotel. It was tempting. He was tired of fighting the storm, and it was still a little chancy to head out into it even with ropes and landmarks. But the children looked at him earnestly, silently telling him they wanted to go home. So he would fulfill his promise to Mykaela and take them home.

When he returned from getting the ropes, he wanted to head right out -- getting warm and then facing the cold again was torture. And the kids were eager to get going as well.

101

Dana-Sue Urso

"I still think you're making a mistake," the sheriff said as he walked them out. "But I guess I understand." Holding out his hand, he wished them God-speed. Jax shook his hand and thanked him. Ten minutes later, he was wishing they were back at the store. They had reached the edge of town by the woods, and he knew they were facing the cabin. The blizzard was so bad that he couldn't see his hand unless it was so close to his face that it touched his nose. And forget about actually seeing the children with any clarity.

Carrying Rachel, he led Ryan a few feet into the woods which allowed him to blurrily make out his outline. Putting his mouth close to the boy's ear, he shouted to him that he would have to let go of his hand for a moment while he tied the rope to the tree; Ryan was to hold onto his coat and not let go. The boy nodded his understanding.

The wind did everything it could to whip the rope from Jax's hands. Grit and determination were all that kept him from losing hold of it. He had mentally calculated the distance from the forest to the front porch and came up with a tentative 200 feet, the length of all 4 ropes. With his most fervent prayer yet, Jax prepared to guide the children on the last leg of their journey.

Mykaela tried not to watch the clock, but she felt an almost overwhelming need to check it every few minutes. Allowing for the struggles he would have in the ferocious wind and blinding snow, she figured he'd be gone a couple of hours at the very least. Pacing the small cabin didn't help her piece of mind, but she couldn't get herself to do much else the first hour he was gone.

Legacy of Love

Finally, she sternly told herself she needed to be busy and set herself the tasks Jax had mentioned. She hung a line in front of the fireplace and draped several quilts over it, then built up the fire. She also kept a pan of milk handy in the lean-to ready to heat when they got home. And the question was when, not if. She refused to dwell on the negatives, distracting herself by taking down the dried linens that she'd hung across the kitchen, folding and stacking them, then bundling them ready for delivery.

She tidied up the cabin. She got the kids' pajamas and hung them over the line. She braved the fierce storm and went to the barn to feed the animals although it was a little early. By the time she returned to the cabin, a feeling of despair washed over her. The blizzard was wild and crazy; it seemed almost alive. She'd had a difficult time keeping hold of the clothesline Jax had hung between the house and barn. The violent wind kept trying to blow her off her feet, and she staggered most of the way to the barn and back.

She knelt in front of the fire to rake the logs with tears leaking from her eyes. She didn't want to cry because that would mean all hope was lost. She prayed often throughout the rest of the afternoon, begging God to bring her children and Jax home safely.

By the time the 3rd hour had crept past, Mykaela had given up finding tasks to do and sat curled up in her chair, trying to stay calm. Several times, she almost headed out into the storm, but logically she knew that was the worst thing she could do at this point.

Suddenly, the blizzard was in the house. Almost falling out of her chair in surprise, Mykaela hurried to take Rachel from Jax's arms; the little girl threw her arms around her mother and hugged tight, but not saying anything. Mykaela set her down in front of the fireplace. Jax followed her with Ryan and then followed her lead by helping him off with his outer garments. Snow was encrusted in their hats and scarves as well as caked on their mittens.

Mykaela shook out their coats and accoutrements, hanging them in their usual place by the door. No one spoke as the children were dressed in warm pajamas and socks, wrapped in warmed blankets, and tucked close to the fire on pillows. The kids were basking in the warmth, shivering a bit. Mykaela knelt next to them and put a hand on their still cold faces.

"Are you two alright?" she asked with concern.

"W-we're OK, M-Mama," answered Ryan. "J-just a little cold, b-but the fire f-feels good."

Rachel looked at her mother with a serious expression. "I t-told Jax that you would m-miss us. And he said th-that he w-would bring us h-home. And he d-did!" She finished with a flourish, smiling her tooth-gapped smile up at Jax.

He was taking off his own apparel feeling like a block of ice; he couldn't remember when he'd been so cold. Or so tired. All he wanted to do was sit down and put his feet up. But he looked down at the little girl and winked at her.

Mykaela waited until he also wrapped up in a blanket then settled in the chair by the fire, propping his stocking feet on the hearth.

"Thank you." She simply said, afraid to say much more at the moment, tears pricking her eyes.

Jax nodded his head at her. "I have to tell you, they were very brave." He then proceeded to tell her all that had transpired since he'd left to go look for them. Ryan and

Legacy of Love

Rachel butted in now and then with some details which made the tale all the more interesting. At story's end, Mykaela hugged her children, telling them how proud she was of them.

"We're just glad to be home, aren't we Rachel?"

She nodded. "Uh huh." Then a huge yawn. She leaned her head on her mother and closed her eyes. "I'm sleepy." Mykaela felt her daughter shiver a little, still somewhat chilled.

"You need to drink some warm milk." She informed them and went to the kitchen. She quickly heated up the milk, put some Cocoa in it, and brought the children each a cup. She handed Jax a cup of coffee.

Grateful, he smiled his thanks and gratefully sipped at the refreshingly hot beverage.

Mykaela set about filling supper plates with the Shepherd's pie and having everyone eat in front of the fire. While she worked, Jax unobtrusively checked the children for signs of frostbite. With great relief, he noted that their hands and feet, although pale from the cold, were not blood white, a sure sign of frostbite.

They all settled down to eat with relish. Jax felt like he could eat an entire deer and still not be full. Fighting the blizzard had worked up quite an appetite, and he didn't say no to seconds.

It wasn't long before the kids fell asleep soon after finishing their supper. Mykaela carried Rachel to her bed, wondering how she was going to manage her heavier son. But Jax came in behind her with Ryan and put him in his bed. He left Mykaela to finish tucking them in and went out to prepare to head to the barn for the evening chores.

Mykaela came out soon after, closing the door behind her.

Dana-Sue Urso

Seeing Jax pulling his coat on, she said, "You don't have to go to the barn tonight; I did the chores a little while ago."

"Oh, well, thanks. Thanks a lot." He hung his coat back up. "I wasn't looking forward to going back out there." He admitted with a rueful grin, then ran a hand down his face. Mykaela could see exhaustion etched all over him. Along with his usual 5 o'clock shadow that gave him such a rakish air.

"Why don't you sit down, and I'll refill your cup."

Jax didn't need a second urging. Plopping down with a sigh, he leaned his head back and closed his eyes. The chair he was sitting in was actually fairly comfortable. It was called an easy chair and had fabric similar to the fabric that covered Mykaela's rocking chair on the opposite side of the hearth. Propping up his feet once more on a small stool, covered with a blanket, Jax felt himself slowly relax. The coffee he drank warmed him which made him all the more drowsy. Putting down the cup, he had every intention of going up to his room, but leaned back for another minute. And fell asleep.

Mykaela sat in her chair, knitting. In slumber, Jax's face lost its hard edge, the lines smoothing away. He looked younger and so peaceful. She sat watching him for the longest time, her sewing forgotten. She knew with a certainty that she would never grow tired from looking at him. He'd saved their lives, found her children, and taken on the onerous burden of the upkeep of the farm. All for a lower rent. She shouldn't be charging him anything, truth be told. But she needed the money. The taxes were coming due; she'd been saving a little here and there, but she was short. She'd come close a few times over the last several years of not having the money and losing the farm. She and the children had nowhere else to go so she made an effort to save throughout the year, somehow managing to have the money when it was needed.

Mykaela lost track of time, but probably less than 30 minutes had gone by when a log suddenly fell, knocking another one forward and out onto the hearth. She jumped up to push it back. The noise wasn't that loud, but Jax woke up.

Yawning, he apologized for falling asleep.

"You certainly don't have to apologize," she sternly told him. "You must be completely worn out!"

"I am, but it's OK. It feels good in a way." He yawned again and stretched. "I'm tempted to just sleep right here tonight, the fire feels wonderful."

"You must have been freezing out there," Mykaela observed, frowning.

"I know the kids were really cold," Jax stared into the flames, thoughtful. "I probably should have left them at Sam's. It was risky taking them out in the blizzard."

"I'm glad you didn't," she assured him. "I would have been worried sick."

"But if something had happened . . ." Jax seemed determined to undermine what he'd done.

"But nothing did," Mykaela reminded him firmly. "God was watching over you the whole time." She sounded so confident that Jax looked over at her.

"I believe He was," he agreed softly. They continued to look at each other for a moment, each lost in thought. Jax was deeply touched by her confidence in him, her readiness to let him take charge when he felt it was best; yet her faith in his ability to come through was humbling. He couldn't help feeling that he would end up letting her down some day.

For her part, Mykaela had never known what it felt like to have someone help her in a time of need. Her father certainly had never been there for her, and Danny usually left her to handle everything on her own; he'd rather go into town to meet his buddies at the saloon then spend a lot of time with her or the children. But the guilt she felt about all the work Jax did around the place, doing more than was required by their agreement, overwhelmed her. She never wanted him to think she was taking advantage of him or relied on him all the time.

Another falling log broke into their thoughts. Mykaela gathered up their cups to take to the kitchen. Jax folded his blanket and took down the line for her before heading to his room for some much needed rest. Mykaela stopped him with a hand on his arm. Looking up into his eyes with those warm chocolate eyes sparkling with unshed tears almost did him in.

"Thank you seems so inadequate for what you did today," she said in a husky voice. "But I will always be so grateful to you for bringing my children home safely."

As Jax gazed down upon her, he felt a sudden urge to kiss her. It was so strong, that he actually started to tilt his head down. And from the look on her face, Jax thought Mykaela wouldn't be protesting. But common sense prevailed, and he stopped himself before it was too late. Instead, he reached a hand up and gently touched the side of her face.

"You're welcome," he replied softly and went up the stairs.

Mykaela went into her own room, her heart pounding. She'd been so sure Jax had been going to kiss her. She thought about that as she quickly undressed in the chilly room. He had stopped himself which was a good thing, surely. *I mean, the children were in the next room, and he was her boarder*, she berated herself. *It wouldn't be right.* But as she climbed under the covers, pressing her feet up against the warm brick, she couldn't help wishing that it *was* right.

CHAPTER 8

The blizzard blew itself out sometime through the night. The cabin's occupants got up to the sight of fresh glittering snow with drifts piled higher than their heads. Jax rose very early and spent over an hour digging a path from the back porch to the barn and then another hour clearing away the 6 foot high drift in front of the barn doors. By the time he went back in for breakfast, he was exhausted, and the day hadn't even started yet. Mykaela could see his fatigue, knowing that he hadn't gotten enough sleep last night to make up for the hard day he'd had. And she felt bad.

"Why don't you stay home this morning, catch up on some sleep?" she suggested.

He shook his head. "Can't." He yawned and swallowed a mouthful of stimulating the hot coffee. "I want to go into town and see how everyone fared. See if the sheriff needs help looking for anyone who might be missing."

Mykaela marveled at how much this man, a virtual stranger to her town, could care so much about virtual strangers. That's the way a doctor should be, she told herself, but believed he went above and beyond. If she hadn't known it before, she knew now; Jaxon Dumont was NOT a murderer.

The children came to the table, bright-eyed and bushy-tailed, none the worse for wear. Jax could only wonder at their energy . . . and wish he had half of it. Finishing his coffee, he stood up and said his good-byes; he'd be back in time for the evening chores.

Today was a holiday for the kids, but Mykaela didn't want them outside so soon after their ordeal yesterday, afraid they might get sick. She was supposed to work at the *The Fabric Shop* since it was a Friday, but she had switched days and was going to work Monday instead while the kids stayed with Tina Michaels.

Mykaela kept them busy. They went with her to town to drop off her load of linens and pick up the next one. The trip took twice as long because of the deep snow so they didn't linger. Plus, she wanted to do some baking. With Jax's rent, she was able to buy a 10# sack of flour, a pound of brown sugar, a can of baking powder, a small tin of cinnamon, and a pound of coffee.

Ryan and Rachel enthusiastically pitched in helping her bake some bread and apple muffins. They got more on their clothes than in the pans, but they had fun doing it. Mykaela was glad of the time she was able to spend with them, but found herself thinking of Jax, wondering what he was doing.

Knowing he would have had a long day, Mykaela went to the barn after supper to do the evening chores a little early so he wouldn't have to. Sitting on the milk stool, she hummed to Josie as she squirted milk into the bucket; the placid old cow blinked at her while she chewed some hay. Seeing a little field mouse peeking at her from the corner of the stall, Mykaela took careful aim with one of Josie's teats and sent a stream of warm milk towards the furry creature. A direct hit. Laughing, she watched the mouse scurry around in circles, then sit up on its back legs and swipe at its face with its front paws, whiskers quivering with indignation.

"Not too bad," drawled a deep voice behind her. "For a girl."

Startled, Mykaela turned to see Jax leaning on the stall's frame, arms crossed over his chest, a tired smile on his face.

"Oh yeah?" she responded with a smirk. "How 'bout this?" She quickly and accurately aimed another stream of the foamy milk, this time right on Jax's boots. He jumped back in surprise.

"Hey," he cried good-naturedly. "Unfair! I don't have a weapon." He swung his arms wide, deliberately looking helpless.

She aimed the teat at the center of his chest. "Say I'm as good as any man, and I'll stop the attack."

Jax grinned, throwing up his hands in mock surrender. "OK, you win. You are as good as any man. But boy am I glad you're a woman." Now where had *that* come from? he wondered, his smile slipping. She was looking up at him with an expression that could only be described as appreciative.

"I am, too," she agreed softly, still looking at him. He swallowed. Hard. They continued to watch each other, the only sound coming from one of the horses as it snorted and a faint scratching sound that could only be the milk-covered mouse.

Mykaela felt as though she were caught in some ancient spell, one that kept her frozen, her pounding heart the only sign of life. Something indefinable floated between them, and her breath caught in her throat. She was really coming to care for this man, she realized, and if she wasn't careful, she was going to have her heart broken when he left come Spring.

Josie shifted her weight and almost knocked over the bucket of milk, effectively breaking whatever sort of trance the two humans had been in. Jax cleared his throat and mumbled something about feeding the animals while Mykaela turned her attention back to her milking. She had a difficult time getting back into the rhythm because her hands were shaking so badly.

Jax climbed up into the loft to fork down fresh hay, but had to take a minute to get himself together. He wasn't sure what just happened, but he had been more aware of her as a woman than he'd ever been before. She'd looked adorable perched on that stool, her mouth curved into a devilish smile as she shot the milk at him; her hair was escaping from her usual braid, wisps of it framing her face, a piece of straw clinging to one end. He thought she was more beautiful with each passing day.

He suddenly realized he was standing there, leaning on the pitchfork staring off into space. If anyone had seen him just then, they would have thought he'd lost his mind. As he began to pitch down the hay, the thought struck him that he was coming to care for his sweet landlady more than he ought, and that Spring was going to come along much too quickly!

The next morning dawned bright and clear, a gorgeous fall day. It was apparent that if the sun continued to shine like this for several more days, the snow would soon be nothing but slush. Ryan and Rachel were eager to take advantage of the newness of it before this happened.

Jaxon came out of the barn and laughed as he watched them attempt to roll a large mound of snow into some semblance of a snowman's body. Rachel really wasn't much help, and she kept losing her footing. Frustrated, Ryan explained to her more than once how to properly roll the snow and to quit slipping. Soon, they were engaged in battle, shouting and flinging handfuls of snow at each other.

Trying to contain his laughter, Jax walked over to them and demanded a truce.

"What's a truce?" Rachel wanted to know.

"You don't know *any*thing!" admonished her brother with disgust.

"Do *so!*" she yelled at him, hands on hips. Jax thought she looked like a mighty warrior ready to right a wrong. But before all out war broke out, he offered to help them with their snowman. This effectively stopped their arguing.

Mykaela heard most of the exchange from the front doorway. She was impressed out how easily Jax had handled the kids' tiff, like he'd been doing it all his life. Again, she wondered about his family, and his estrangement from them.

With Jaxon's assistance, Mr. Snowman, came to life, so to speak. He stood at the edge of the half-drive by the road, standing straight and tall. Two mismatched black buttons from Mykaela's button box were his eyes while a small carrot stood in for his nose. Several smaller, multi-colored buttons curved unto a smile and long stick arms poked out of his sides. Ryan wrapped his scarf around the snowman's neck and declared him ready for guard duty.

"He doesn't look too bad," praised Jax, head to one side as he studied the huge blobs of snow before him. "My brother and I used to make snowmen all the time."

"You have a brother?" asked Ryan as if surprised.

"Yeah, I do. His name is Jarrod, and he's two years older than me." Jax paused as he thought about him, found that he missed him; the pain struck him then, and he frowned, not willing to acknowledge it.

"Does he think you don't know anything either?" asked Rachel, eyeing her brother with a steely look in her eyes.

"Sometimes," he replied, smiling a bit ruefully. "But we had lots of fun together, and we would fight, but then we would make up and be friends again."

Rachel frowned as she thought about this, not sure if she believed him. Ryan chose to ignore his comment and asked him if any of his snowmen were as great as theirs was.

When Jax assured him that no snowman had ever been built as grand as theirs, Rachel marched up to him and wanted to know if he had any sisters. Squatting down eye to eye with her, he told her he did.

"Her name is Jenna, and she is 6 years younger than me."

"Can she build snowmen?"

"She tried. She always wanted to be able to do everything I could do so she was right there with us most of the time."

"I'll bet she was a pest, too" this from Ryan, rolling his eyes.

"Sometimes, but then what girl isn't?" Jax was only teasing because he liked to see Rachel with her hands on her hips, eyes snapping with indignation. He tapped her nose and opened his mouth to tell her he had been kidding when suddenly a ball of snow exploded in his face, filling his mouth. Sputtering with surprise, he rose to his feet, swiping at his face.

Blinking, he looked around and saw Mykaela calmly patting another snowball into shape, watching him with an innocent expression. But her eyes were dancing with mischief.

"Oh, I'm so sorry," she said, too contritely. "Did that hit you? I didn't mean to be such a pest." And then she fired, taking him completely by surprise. Again! Jax had been confident she wouldn't really throw another one at him, so he'd stood there like a large idiotic target.

"Ooo, good one, Mama," cried Rachel, clapping her hands in delight.

Ryan, eyes wide, watched Jax intently.

Jax very carefully and methodically wiped snow from his face. Again. He smiled very pleasantly at Mykaela. "Good shot. You must practice your aim quite a bit. Or is it a natural talent?"

Mykaela also remembered the night before and laughed. Putting her hands up this time, she said, "I think I've salvaged the pride of all non-pesty woman everywhere. Truce?" She stuck out her hand towards him. Jax ignored it and took a step towards her instead. Mykaela decided she did not like the gleam in his eye. She took a step back.

"You know," she began conversationally. "I do think that it takes a big man to forgive and forget, don't you?"

He took another step forward. She took another step back.

"What's to forgive? You were defending women everywhere. A noble cause to be sure."

Another step forward, another back.

"Well, then, I'm glad that's all settled. I have some work to finish inside, so . . ." she suddenly whirled and headed for the door. She hadn't taken two steps before she realized that she'd never reach it in the two feet high snow. So, she veered to the right and ran towards the barn using the cleared path Jax had shoveled yesterday.

Rachel squealed, "Run, Mama, run faster!"

Ryan shouted, "Get her, Jax!"

Mykaela yelled back, "Hey, where's the loyalty?'

Legacy of Love

Jax called out, "We men must stick together." He let her run, enjoying her strategy. Instead of wasting time opening the barn doors, she veered again, to the left this time, and disappeared around the corner of the barn. She was hampered by her skirts which not only slowed her down, but made her work harder. He caught her at the back corner of the barn. He snaked an arm around her abdomen, effectively stopping her mad dash for safety.

Laughing and trying to catch her breath, Mykaela struggled uselessly. Jax wrapped his other arm around her torso, capturing her arms. Holding her close, he asked her to admit defeat.

"Never!' she cried, struggling anew, but again, wasted effort. Ryan came up, dancing happily. Rachel demanded he let her Mama go.

"Not until she admits that women are pests," Jax said, quite enjoying how this was playing out, content to hold her in his arms.

"I will never admit defeat; women are just as good as men, better really," Mykaela retorted stubbornly, her face red with her exertions.

"Yeah!" Rachel cried, crossing her arms over her chest, head held high.

"Uh oh, Ma," warned her traitorous son gleefully. "You're in for it now."

Before she could respond, Mykaela felt herself being lifted up and over Jax's shoulder, her head hanging down. He swung around, and her children's faces came into view.

"Mama, what's he gonna do?" Rachel asked breathlessly, eyes wide with wonder.

Mykaela braced her hands on his back and pushed, but to no avail. It was like pushing on a boulder. He had a vice grip on her, and she wasn't going to be able to budge him.

Again, she felt herself lifted, but this time she was actually flying -- or so it seemed. The sky came into view as she fell backwards . . . . . Whoompf! She landed in a huge pile of snow that was actually a 4 foot high snowdrift against the paddock fence. As she sank down, snow caved in around her, burying her. But she didn't have time to panic about being smothered because Jax had been careful to ensure her head was at the very edge of the drift; only a little snow actually fell into her face.

But the rest of her was covered. Jax stood over her, grinning in triumph.

"What were you saying about women and men and who's better and who's not?"

Rachel came forward slowly, staring at her mother.

"Mama, you're covered in a snow blanket."

"You look like a snowwoman," observed Ryan, grinning approvingly.

"Come here, both of you," Mykaela said. "I have a secret to tell you."

Jax's grin slipped as he watched her whisper in their ears; this didn't bode well for him, he was sure, but felt like grinning again because it felt so good to be playing like this. He truly could not remember the last time he'd had fun. Whatever they had in store for him, he would go along with it.

Both kids were now looking at him with what he would swear were calculating looks. *Was that even possible in children*? he wondered. Then they were on him. Ryan made a flying tackle at his legs while Rachel pulled on one of his arms. They weren't strong enough to actually push him down, but he got into the spirit and fell over with a dramatic cry. Landing with arms and legs spread-eagled, he allowed them to 'hold' him down while Mykaela managed to fight her way out of the drift. Now *she* stood over *him*, a double-sized snowball in her hands. They both knew that he could 'escape' anytime he wanted, but she was touched that he played along, making it more fun for the children.

Holding the snow over his head, she intoned gravely, "Now, women or men? Which one is better?"

"Well, now, you have me at a distinct disadvantage," he remarked, "struggling" to free himself. "If I say women, then I'm a traitor to my own kind. If I say men, then I get a faceful of snow."

Rachel giggled.

"Don't wimp out now," Ryan told him.

"Look who's talking, Benedict,"

"Who's Benec-dit?"Rachel wanted to know. Mykaela worked hard not to laugh.

"Nobody important, sweetie. Just a guy who thought he was better than everyone else, but ended up getting into a lot of trouble." She hefted the snow higher. "So. What's it to be? Your honor or your face?"

"The only thing I can do is be completely honest," Jax said. "Some men are better than some women, and some women are better than some men."

Mykaela tilted her head, eyes sparkling with laughter.

"OK, you win. AND I win," she declared, dropping the snowball. "Let him up, kids; a truce has been declared and the war is over." She suddenly shivered. "I don't know about the rest of you, but I'm cold. Who wants hot cocoa?"

Dana-Sue Urso

The answer was unanimous and soon the four-some were in front of the fire, mugs in hand. Jax didn't stay long. He was planning on fixing a portion of the fencing that had come loose in the blizzard. Then he had to go to the feed store and work the rest of the afternoon. Mykaela and the children spent the day doing chores, an unwelcome yet necessary evil in the household every Saturday.

By the end of the day on Sunday, the snow was definitely losing the battle with the sun. Slush puddles abounded, and Mykaela spent a lot of time sweeping muddy water from the floor of the cabin that was tracked in by all of them.

She was puttering around the kitchen waiting for Jax to come in from the barn so she could do a final clean-up when he came in the front door, Doctor Greene with him.

He accepted a cup of coffee and sat down with her while Jax brought in wood. The kids were playing Tiddly-Winks near the fire.

"The reason I stopped by, Mykaela," began Dr. Adams. "is to give you a message. From Tina Michaels." He paused to sip his coffee.

"I hope everything's all right," Mykaela said with concern.

"It will be. The kids have the Mumps."

Mykaela raised her eyebrows. "All four of them?"

The doctor nodded. "Yep. Right down to the baby." Who was actually just over a year old. "And since yours haven't had them . . ."

"They can't go over tomorrow," finished Mykaela. Jax leaned a hip against one of the kitchen counters, sipping at his coffee.

"What's the problem?" he asked.

"Ryan and Rachel were going to stay with them tomorrow while I went to the The Fabric Shop. This was a 4 day holiday weekend," Mykaela frowned. "Now that I think about it, I don't remember seeing them at church this morning."

"Yes, they were all giving each other the mumps. Well, I'd best be off," the doctor stood up. "I need to check on them before I head home. Thanks for the coffee."

After he left, Mykaela sat at the table with a frown of concentration.

"I guess I could take them with me to the store," she mused out loud. "Or maybe I could ask the Harrison's in the morning; their son Tim and Ryan are friends although I don't know his parents very well."

"I'll watch them," Jax offered, picking up one of the kitchen chairs and turning it upside down on the table. He was going to fix a wobbly leg.

"That's very kind, Jax, but I wouldn't want to trouble you."

"It's no trouble, Mykaela," he assured her sincerely. "I don't work at the feed store tomorrow, and I was just planning on fixing the rest of the fence. They can stay outside with me and play."

"Can he, Ma, can he?" Ryan was standing next to her chair, bouncing up on his feet. "I promise to be nice to Rachel.'

"Me, too," piped up the little girl, not to be outdone. "I pwomise not to be a pest."

Jax saw Mykaela's hesitation and felt bad for putting her in this position. It was pretty obvious she didn't trust him fully, and he couldn't really blame her. Feeling embarrassed, he opened his mouth to retract his offer when she spoke to her children.

"Well, if you both promise to behave and not cause Jax any trouble whatsoever . "

"Oh we do, don't we Rach?"

She nodded emphatically. "Uh huh."

"I guess it would be OK," she turned to look at the man standing opposite her. "But are you sure? I mean, it would be easier for you to get your work done without them underfoot."

Relieved, he replied, "It's no problem, really. I'll enjoy the company."

"Can I help fix the fence?" Ryan asked eagerly.

Jax finished tightening the leg and put the chair down.

"Sure!"

"Really?" cried Ryan. "Oh boy!" He grabbed his sister's hand and pulled her back to the hearth to continue their game.

Jax watched him, puzzled.

"Well, I can honestly say that he's the first kid I've ever known who was excited at the prospect of doing something as mundane as fixing a fence."

Mykaela also watched him, a sad smile on her face.

"That's because his father never let him help him do any of those kinds of things. Not even simple chores."

"You're kidding?" Jax was surprised. A young boy should be helping out with the farm's chores, learning the things he needs to know to survive.

"Danny was very impatient," Mykaela went on. "He liked to do things a certain way, and he didn't want to deviate from it. Not even to show his son the things a boy should know," she fiddled with the handle of her coffee cup, speaking in an undertone. "He and I used to argue a lot about that. He just

Legacy of Love

didn't want to be bothered with being a parent, and I found that unacceptable. He would just brush him aside like he was a nuisance. And he never played with him or Rachel."

"You have terrific kids," Jax told her. "Your husband was missing out on something pretty great by not getting to know his own children."

Mykaela smiled at him with gratefulness.

"Thanks! And thank you for being so nice to them."

"It's not a hardship, I assure you," he grinned back, then as if to prove his point, he played a rousing game of Tiddly-Winks with them. As Mykaela watched the three of them together, it occurred to her that in the short time he'd been with them, Jaxon Dumont acted more like a father to them than Danny had in 6 years. Her heart filled with warmth as she watched him playing; he looked so young and carefree, not at all like the man she'd first met. *Which just proved that appearances could be deceiving.*

In fact, she liked the way he looked, the way his hair fell down over his forehead, the way his mouth curved up at the sides as he smiled over the kids' antics, the way his eyes had looked last night in the barn . . .

It suddenly occurred to her that what she felt for him at this moment was way stronger than what she'd ever felt for Danny. She frowned into her cup. *Was that fair to think that way?* she asked herself. She forced herself to remember what she felt when Danny had died; she had been saddened that a young life had been cut short and, if she was honest, she'd felt a little angry that he'd left her to fend for herself. But had she felt pain and remorse that her husband was gone? She sat up straighter, thinking hard. No, she hadn't because her husband had left her a long time before that. She had been so caught up with allowing him to take her away from her father that she'd never really stopped to see what kind of man he was until it was too late. It all came to light after they were married.

She looked over at Jax. How would she feel when he left in the spring? Pain sharp and fierce pierced her chest, the sensation so strong that she barely managed not to draw attention to herself by grabbing at her chest; instead she clutched the edge of the table. Closing her eyes, she let herself think about how she was feeling and more importantly why. She would be beyond sad when he left, she realized. She would be devastated, and the reason became as clear as if she was reading it on a piece of paper.

She loved him. Plain and simple. In the span of a few short weeks, she had allowed herself to fall in love, albeit without meaning to. Feelings of love and warmth spread through her filling her with a quiet joy. THIS was what being in love was like. She was ashamed to admit that she had felt nothing like this for Daniel, not ever; in fact, she knew in her heart of hearts that she'd only married him to get away. But these feelings for Jax were new and somewhat scary because they'd come on so fast. Her heart was pounding with excitement, and she wanted to tell him how she felt.

But she stayed still and quiet. The last thing she would ever want to do was embarrass him. Instead she sent up a simple prayer to God that she hoped it was His will that Jax should fall in love with her. And that she would be able to accept it with dignity if he didn't.

CHAPTER 9

Monday afternoon found Jax halfway down the pasture, trying to get a broken fence post out of the ground. The temperature was in the mid 50's and the snow nothing but muddy slush, but the ground underneath was still somewhat frozen; the post wouldn't budge. He sent Ryan back to the barn to bring him the pick so he could loosen the dirt a bit if it was even possible. Which he doubted. Rachel spotted a winter hare and began chasing it, zig-zagging this way and that, slipping and sliding in the snow-muddy field.

Blackjack, Maestro, and Velvet were mid-field, scrounging around for any grass that may have survived the blizzard; they had churned up quite a muddy swath. Wiping sweat from his brow, Jax shrugged out of his coat, the sun beating down.

Just as he spotted Ryan coming toward him with the pick, all three horses suddenly whinnied, high and loud, before turning tails and heading for the barn in an all out slippery run. Jax stared after them, frowning. Even Ryan slowed down to watch them. *What on earth?* Jax thought to himself. Then the hair on his neck stood up, and goosebumps broke out on his arms. Whipping his head around towards the direction Rachel had run, his heart skipped a beat. The fence line ran parallel to the woods, the two edging closer to each other the farther downfield they went. A huge tree loomed over the fence about 50 yards away, its branches reaching out over the top of the fence into the field. And on one of those branches crouched a cougar. It was very still, tail barely flicking, its eyes focused entirely on the little girl 30 yards ahead, 10 feet down. It would be a fairly easy jump for the big cat.

Later, Jax would swear that time actually slowed down over the next few seconds. As he reached for his rifle (which thank God he always had with him when away from the house), Rachel -- who had been standing with hands on hips, staring in exasperation after the fleeing rabbit -- turned around and locked eyes with the big cat. She screamed and started to run, but slipped and fell. This was the cat's cue. He tensed his muscles and leaped, forelimbs outstretched, razor-sharp claws extended. Still screaming, Rachel scrambled backwards as Jax fired off a shot.

He hadn't had time to sight accurately; he had to get the cat's attention away from the little girl. The bullet hit the cougar in its right hindquarter causing it to howl in fury and pain. Landing short of his goal, the injured animal twisted around to try and get at his hip. Jax fired again, hitting it in the left shoulder. The mountain lion decided to change tactics; he spied the man running towards him and in a mighty leap, despite his injuries, managed to actually reach Jax. But Jax was able to get off a third shot, the angle much better, hitting the cat in the chest as he leapt at him.

Jax took the full force of his weight, and they both went down in a heap. For an instant, Jax expected to feel the cat's jaws around his throat, but then realized that its body was limp. His last shot had been true; the cougar was dead. With a heave, he shoved the large feline off him and sat up. Blood from the animal was splattered down the front of his shirt.

Ryan was kneeling beside a distraught Rachel, his arm around her. Rachel threw herself in Jax's arms, sobbing. He held her and murmured soothing words to her. He couldn't remember what he'd said, but she eventually calmed down. Sniffing and wiping her nose, she tucked her head into Jax's shoulder.

"T-that was a b-bad k-kitty," she said in a wavering voice.

"Yes, it was," he agreed. He noticed how white Ryan was as he looked at his sister, his eyes big and round, shiny with unshed tears of his own. Jax reached out and squeezed the boy's shoulder, smiling encouragingly.

"That was . . . scary," the boy barely got the words out. Clearing his throat he tried again. "I thought cougars lived up in the mountains."

"They do," affirmed Jax. "But I suspect that he was hungry. Maybe starving."

He confirmed this moments later when he examined the cat. He looked to be fairly young although large. One of its legs was deformed, and he had a lot of scarring along his body; it was obvious he'd been in many fights. The thinness of his body revealed that he was probably starving due to his having trouble hunting for food because of his deformity. He probably came down from the hills to try and find an easier meal. Jax kept these thoughts to himself.

"Hey," cried Ryan. "Your shirt's torn."

Jax glanced down at his right arm. His shirt was ripped near the shoulder and, yes, that was his blood staining the cloth. Suddenly his arm felt like it was on fire; the cat had managed to claw him after all. Pulling the shirt away, he saw claw marks 3 inches long that were still trickling blood. *Terrific,* he thought. Not wanting to upset the children even more, he covered the spot with his hand, needing to let go of Rachel in the process.

Dana-Sue Urso

"Come on," he said, standing up. "Let's get to the house. We all could use a good clean up. The fence can wait." Truer words were never spoken. All three of them were filthy from head to toe. Mud and dirty snowy water were plastered over pants and skirt as well as splattered onto coats and Jax's shirt.

But both Ryan and Rachel were staring at his bloody shirt in fascination.

"Does it hurt?" the little girl asked.

"Do you think you'll have a scar?" asked Ryan, eyeing the blood trail avidly. Jax wasn't sure whether to be relieved that they weren't upset at the sight of blood or not. Their interest seemed a bit macabre.

"Yes, it hurts. And yes, it'll probably leave a scar," he answered honestly, leading the way back towards the cabin. He didn't notice the tears gathering once again in Rachel's eyes. They were just going through the gate when the backdoor opened, and Mykaela stepped out on the porch.

Ryan spotted her first and ran to her, trying to tell her what happened. Rachel ran up to her, crying again. All Mykaela could make out from Ryan's excited chatter was 'mountain lion' and 'Rachel.' Her heart in her throat, she gathered her daughter to her, quickly assessing her for any injuries.

"Ma-you-shoulda-seen-him-he-was-huge-and-he-was-hungry-and-he-thought-Rachel-was-a-snack-and   .   .   .," Mykaela lifter her hand to stop him. Picking up Rachel, she looked to Jax for the full story. She was having difficulty concentrating as she knew from Ryan's disjointed ramblings that Rachel had been in danger.

Jax looked her right in the eyes.

Legacy of Love

"She's fine," he reassured her quietly. "The cat never touched her."

Mykaela nodded, then noticed his shirt and arm. "But your hurt." She cried.

"M-mama," sniffled Rachel. "That bad k-kitty scratched Jax."

"I can see that. Come on, let's go in so I can take a look at it."

She put water on to warm up and gathered up her bag of clean cloths she used for bandages as well as some salve. Jax told her that he could clean the wound himself, but she overruled him; staying busy would keep her from reacting to the fact that her little girl had been in mortal danger. She made him sit at the table and hold a cloth to his arm while she instructed the kids to wash up in their room and put on clean clothes, this after she comforted Rachel for a few minutes first.

When she came out of the kids' room, she saw that Jax had taken off his shirt and was dabbing at the wound. She picked up the basin, rounded the table behind him … and came to an abrupt stop. She couldn't help the gasp from escaping. Five long ugly-looking scars criss-crossed Jax's back, three diagonally from shoulder to low back and two straight across his mid-back. They were white and puckered, obviously old and well-healed. But to leave such terrible scars meant that the original injuries must have been from a horrifically brutal beating. Maybe more than one.

Jax heard her gasp and looked over his shoulder. He saw her staring at his back and wanted to curse in frustration. He'd taken off his bloodied shirt as that made it easier to get to the wound, but he'd completely forgotten about his scars. He turned away before he saw revulsion in her eyes. Feeling shamed and embarrassed, he grabbed up his shirt and started to pull it back on, uncaring that his injured arm was hurting something awful.

Then, he felt her touch one of the scars so lightly and quickly that he couldn't really be sure she'd touched him at all.

"What terrible pain you must have suffered," Mykaela murmured sympathetically; Jax had to strain to hear her. She came around in front of him. "How awful for you." She set the water down and began pulling cloths from her bag.

Jax stared at her in amazement. She didn't sound as if she was repulsed by his scars. In fact, he could actually feel her empathy, and it tugged on his heart like nothing ever had. And she had physically touched him. Had actually touched one of those hideous scars.

A huge weight he hadn't even been aware of suddenly lifted off his shoulders. He'd carried the memories of that dark time in Andersonville around for so long, and then been incarcerated yet again, believing he'd never be free, followed by the worst thing that had ever happened to him -- the rejection by his family -- all of it had worked together to create a wall around his heart. And now, little by little, living here with this amazing woman and her children had caused that wall to crack. He had never known such peace and contentment as he felt here. All the traveling he'd done, all the things he'd seen, everything he'd been through, had led him to this one place and moment in time.

And as Mykaela leaned over him and began wiping the blood from his arm and shoulder, he knew without a shadow of a doubt that he loved her more than life itself. He watched her as she worked, memorizing every facet of her face. And if she was aware of his intense scrutiny, she never let on.

She continued to carefully and gently care for his wound. As the blood wiped away, she could clearly see the claw marks. There were 4 of them beginning at the shoulder joint and traveling halfway down his upper arm. The two inner ones were still seeping blood, and she pressed a folded cloth against it, applying pressure.

"I think they need stitches," she remarked, looking directly at him. Their faces were inches apart. Mykaela felt her breath catch in her throat at the way he was looking at her, his eyes filled with . . .something. Suddenly nervous, she licked her dry lips unaware that the simple gesture caused a wave of desire to shoot through Jax like an arrow. Needing distraction, Jax put his hand over hers to lift away the cloth so he could see the wound.

"Well, Nurse," he said, striking a jovial tone. "You may be right. The two in the middle could probably use a few stitches." He dabbed at it while she got another wet cloth ready to continue cleaning the wound.

"Where's the cougar now?" she asked steadily though her hands were shaking. Jax quickly explained what had happened, downplaying his part in it, ending with,

"Mykaela, I'm so sorry for the danger I put Rachel in." He had such a look of guilt that Mykaela actually got mad. Putting her hands on her hips, she said very clearly,

"From what I can see, you not only saved her life, but risked your own life to do it. All I can say is Thank God you had your rifle. And," she paused to take a steadying breath, "thank you for saving her." Her voice caught, and she couldn't prevent the tears that came to her eyes. Sitting down, she picked up one of the clean cloths and swiped at them.

Jax tilted his head to one side and smiled at her.

"Now I know where Rachel gets her cockiness from. She puts her hands on her hips the exact same way you do."

Mykaela gave him a watery smile.

"She is definitely her mother's daughter," she agreed before proceeding to bandage his arm. "You'll need to go see Doc Greene."

Jax studied his bandaged arm.

"You know, you make a pretty good nurse," he complimented her. "In fact," he stood up and stepped towards the stairs. "you'd probably make a pretty good doctor, too. For a girl."

Mykaela threw a bundle of cloths at him while he laughed and headed up the steps. Smiling at his playful attitude, especially in light of all that had happened, she started to clean up.

She threw the bloodied bandages into the fire and put away the cloth bag. Turning, she spied Rachel standing in the doorway of her room.

"Mama?" she said quietly. "Is Jax gonna be OK?"

Mykaela held out her arms, surprised when the little girl walked very slowly towards her.

"Yes, sweetheart, he'll be fine. He's going to go see Doc Greene for a few stitches, but that's all."

Rachel suddenly burst into tears. Running to her mother, she threw her arms around her waist.

"It's all m-my f-fault that J-Jax got hurted," she wailed.

Mykaela squatted down and put her arms around her daughter.

Legacy of Love

"No, Rachel, it wasn't your fault," she insisted, unsure of where this was coming from. "It wasn't anyone's fault. Sometimes bad things just happen."

Rachel leaned back, sniffling. "B-but if I hadn't ch-chased the wabbit, the kitty wouldn've tried to eat me."

Before Mykaela could think of an adequate reply to allay her daughter's guilt, Jax was there. Kneeling beside them, he cupped his hand behind Rachel's head, gently forcing her to look at him.

"I want you to listen to me very carefully, Rachel," he began, speaking quietly yet firmly. "Cougars don't usually bother with people at all. They stay far away from us. But for some reason, the one today came right up to where we were, probably because he was very hungry and was getting desperate. Chasing that rabbit had nothing to do with his decision to attack us. If we hadn't been there, he would have gone after the horses. *You* are absolutely, positively not to blame for my getting scratched; in fact, I should have known better than to get too close so it's really my fault I got hurt."

Mykaela suspected that he got 'too close' in order to protect Rachel, but didn't dispute his claim. She watched the two of them standing so close together, her heart full of love and gratefulness. She almost started crying when her daughter hugged Jax as hard as she could, and he hugged her right back, his eyes closed.

Jax's throat suddenly ached as he struggled to maintain his composure. He hadn't thought twice about saving Rachel from the mountain lion because he had come to love her and her brother. How he wished he could be an actual member of this little family.

Pulling back slightly, he pressed his forehead against Rachel's and said, "Now, no more talk of who's at fault. OK?"

" 'K," she agreed before kissing his cheek. That nearly did him in. He stood up and mumbled something about getting his arm sewn up, then walked quickly out the front door. Mykaela smiled secretly knowing that her family was getting to him. Maybe, just maybe, he wouldn't want to leave when spring came.

It was about 9 pm. Jaxon had come back with a total of 8 stitches, ate supper, then went to dispose of the cougar's body before the evening chores. Mykaela finished putting the children to bed and sat down to try and see if she could salvage Jax's torn shirt. He came in from the chores, threw some wood on the fire, and sat opposite her with his rifle and cleaning kit. Mykaela eyed the gun and remarked, "I'm very glad you carry your rifle with you."

"So am I," he agreed wholeheartedly. "I learned to always have it with me when I was growing up. My father made sure my brother and I learned how to shoot when we were barely out of diapers, or so it seemed." He smiled at the memories.

"I remember you telling me you grew up on a ranch. Is it close to here?" Mykaela deliberately keeping her tone light and casual.

He shrugged. "Between Boulder and Denver."

She noticed that he was rubbing the barrel a bit more vigorously that was warranted, his mouth in a hard line. But whether from discomfort from his injured arm or from unpleasant memories, she couldn't be sure.

Legacy of Love

Still feeling her way, she asked tentatively, "You never told me about prison, why you were sent there. Do you mind telling me now?"

Jax shook his head. "No, I don't mind. I told myself I'd tell you the whole story when you asked."

He told her about the poker game, the argument and threats, the fight the next morning; he left out his spending the night with the saloon-girl.

"When the judge sentenced me to life in prison, it was worse than death. Or so I thought. Knowing I'd never be free, well, after Andersonville, I truly wished I'd received the death sentence."

"Oh, Jax, I'm so sorry," Mykaela's heart went out to him.

"You're probably wondering whether or not I wrote to my family. The answer is yes and no. I wrote several letters during the first year, but I never sent them." He paused here, gathering his thoughts. "I knew that by now, they must have thought I had died in the war. To have them know I was alive but trapped in a prison where I would never be able to be with them ever again seemed somehow worse." He swallowed hard, not looking at her. "To be honest, I wasn't at all sure I would be able to handle it, seeing them if they came on visiting day, and then watching them walk away. So, I never told them where I was."

Mykaela replied gently, "I think I understand. I know it must have been so hard for you."

Jax worked on cleaning the inside of the barrel for a moment before answering somewhat bitterly.

"What was hard was knowing that if I had just notified them upon my release from Andersonville, I wouldn't be spending the rest of my life in prison."

"Yet, here you are," Mykaela pointed out. "Not in prison."

Jax smiled ruefully. "You're right. And, no, I'm not an escapee."

Mykaela shot him a frigid look at his joke. He ignored it and went on with his tale.

"I spent the first six months in prison defending myself. Inmates tend to create little cliques that they feel comfortable in. I just wanted to be left alone. But inevitably, I had to make some choices and become friends with some of the other inmates if I was to survive. But even so, there were quite a few fights, and I spent time in solitary which wasn't all that bad really. That's where I first met Sheriff Hoskins. He was the lead guard for solitary confinement. He didn't like me, but he wasn't cruel, and he treated everyone fairly." He thought for a moment. "There was this huge fight that broke out between some of the more violent inmates and the guards. One of the guards got stabbed in the belly with a butter knife that had been filed down into a sharp point. No one was helping him. All the other guards had their hands full keeping everyone under control so I did what I could to stop the bleeding." He paused again. Then, "The prison doctor and warden knew I had tried to help him. They knew from my records that I was a doctor and arranged to have me work in the infirmary three afternoons a week. I was glad to have something constructive to do." He didn't mention that the rest of the time when he wasn't in the infirmary was spent at hard labor, something he didn't rebel against because the hard physical work enabled him to sleep at night with fewer nightmares. It was also a good way to work off the anger and frustration that were a daily part of his life.

However, working at the infirmary had its perks including the fact that the other inmates began to trust him so much so that they quit picking fights with him and left him alone.

"Working at the clinic got me through the second year, and I started to think I might actually survive after all. One day at a time."

The nights were the worst; he didn't tell her about the nightmares or the fact that he had trouble sleeping if he didn't exhaust himself. He did tell her that his lawyer showed up one day with his release papers.

"My lawyer never gave up on me, always believing I was innocent." He broke off, remembering his lawyer with something akin to amazement.

"So what happened?" Mykaela was listening with rapt attention.

"Well, apparently, there *was* a witness to the fight and shooting."

"And he took over two years to come forward?" Mykaela was indignant.

"It was Judge Waverley, the boy's father." He watched with some amusement as her jaw dropped opened. "I had a similar look on my face, believe me." He went on to explain that the judge not only witnessed what had occurred that fateful morning, but had snatched up the knife as well. Without it as proof of Scott's attack on him, Jax hadn't stood a chance in court. The judge had always known his son had a mean streak in him, gambled too much, got into too many fights, but he always looked the other way. And with his death, he didn't want his son remembered as a bully.

"But apparently the guilt kept eating at him. That's why he spoke up on my behalf at the trial, convincing the trial judge not to impose the death penalty which is normal in murder convictions. Two years after the trial, the judge found out he was dying from a rare blood disorder. Probably cancer. Anyway, over the next few months, I guess the guilt ate at him, and he finally decided that he didn't want to die with a guilty conscience so he wrote out what really happened that day, called the trial judge, the prosecuting attorney, the jury foreman, the sheriff, and my lawyer to his bedside, and told them everything."

"Thank God," breathed out Mykaela, fascinated by his story.

"He even gave over the knife," Jax explained. "It matched my description exactly. All six of them agreed to turn over the conviction, and my lawyer headed off to Jefferson City as quickly as he could." Jax wanted to tell her how he felt upon his release as he walked out of that prison a free man, but couldn't find the right words. "Relief just isn't strong enough to describe my emotions that day." Was all he could come up with.

"I can only imagine," Mykaela said. "But thankfully the judge -- the father -- did the right thing in the end although you lost over two years of your life."

"Sometimes I think it's a just punishment for provoking the boy in the first place. I had so much anger bottled up inside from the war . . . . . I was always looking for some way to vent it, unfortunately." He didn't mention that the venting was usually done in a saloon-girl's room or with a bottle. His time in the penitentiary had helped him come to terms with a lot of his anger and frustration. When he left the prison, he decided that his life had to change, that he had to try and gain some self-respect. Although in his heart of hearts, he hadn't believed that would ever be possible. But sitting here with this amazing woman, being accepted by her, living with such peace and calmness, he couldn't help thinking that maybe things could be different.

They were both silent for a time, each working quietly. A log fell over, crackling and sending up a shower of sparks. Finally, Mykaela declared that his shirt was a lost cause.

"Even with patches, it just wouldn't look right."

"That's OK. Thanks for trying to repair it."

She planned on sewing him a new one; it was the least she could do although she didn't tell him. The fabric was flannel, and she had several stacks of it that she used to make blankets and the occasional piece of clothing. She would use the torn shirt for sizing.

Jax finished cleaning his rifle and stood up to stretch. He hadn't realized how tense his muscles were; his right arm was sore although Doc Greene had done a good job sewing him up. It was going on 10:00, and though it had been a long day, he was restless and full of nervous energy.

"Do you want to let me beat you at a game of checkers?" he challenged Mykaela.

Calmly looking up at him, she replied, "No thank you. But I'd be happy to beat the pants off of you fair and square."

"Not literally, I hope," he said teasingly, then grinned when she blushed; he thought she was adorable.

"Just set up the board," she ordered mock sternly to hide her discomfiture.

An hour later, they both had each won a game and tied twice, then agreed to call it a night. As she stood up from where she had been curled in front of the fireplace, Mykaela didn't realize her left leg was numb from sitting in one position for so long. It wouldn't hold her weight, and she began to topple over sideways towards the fireplace. But Jax reached for her, dropping the board and checkers in the process. Neither one of them noticed. As he held her and prevented her from falling, Jax drew her a little closer.

Mykaela, feeling content in his arms, whispered, "Thank you."

"You're welcome," Jax whispered back just before he settled his lips over hers. Her lips were soft and warm, tasting slightly chocolaty from the cocoa they'd drank during their games. She fit perfectly in his arms, and he pulled her closer, gratified when she didn't resist.

Mykaela had never been kissed like this before. Danny's lips had usually been cold and unyielding, demanding and pushy. But Jax was patient and gentle, asking but not demanding. She felt a pinging in her blood and wished the feeling could go on forever.

But Jax had a slightly clearer head. He knew if he didn't stop right now, he might make a huge mistake. And the last thing he would ever want to do was to take advantage of this amazing woman. So he slowly, reluctantly, drew back. He gazed down into her liquid brown eyes that were slightly glazed over, his own eyes smoky gray.

"Mykaela, I won't say I'm sorry for what just happened, because I'm not, but I promise I won't ever take advantage of you or hurt you," Jax told her from the heart.

Mykaela nodded, and tried to form a coherent sentence. It took her two tries.

"Just so you know, I'm not sorry either," and with that, she stepped out of his arms and headed for her bedroom. She knew she should stay to clean up, but she was afraid she would throw herself back into his arms and beg him to kiss her again.

Jax watched her go, a silly grin on his face. He knew she'd been affected by their kiss, had seen her struggle to get herself under control. As a normal red-blooded man, he felt a little proud and smug. But as a man who wanted to do the right thing, he could only hope that her positive response was a sign that maybe she was coming to care for him as much as he was for her. Whistling softly, he cleaned up the checkers, banked the fire, and went up to bed.

CHAPTER 10

The next two weeks went by with no excitement, a good thing in Jax's opinion. He had settled into a routine that he found calming in its normalcy. He worked four days during the week at the feed store with the occasional Saturday. On his days off, he still found plenty to do around the farm especially since the weather was holding. There were always the chores to do and something to repair, and it felt good to actually be accomplishing something, to provide and help this little family who had come to mean so much to him.

He liked the evenings best of all. Because he could spend them with Mykaela. He looked forward to the time after supper when she would help the kids with homework, or he would play a simple game with them. After she put the children to bed, she would sit in her rocker by the fire, usually with a cup of hot cocoa, and work on a sewing project. She had already knit him a couple pairs of socks, and she mended his clothes as well. She had even knit him a scarf, warm and fluffy, blue with black edges; he was touched beyond words as it had been so very long since anyone had given him a gift. He wished he could afford to buy her a new cloak, but just didn't have the available funds which was ironic, really. But he was saving every bit he could, determined to buy her a new cloak by Christmas.

It gave him pleasure to sit across from her working on one of his own projects such as cleaning his gun, oiling his saddle, or fixing something around the cabin that was broken. It gave them time to talk or just sit quietly, enjoying each other's company. He found it very soothing that they could be silent yet comfortable with each other at the same time.

The not quite two months he'd been with the Caldwells had eased some of the tension and frustration he'd been carrying around for so long; he felt less discouraged when he thought about his family. The harmony in this household, his having a purpose for his life, and his growing closer to God had helped to begin healing some of his inner wounds.

For Mykaela's part, she thanked God every night for bringing Jaxon Dumont into their lives. His rent and the way he took care of the farm helped to ease the burden *she'd* carried for so long. And even though she knew it wouldn't last longer than another 2-3 months at the most, she would be grateful for the time that he was there. That didn't mean that her financial worries were over. Far from it. She wasn't sure if she would have enough money saved to pay the taxes that would come due at the end of December. She had been scrimping and saving all summer. If nothing major occurred and if she could start putting aside some of Jax's rent, then she may just have enough, but nothing was guaranteed. And even if she came up with the correct amount, Christmas would be very slim and disappointing as usual. In the back of her mind, she knew she could always sell one of the horses although she wouldn't do that just for presents, only if she needed money for the taxes.

At least the cabin and property were paid for, had been before she'd married Danny. She had actually sold a total of 190 acres since his death, to pay the taxes. One of the ranches abutted her property line way to the north toward the mountains; the owner had bought most of the land turning it from crop planting to grazing. All that was left was the 10 acre pasture she needed for the animals as well as about two acres of the forest that stood between the back property and the front. She had run out of options and prayed often to God to show her what she was to do.

She didn't want to burden Jax with this problem so she never shared her worries with him. She trusted God that everything would work out in the end.

October segued into November with little fanfare. The weather continued to stay warm, relatively speaking -- 40's during the day. Mykaela saved most of the rent money for the taxes, built up her account at the general store by selling eggs and milk, and used her wages from the laundering she did for the hotel to pay for needed grocery items and other essentials like kerosene and shoes.

Shoes were an item that were absolutely necessary yet the children, especially Ryan, grew out of them so quickly. He was now beginning to complain that his shoes were pinching his feet; she'd just bought them mid-summer. She didn't want to dip into her tax-savings, but she also didn't have enough money to buy new ones. So she went against Ryan's wishes and found an adequate pair from the donated clothes that Misty Brooks routinely gathered from the community.

Mykaela tried to buy a new pair at least once a year and had explained to Ryan why he had to have used ones this time out. He never complained, but she knew he was somewhat embarrassed and hoped no one at school would notice. Watching him take the pair into his room, she heaved a big sigh. Yet again, she felt inadequate because she couldn't provide for her children as well as she liked. But Ryan also had to learn to make do and that it really wasn't the end of the world not to have new. She rarely ever picked through the used clothes barrel for more than shoes because Miss Hanks let her have cloth and material in exchange for wages so she could make most of their clothes rather than having to buy.

One bitterly cold evening the second week in November found Jax in the barn affixing new strips to the wagon wheels -- he'd found the strips under a tarp covering an old wheel. They were brand new, but had never been used. A complete waste because Mykaela's wagon had probably needed new stripping for quite awhile.

Jax heard the door open and watched Ryan amble in. He was shuffling, kicking his feet which usually always meant he was worried or upset.

"Hey," Jax greeted. "You're just in time to help me set this wheel."

Ryan shrugged, barely looking up. Narrowing his eyes thoughtfully, Jax said,

"You know, I find it hard to believe it's really that bad."

That caught Ryan's attention, and he looked up with a puzzled expression.

"What's that bad?" he couldn't help asking.

Jax leaned an arm across the wheel.

"The down-in-the-dumps look on your face."

Ryan slumped even more.

"Oh."

"Come on. What gives?" Jax urged him gently.

"Nothin'" A pause. Jax waited patiently. "It's just that . . . well, my Ma gave me some new shoes only they aren't really new." His voice lowered. "They're *used*." He said it like it was a bad word.

"Oh, I see. Well, I had the blacksmith put a horseshoe on Blackjack once that I'd found in the road which was lucky for me since I didn't have the money to buy a new one."

"No one can see his shoes." Ryan pointed out despondently.

"That's true. But the way I see it is that you needed new shoes, and God provided a way for you to get them. What if there hadn't been any in your size?"

"Then Ma would've had to buy them." Ryan stubbornly crossed his arms.

"Don't you think she would have bought them if she'd had the money?"

Agitated, Ryan flung his arms up into the air.

"She does have the money. She's *saving* it!" He spit this out.

"Saving for what?'

"The stupid taxes," Ryan muttered, sprawling down on a bale of hay sitting near the chicken pen.

Jax frowned. He knew the farm was paid off since Mykaela told him Daniel had owned it for about 15 years before they were married; she'd said that Danny had been about 10 years older than her and had lived by himself a long time. But the taxes were something he'd not considered, probably because he'd never had to pay them.

Still trying to be logical, he remarked, "What would happen if your mother didn't have enough money to pay the taxes?"

Ryan was silent for a moment, then heaving a sigh, he reluctantly replied, "I guess we'd lose the farm."

Jax let that simmer for awhile as he set about finishing his self-appointed task. After a few minutes, the boy wandered over. He ran his hand down the wheel feeling the smoothness achieved by Jax after he'd sanded it.

"Jax, do you ever wish you had more money? You know, enough to buy anything you want?"

Careful here, Jax thought to himself. *I don't want to lie.* Aloud, he said, "Well, to be honest, I grew up in a pretty nice house. And we had some pretty nice things. But do you know what I remember most about my childhood?" He stopped what he was doing to give Ryan his full attention. "I remember the times my mother baked cookies. I remember playing hide and seek with my brother and cousins in the barn. I remember my father teaching me how to ride a horse and me teaching my little sister. But right now, if you asked me, I couldn't tell you what any of my birthday gifts were or what presents Santa left in my stocking. **Families** are what make up happy memories, Ryan, not **things** that can be broken or lost. And even though it is nice to have new things, they don't bring happiness. And it's important to realize that there are some people who don't even have a used pair of shoes to wear."

Going back to his work, Jax watched Ryan out of the corner of his eyes. The boy looked very thoughtful, mulling over what he'd said.

"Ma hasn't baked cookies in a long time," Ryan said slowly. "But she always has cocoa, and I love hot chocolate." He ducked his head. "I'd like to learn how to ride a horse some day." He gave a sideways glance towards Blackjack who was in the stall behind him, munching on some oats.

"Maybe I can teach you come spring," Jax offered.

"Really? Truly?" Ryan beamed up at him.

"Sure thing," Jax assured him with a smile.

Then Ryan asked if he could help him with the wheels, and the two spent a pleasant hour together, Jax's affection growing ever stronger for this young boy as Ryan's was for him.

The next morning, Jax hooked up the wagon and drove everyone to town. The kids had school, and Mykaela had her laundry delivery and pick-up to make; Blackjack was tied to the back. Jax had to ride to Pagosa Springs as a favor for the doctor. The train was going to be a few days late because of some rail problems further up the line, and on it was some medicine that the doc needed somewhat urgently for one of his patients. He had asked Jax to go by horseback which would allow him to get there and back in one day; Doc Greene was too old to travel all that way on the back of a bobbing horse and would pay him for his time, but Jax had no intention of accepting what amounted to a small favor for a friend, especially a favor that was a medical need.

As Jax set the brake near the hotel, the hairs on the back of his neck stood straight up. The last time he'd felt it was the morning Scott Waverly attacked him. Looking around, all he saw was a few townspeople going about their daily business. He didn't see anyone who looked suspicious or who was watching him.

Shrugging it off, he helped Mykaela down. She thanked him and told him to be careful. He grinned.

"You sound like a mother."

"That's because I am," she responded primly. "Just not yours."

Legacy of Love

Jax grew serious. "No. You're not." He gazed expectantly into her eyes, wishing he had the right to just lean down and kiss her goodbye.

I wish he would kiss me goodbye, Mykaela thought to herself as she looked into his extraordinary smoky eyes.

Loud laughter broke them apart. The barkeep of the saloon next door was talking to the telegraph operator who wore a huge grin although neither were paying them any attention.

"I'll see you tonight," Jax said as he untied his horse. "I expect I'll be late, probably after the kids are in bed; I'll use the outside door up to my room."

"You don't need to do that," she told him, following his movements as he swung effortlessly up onto Blackjack. "And don't worry about the chores; Ryan and I will do them."

Jax nodded and gave her a wave goodbye. As he set the horse in motion, he again had the feeling he was being watched. Trying not to be so obvious this time, he attempted to see if there was indeed someone watching him. But again, nothing. Figuring he was just being jumpy for some unknown reason, he cantered out of town, following the railroad tracks north.

Mykaela spent a long day washing, scrubbing the cabin's floor, and baking bread. By the time the children came home, she was tired. But if was the good kind from knowing you worked hard for your family.

She had put pinto beans on to soak that morning, but after mixing up some cornbread batter, she decided the beans needed another hour. The sun was just starting to disappear over the mountains as she went to the barn to do the chores.

She liked to get them done early when Jax wasn't home. Ryan usually helped, but today, he had a lot of math problems to work, so she had him stay in the cabin to work on them. And to keep an eye on Rachel who was copying her spelling words.

When she opened the barn door and stepped into the shadowy building, she lit the lantern that hung on a hook between the door and the indoor chicken coop on the right. Weak light came through the windows, but would soon fade as the sun continued its journey west.

As she rehung the lantern, goose bumps broke out on her arms. Frowning, she turned and looked around, but all she saw was the usual: chickens clucking around, the newly cleaned open area to the left of the door (Jax had spent an afternoon clearing away old junk), newly waxed wagon strips leaning against the first stall, Maestro and Velvet shuffling around in the two stalls next to the chicken coop. Nothing out of the ordinary. Nothing to explain the sudden wariness that crept over her.

Mykaela was rarely nervous being alone, probably because that's how she'd spent much of her life. Up until last Spring, they'd had a watchdog; she knew she should get another one, but that just meant another mouth to feed, and she'd never really seen the need. Barn cats on the other hand were useful, but their's had run off a few months ago.

Uneasy, she scooped up some chicken feed and quickly scattered it inside the coop. Then she headed for Maestro who gazed placidly at her over his stall door. As she prepared to enter the stall to fill the oat bucket, she heard a noise behind her. But before she could turn, an arm came around her waist grasping her tightly while a large hand clamped over her mouth.

Legacy of Love

Struggling, Mykaela tried to dislodge the hand; a chilling chuckle resounded in her left ear.

"Go ahead and scream," a deceptively soft raspy voice said. "I'm shore those kids up in the house'll come runnin to see what's what."

Dear God, the children! Mykaela immediately quit moving and stood still. Her heart pounded so hard, she wondered why it didn't just beat itself out of her chest. She had never been so frightened in her life, and she couldn't help trembling as she stood in this horrible man's embrace. He slowly lifted his hand away from her mouth, and when she didn't yell, he turned her around.

Mykaela found herself staring into the coldest pair of eyes she'd ever seen. The wild thought came to her then that she'd thought Jax's eyes were cold when she'd first seen them. How could she have been so wrong? This man's eyes held no emotion whatsoever; they were like two pieces of green ice, glittering shards of glass. Her fear jumped up a notch which he must have noticed because the grin he gave her was full of malevolence. He had dirty, broken teeth and fetid breath that nearly choked her. He was filthy and unkempt with long greasy hair. Foulness emanated from him, and Mykaela knew that she was in grave danger.

"You shore are a purty little thing, aint ya?" the man said, eyeing her up and down. "It's been awhule since I had me such a purty woman." His intent was plainly obvious, and Mykaela panicked. She kicked out at him and twisted away for a few precious seconds, but he caught her several feet from the door, pulling her to a stop by her braid. Latching his arm around her again, he whipped out a knife and placed it against her throat. She couldn't honestly say what frightened her more: the coldness of the steel or the coldness of his eyes.

Then he whispered, "If you do that again, I'll knock ya out and introduce myself to those young-uns."

Mykaela believed him. She had no choice. Seeing the knife and thinking about what this man could do with it intensified her fear to the point that she was afraid she would pass out.

"P-Please don't hurt them," she cried. "I-I'll do anything you want, but p-promise you won't harm them."

He chuckled again. "Waal now, let's just see how things go from here on out, shall we?"

He began to pull her back towards the pole that made up one side of Blackjack's empty stall. Jax wasn't due back for several more hours which meant that Mykaela was completely at this man's mercy without hope of reprieve; it was all she could do not to lose control and scream out her fears and frustrations.

Releasing her, he stepped back and ordered her to take off her cloak. Tears welling up, she shrugged out of her wrap, having a sudden urge to throw it at him and try to get away. But then what? It wasn't like he couldn't catch her before she could get the kids to safety. Sending up a fervent prayer, she threw the wrap to the side.

The man pulled out a length of her own clothesline, grinning when he saw her flinch.

"Unbind your hair," he ordered next.

Swallowing against the rising panic, she did as she was told.

He reached out with the knife and wove it through the long strands.

Legacy of Love

"Real purty. Nice and shiny. Now sit."

"M-my husband'll be home any minute now," she boldly lied, desperate.

"Really?" he responded slowly. "I saw'm ride out earlier today, to Pagoda Springs if the storekeeper can be believed. 'Sides, iffen he does get back afore we're done, he can watch." He let out a chuckle that made her skin crawl.

"What are you g-going to do?" she asked, not moving, her eyes wide and bright with unshed tears. Suddenly, pain exploded in her skull as he backhanded her across the face, hard enough that she stumbled and fell. Quick as a snake, he was pulling her hands behind her and tying them to the post, leaving her in a half sitting/half reclining position.

Trying to clear her head, Mykaela worked at getting her breath back. She tasted blood at the corner of her lip, and her head felt like it was going to explode. A few tears tracked their way down her cheeks.

"Waal now, that's much better," he told her, squatting next to her. "And in case ys didn't get it yet, no more talkin'"

He ran a grubby hand through her hair, rubbing his unshaven cheek against it, admiring it in a way that made Mykaela's blood run cold. Then he suddenly leaned forward and smashed his lips on hers. Disgusted, she couldn't help but struggle, although futilely. He pulled back slightly and laughed.

Then he kissed her again and ran his fingers along the top of her bodice before cutting the buttons off one at a time. She silently prayed over and over as she sat helpless in this wicked man's power unable to prevent the horror that was coming.

153

Dana-Sue Urso

Jax rode back to Riverton like a tornado was chasing him. He had spent most of the day waiting on the stage (it had picked up the medicine from another town where the train was stopped), fretting about . . . . . . something. All he knew was that ever since he'd left for Pagoda Springs, he had the nagging feeling that something was wrong. That he had to get back as fast as possible.

So here he was, riding like the wind and didn't know why. As the town came into view from atop a hill, he felt calmer. Soon he'd be back at the cabin, having a pleasant evening with the woman he loved. Albeit, it would be even more pleasant if she loved him back, but that wasn't to be. At least not right now.

He trotted down Main Street towards Doc Greene's clinic. Everything looked as it usually did: a buggy or two making their way down the street, a couple of cowhands tying their horses in front of the Silver Dollar Saloon, Sam sweeping the boardwalk in front of his store. Waving to him, Jax rode on, stopping at the clinic.

After delivering the medicine, he declined the doctor's offer of a cup of coffee, insisted that he didn't want paid, and again feeling an urgency to get home sooner rather than later. As he strode back out, he came face to face with the sheriff.

"Evenin' Dumont," the older man greeted cheerily.

"Sheriff."

"How 'bout a drink before you head home?"

Jax hesitated. It still surprised him that they could have a normal relationship, some might even say a friendship. Not wanting to cause a division in their fragile rapport, Jax opened his mouth to accept. But he was suddenly overcome with another overwhelming desire to get home; the feeling was so strong, he actually turned toward his horse before remembering to answer.

"Thanks, but can I take a rain check?" he said, actually feeling more and more anxious to be on his way.

"Sure! I know you must be tired. Say hello to Mykaela for me."

Jax nodded and leapt into the saddle. Spurring him on, Jax guided Blackjack out of town. As he approached the end of the tree line, he instinctively slowed the animal to a walk. They came around the corner, and there stood the cabin, unchanged, the same. Smoke rose lazily from the chimney, nothing moved. In the fading light, he could see the barn door stood slightly ajar which meant Mykaela was doing the chores early as was her want.

But as he continued to head toward the building, the hairs on the back of his neck stood up again.

Frowning, his heart thudding with anticipation, he looked all around him as he climbed down and pulled his gun from the holster. Quietly, he walked to the front windows of the cabin and peered in. Ryan and Rachel were sitting at the table, their hands busy with some project; that was one concern out of the way.

He crept toward the barn, cocking the hammer on the gun, straining to hear something, anything, but all was silent. However, as he neared the door, he heard a muffled shuffling sound, then an almost inaudible human voice. *A male voice.* Gripping the gun securely, he edged his way into the doorway. And the sight before him scared him more than anything else in his life ever had.

A very large man was kneeling beside Mykaela, much of his body obscured by her, half his face showing above her right shoulder. But it was the wicked-looking knife that held Jax's attention. The blade had to be at least 4 inches long with a base that was a good two inches wide. The curved point, glinting in what little light there was, pressed against her throat.

"Waal, now, look whose come to join the fun." The man said with a vicious chuckle.

Aiming the gun at his head, Jax said firmly and clearly, "Let her go, or I'll blow your head off."

"D'ya really wanna risk hitting this purty little thing?" he asked quite casually. "Even at this close range, I doubt ya'd be able ta miss 'er."

Unfortunately, he was right. Jax was a decent shot, but the man was too close to Mykaela.

Trying another tactic, he taunted,   "Hiding behind a woman just proves how much of a coward you are."

The stranger just smiled and maliciously made a small knick in Mykaela's neck; she couldn't help flinching. Jax's heart leapt up to his throat, and he automatically took a step toward them.

"I wouldn't do that," he waved Jax back with his head. "One more step, and I'll slice her up good."

"Then your shield would be gone," Jax pointed out, wanting so badly to look at Mykaela, but knowing he had to keep his focus on the man.

"Nice try, cowboy, but I know how ta slice without killin'. D'ya wanna see?" he moved the knife slightly.

"No, don't," Jax couldn't help crying out. He stepped back.

That's better, but ya got 10 seconds to throw that peacemaker over inta the stall. One . . ."

Legacy of Love

Jax risked glancing at Mykaela. She was watching him with overly bright eyes. Fury filled him as he noted the dried blood on the side of the mouth and the bruise forming along her jaw line.

"Three, Four . . ."

Her hair was unbound and disheveled, the front of her bodice torn open. Her hands looked to be tied behind her, and she was trembling.

"Six, Seven . . ."

But the look in her eyes was what nearly did him in. They were full of trust and hope; she fully believed he could save her. He felt like a failure because for the life of him, he didn't know what to do.

"Nine, . . ."

"OK!" Jax practically shouted. "You win." *For now*, he echoed in his head before resetting the hammer and tossing the gun over the man's head into Blackjack's stall.

He stood there, fists clenched, praying that the man would leave Mykaela alone. The stranger smiled malevolently and kept his eyes on Jax as he ran his free hand down Mykaela's hair and across her chest. Mykaela tried hard not to react, but she had an overpowering urge to vomit. Swallowing hard against the bile rising in her throat, she stayed still, not wanting to be a distraction to Jax who stood frozen, not saying anything, his rage building; one good thing had come out of his times of imprisonment: he had learned the art of patience and had the ability to keep his emotions under control during times of great stress.

"I'm not so shore having yur man watch is all it's cracked up to be," her attacker whispered softly. "I think I'll just kill'im." And with that he jumped out from behind her and threw himself at the smaller man, his knife pointed straight at him.

Two things became very clear to Jax at that moment. One, the would-be rapist moved fast for someone so big -- he as at least 2 inches taller than himself -- and two, he, Jax, was in trouble. He hadn't anticipated the man's attack soon enough. He'd figured the man would want to draw out Jax's torture for awhile.

Reacting on adrenalin and instinct, Jax threw himself to the side just in time, but gained a knick in his right arm. The attacker whirled quickly, lashing out with the knife. A sense of déjà vu washed over Jaxon. *Why did everyone attack him with a knife?* was his irrational thought.

It took all of his wits to stay clear of that knife. He knew there was nothing near enough to use as a weapon; he'd done too good of a job cleaning out the old junk. He got backed into a corner which caused his attacker to slow up, thinking he had him cornered. He grinned, enjoying his triumph. Jax took advantage and whipped off his coat, throwing it at the larger man. It distracted him enough that Jax risked leaping forward and grabbing the arm holding the knife.

This infuriated the knife-wielder. Growling in anger, he dove his fist into Jax's side, once, twice. He had a mean fist, and Jax felt each hit, but he was determined not to let go. He had both of his hands wrapped around the man's wrist, trying to wrestle the knife away.

But Mykaela's assailant was just as determined not to let go. They danced around the floor, struggling for possession of the knife. Then, Jax slipped on his own coat and started falling, drawing the big man down with him. Unfortunately, the other man landed on top of him and took full advantage.

Legacy of Love

He straddled Jaxon and leaned his weight on his knife arm. Jax's only option was to brace his elbows on the floor and lock them. The knife point was a hair's breadth from his throat. He jerked the man's arm this way and that, but couldn't loosen his hold. Sweat dripped off both of them as they thrashed about.

Then, the attacker let up slightly, but only so he could lift off the floor and then smash down onto Jaxon's midsection. Hard. Breath whooshed out of Jax, and he felt his hold weaken. The man did it again. In desperation, Jax risked lifting one of his elbows and banging it into the man's shoulder. It threw him just enough off balance that Jax was able to flip their positions.

But he'd made a grave error. As he came around on top, he wasn't straddling the other man which allowed his opponent to lift both legs and slam his feet into Jax. He not only lost his hold, but he flew back several feet. His head hitting the wall stopped his momentum; his vision went black for several seconds, and he fought not to pass out. Shaking his head, he tried in vain not to fall, but his legs were buckling; he couldn't clear his head and could feel himself beginning to lose consciousness. The finality of the situation swept over him, and he realized he'd failed Mykaela. Just as he'd failed his family. Just as he'd failed that young soldier.

Through the gray haze of his vision, Jax saw the other man moving in quickly, grinning in victory. Jax braced himself for the knife thrust as he continued his fight to remain conscious.

From behind the man, Jax saw Mykaela raise her legs and kick the man over to the left. It happened so quickly that her attacker wasn't able to stop his forward momentum and stumbled into the wall next to Jaxon.

Enraged, he cried out, "I warned ya! Now yu'll pay!" He jumped at Mykaela in a fury, the knife raised ominously. She curled her legs and turned to the side with a terrified cry.

Nothing could have cleared his head faster than seeing Mykaela in immediate, mortal danger. With a furious shout of "NO!" he dove for the other man. Grabbing him around the legs, Jax knocked him sideways to the ground, about a foot from Mykaela; his fear for her gave him added strength. Planting a knee into the attacker's back, Jax quickly tried to grab hold of the knife arm.

But something was wrong. The other man didn't struggle, not one iota. His knife hand was trapped under his body and with a feeling of dread, Jax slowly, cautiously, turned him over, making sure to have both his hands at the ready to grab the knife. But the precaution wasn't necessary. The knife was buried in the other man's chest, up to the hilt. There was very little blood. It had entered at a downward angle just above his 5th rib on the left side. Jax knew that it must have punctured his heart before ending in his lungs. Frothy sputum bubbled around his mouth as the man tried in vain to pull the knife out. He looked at Jax in stunned disbelief before his eyes glazed over. And, just like that, he was gone.

Putting his hand up to close the man's lifeless eyes, Jax closed his own eyes and tried to take a deep breath; his ribs hurt, but not as much as his head. He still felt a little fuzzy as a wave of nausea swept over him. But the danger was over. He would gladly endure anything as long as Mykaela was safe.

Legacy of Love

He opened his eyes to see her staring in horror at the dead man. Jax carefully knelt beside her and carefully turned her head toward him.

"Don't look at him," he said. He untied her hands, then gently rubbed her wrists where red marks were indented in the skin.

"H-he was w-waiting," he heard her say in a wavery voice. Looking up, he saw glistening tears sliding down her cheeks. "He knew you were g-g-gone. He . . . snu-snuck up behind me. He-he was g-going to . . ." she broke off with a sob, unable to say it.

Jax finished it for her in his mind: the man had been on the verge of raping her. A white-hot fury filled him, and he wanted to pull the knife from the man's chest and stab him over and over to vent his frustration. Instead, he gathered her in his arms, encouraging her to cry out her fear. But a child's voice came to them from just outside the door.

"Ma? Jax?" Ryan's voice effectively shut off Mykaela's tears.

"Oh no, we can't let him see . . ." she began, pulling away, swiping at her cheeks, looking toward the body.

Jax nodded and called out, "Ryan, just stay out there. Don't come in."

"Why not?" was the boy's natural query.

"I'll explain in a minute. Just stay put." Jax's no nonsense tone made it clear he was to be obeyed.

After a quick discussion with Mykaela, he covered the body with a saddle blanket and helped her into her wrap. They were both starting to feel the cold. Shoving his own coat on, Jax led her to the door. Mykaela was furiously trying to wipe off all traces of her tears before facing her son.

Thankfully, the light had faded enough that Ryan couldn't see her face very clearly.

She agreed to let Ryan go into town with Jax to get the sheriff, Jax promising to tell the boy an abbreviated version of what happened. Mykaela went into the house to wash her face and change clothes. She told Rachel that she'd had a little accident which explained her bruised and swollen jaw. As she stood in front of her washstand, she wanted nothing more than to take a bath and scrub herself clean from head to toe. She felt dirty, violated, even though he hadn't really done anything to her. It was the fact that he had touched her at all. With a shudder, she tasted bile and had to throw up.

"Mama, are you OK?" came Rachel's concerned voice from outside her bedroom door.

"Yes, sweetie, I'm fine," Mykaela lied. "I'll be out in a minute."

She took one last look in the mirror, fought back the urge to cry, and went out to sit with her daughter while she waited for "her men" to return.

CHAPTER 11

When Jax returned with the sheriff, Mykaela was dressed in another dress and had pinned her hair into a loose knot at the back of her head. She waited in the house with the children while Jax took the sheriff and the deputy to the barn. Ryan had been told that a man had tried to rob them and had fallen on his knife. Ryan wanted to see the body, but Jax nixed that.

As Jax stood beside the sheriff and the deputy, he explained what had happened as quickly and matter-of-factly as he could. Then he watched the two men study the body while another wave of déjà vu came over him. An illogical desire to turn tail and run was strong enough to actually have him turning toward the door. He stopped himself, knowing that what had happened in Glendale and what had happened here were two totally unrelated events. But he still couldn't help feeling helpless. Just as he had felt standing over that other body. With heart pounding, he waited for the sheriff's assessment.

"I'll need to talk to Mykaela," was all he said.

Trepidation filled Jax as he led the way across the yard to the cabin. He knew he was being foolish; he hadn't done anything wrong. *But then again, you didn't do anything wrong the last time either and look where that got you.* Jax glanced frantically at Blackjack, patiently waiting by the front porch, physically fighting the urge to jump on his back and ride away as fast as he could.

In the end, he had nothing to worry about. Mykaela's story matched his own. In fact, she built him up as quite a hero which he knew he didn't deserve. She had been the one to save his life when she kicked her attacker. He was filled with awe at what she'd done; she'd risked bodily injury to save him. *Was it possible she loved him?* Jax watched her as she spoke. ***Could** she love him?*

The sheriff and deputy were both satisfied. After the deputy left to find some men to help move the body, Sheriff Hoskins looked at Jax.

"Don't worry, Doc. You're off the hook. It's obvious the man's death was an accident although I can't say it wasn't undeserved."

Jax nodded. "Thanks." He responded sincerely, trying not to actually show his relief. But the sheriff noticed. And understood.

"Did I ever tell you I sent for copies of your records from Glendale?"

Confused, Jax shook his head. "Why would you do that?"

"Well, when you first came here, I wasn't real pleased."

"I remember," Jax replied drily.

"But after what you did for Misty, well, I just wanted to know the truth. So, I checked it out for myself. The reports backed up your claim." He shrugged. "I realized that I'd been wrong about you."

And that explained the sheriff's attitude change since he'd first come to town, Jax thought to himself. But he couldn't be upset. In fact, he was glad the air had been cleared between them especially since he found himself respecting and actually liking the older man.

Sheriff Hoskins left with instructions for them to come to the jail tomorrow to sign off on their statements. Then Mykaela kept herself busy finishing supper. Jax completed the evening chores and spent extra time brushing Blackjack; he had done a good job today getting his master home in time. It took him a little longer to finish up as his side was very sore; he was pretty sure his ribs weren't broken, but they were bruised. And his headache had not let up at all.

By the time he came to the cabin, supper was on the table. It smelled delicious, but Jax wasn't very hungry. His head throbbed, and his stomach was queasy; he was sure he had a mild concussion. That meant he probably should stay up until morning and be sure his symptoms didn't worsen.

He noticed Mykaela also picking at her food. He peered closely at her, not liking her color. She looked washed out, drained, a white pallor making a stark contrast to the dark bruise of her jaw. She made a valiant effort to talk to the children who were somewhat excited about the events of the evening. He knew from experience with other victims of violence that she was holding on to her calm demeanor with great will and that eventually, her emotions would engulf her. He could see it in the gravity of her expression, the over-brightness of her eyes, the wobbly smile she gave her daughter.

Although he wanted nothing more than to sit in his chair and lean his head back in an attempt to relieve some of his pain, he instead played a game with the children while their mother cleaned up. The evening seemed to drag on, and Jax's headache continued to beat a steady rhythm inside his skull. Mykaela kept busy with the dishes, cleaning the kitchen area, sweeping the floor, and several other non-vital chores. Jax knew she was trying to keep her mind occupied so she wouldn't have to think about what had almost happened. But it couldn't last.

Dana-Sue Urso

Finally, the kids headed for bed where Mykaela spent extra minutes with them. She needed to reassure herself that they would be OK tonight. Jax tried to relax in his chair after building up the fire, propping his feet on the hearth and tilting his head back. With a loud sigh, he closed his eyes.

Mykaela came into the room, quietly shutting the children's bedroom door. She wanted nothing more than to go to sleep and forget about this day. Her jaw hurt, but thankfully it wasn't broken nor had any teeth been knocked out; Jax had examined her and assured her that the bruise would fade in time; he had had her hold ice to it while he had been with the sheriff (she kept a small block down in the root cellar nestled in a bed of straw).

Too restless to settle down just yet, she walked over to her chair with the thought that she and Jax should talk. She had yet to thank him for saving her life. But he looked like he was asleep, and she didn't want to wake him. So she picked up her sewing and tried to concentrate on it. But as the quietness of the night seeped in around her, she found that her mind started replaying the events of the evening, much against her will. She tried hard to force them out, but they kept intruding. In her mind's eye, she relived the terror she'd felt when her assailant grabbed her from behind. She could still taste the nastiness of his hand over her mouth. She remembered how she had wanted to faint when he cut off her buttons, how terrified she'd been that her children would be harmed. And she could still feel his horrible, cold, slimy lips on hers.

Heart racing all over again, breaths coming rapidly, Mykaela touched her lips and jumped up, her sewing falling heedlessly to the floor. She hurried over to the water bucket sitting by the back door and knelt next to it. With shaking

Legacy of Love

hands, she grabbed the washcloth off the sink, wetted it, and vigorously wiped her mouth with it. As the seconds ticked past, she scrubbed harder and harder, panic welling up in her as she tried to erase the memory of what that man had done to her.

Just before arms came around her for the second time that night, Mykaela heard Jax say her name very softly and sweetly. He caught hold of her wrists and pulled them away from her face, hugging her securely.

"No, don't," she cried trying to yank the cloth away.

"Why?" he asked, not stopping.

"Because I can *feel* him," she burst out harshly as tears of frustration gathered in her eyes. "I *have* to get rid of him, don't you *see*?"

"Tell me," Jax's voice was soft, persuasive.

"He-he was waiting for me, he . . . *touched* me," she cried. "He was g-going t-to . . ." she broke off again, bending over slightly, his arms giving her support. "If you had-hadn't come in, he would have . . .would have . . . . I t-tried to stop h-him, but he threatened the ch-children." She started crying in earnest. "He m-might have k-**killed** them." Sobs racked her body as she finally let loose the emotions she'd bottled up since the attack.

Jax leaned back against the wall, pulling her with him, content to hold her while she got it out of her system, uncaring that her weight pressed on his sore ribs.

She curled up against him and cried her heart out. He gently rubbed her back, comforting her as best he could. It was hard, not because he was holding her -- oh no, that was wonderful. But his head wouldn't let up its relentless pounding, and he constantly had to fight down the desire to be physically ill.

The emotional storm didn't last long, however, and a few minutes later, Mykaela took a deep shuddering breath and relaxed. It felt so good to be in Jax's arms; he made her feel safe and secure, two emotions she hadn't felt with either her father or husband. And certainly not with her attacker. He had saved her, risking his own life yet again. She shuddered as she thought how differently this night would have turned out if he hadn't come home early.

Jax felt her tremble and leaned back to look at her directly. Her color was better, cheeks flushed, and her breathing was under control. Her eyes were luminous and sparkled in the firelight. A wave of protectiveness washed over him, and an icy cold gripped him as he thought about what he would have found if he'd come home too late.

"Better?" he asked her, smiling as she ducked her head in embarrassment.

"Yes, thank you. I -- you -- can let me up now." She told him shyly.

"I'm actually rather comfortable at the moment," he only half teased her. He didn't want the moment to pass, but he knew she really shouldn't be sitting on his lap. The last thing he wanted to do was compromise her in any way. Or make her uncomfortable.

But the look she was giving him made his heart beat faster. Was that gratitude he saw? Or love? Since no woman had ever looked at him either way, he couldn't be sure. Swallowing against his suddenly dry throat, he made an attempt to help her up before he did something he'd probably NOT regret.

Legacy of Love

Once on their feet, Jax tried to take a step forward, but dizziness struck him so hard, he nearly fell over. Mykaela helped to steady him, looking at him with grave concern.

"Are you alright?" she asked, eyebrows knit with worry.

Jax waved off her concern. "I'll be fine. Just a little concussion." He didn't realize that his words were slightly slurred, but Mykaela heard them loud and clear.

With her assistance, she guided him to his chair by the fire. Practically collapsing in it, Jax sat forward holding his aching head.

"Your head hurts," Mykaela made it a statement.

Jax nodded and then winced as the innocuous gesture sent hammers flying all around his skull. He then felt her press the back of his head with a gentle touch, unable to help the flinch when she found the lump.

She gasped. "No wonder you're in pain; that bump's the size of an orange."

"I thought it was more like an apple," he replied, trying to joke it away. He heard her walk away, but she was back within a few minutes. She very gently pressed some ice wrapped in a soft cloth against his injury; the relief was most welcome.

With a sigh, he reached a hand up to hold the ice pack in place and sat back, eyes blissfully shut. He heard Mykaela rustling around, then silence. After a few moments, he couldn't resist opening his eyes to see where she was. She was sitting in her chair, slowly rocking. Although he couldn't see her face very clearly -- the only light was from the fire as she had dampened the two lanterns that were normally lit at night -- but he could feel her watching him.

"You should be in bed," she said in a tight voice.

Dana-Sue Urso

"Can't. Concussion. Need to stay awake 'til morning to make sure the symptoms don't worsen." He closed his eyes again.

"What symptoms? Besides your headache?" Jax hadn't meant for her to know how bad he was really feeling.

Sighing, he simply, said, "Mainly the headache. The ice is helping, though."

"You were dizzy before." She pointed out.

"A little."

"And you slurred your words a few minutes ago."

"Really? I couldn't tell."

Silence, then, "What aren't you telling me? Please, Jax, I *have* to know."

She was actually pleading with him which surprised him so much he opened his eyes and brought the ice bag to his lap. She had stopped rocking and was leaning forward, hands clenched on her lap. He could see her hair, loose once again and flowing around her shoulders, the firelight picking up strands of dark gold.

"Mykaela, I'm fine, really. I appreciate your concern, but I have to ride this out. I hit my head pretty hard, but I doubt there will be any long-term problems."

"But what if you aren't better by morning?" she asked, persistent.

"Then, I'll let Doc Greene have a look at me."

This seemed to satisfy her as she sat back and set the chair to rocking again. Picking up her sewing, she told him to put the ice bag on his head again.

Grinning, he meekly replied, "Yes, maam."

He watched her for awhile, even though he couldn't see her clearly. He liked knowing she was sitting across from him, felt content and peaceful as she worked at taking the hem out of Ryan's pants. Seeing her yawn, he suggested she go to bed.

"I'm going to stay up with you," she informed him matter-of-factly.

"You don't need to do that; I'll be fine."

"But it'll be easier if you have someone to talk to or play checkers with. I can help you stay awake."

It *would* be easier with her help, but still . . .

"You've been through a lot tonight. You need to get some sleep." He insisted.

She shook her head. "To be honest, I'm too wound up to sleep. I --- need to come to terms with what happened first or I'm afraid I'll . . . . . have trouble sleeping."

He knew she was probably fearful of having nightmares. He knew all about those and could sympathize. But she still needed her sleep.

"I'll lie down right after the kids leave for school. I promise."

Hearing the determination in her voice, he settled back more comfortably and prepared to spend a long night with the woman who was quickly coming to mean more to him than anyone else ever had in his life.

"You got back early this evening. Why?" came Mykaela's soft query.

Without opening his eyes, Jax told her about the urgent feeling he'd had that day, about how he felt the strong need to get home.

"I can't explain it. It was just a nagging feeling that wouldn't go away. So I rode Blackjack much harder and faster than I usually would have, and he came through."

"Yes, he did," she agreed. "You both did. You got home

two hours ahead of schedule." A pause, then, "Jax, thank you seems so inadequate for what you did, I .." She broke off as her voice thickened, blinking back tears.

Jax looked at her very seriously and said, "Don't forget, Mykaela, you saved my life in return."

At her questioning look, he went on. "When he shoved me into the wall, I almost blacked out. In fact, I was so weak for a few moments, I wasn't even able to stand upright. If you hadn't kicked him to the side when you did, he would have killed me. It's I who owe you the thanks."

Mykaela set her gaze on the fire, the flames crackling.

"I think we both should thank God for protecting us," she replied softly.

"Agreed." They both fell silent, their thoughts on each other.

As the night wore on, there were times of companionable silences as well as times of talking and sharing; they never seemed to run out of things to talk about. He told her more stories of his childhood antics while she reciprocated with her children's antics as toddlers. She quoted some of the poems from a poetry book that her husband had given her as a wedding gift; he discussed his opinion of Charles Dicken's book *A Christmas Carol*. He expressed his great liking and respect for the Brooks, and she told him of what brought them to Riverton. She asked him questions about medical school, and he asked her how she came to be such an excellent seamstress.

By 4 am, they were both sleepy and drinking their 4th cup of tea laced with lavender; it had medicinal properties that eased his headache and her jaw pain somewhat. His stomach stayed queasy, but the dizziness seemed to have disappeared as he discovered when he filled the wood box beside the fireplace (he did this around 2am when Mykaela had gone to the root cellar for more dried lavender so she wouldn't scold him for getting up).

Yawning and wanting nothing more than to lie down and fall asleep, Jax decided it might be a good idea to tell Mykaela of his estrangement from his family. He couldn't imagine sharing that with anyone else, it was too personal and painful, but telling Mykaela felt right. So when she settled back down in her chair after filling both their cups, he said with some trepidation,

"I'd like to tell you about my family."

She nodded in encouragement.

With a deep breath, he began. "When I was convicted, I went to that prison fully believing that I would be there for the rest of my life. There were times when I wished that they had just hung a noose around my neck."

Mykaela nodded in mute understanding.

"I think I already told you that I wrote several letters to my mother, but didn't mail any of them because I honestly thought it would be better for them to think I was dead than to know that I was rotting away in prison."

"But, surely they believed you might still be alive?"

"Well, I knew that the army had sent a representative to my home after I disappeared. No one knew for sure where I was although having been captured was at the top of their list. But, still, no proof. So I was considered missing. I found out about it after our release from Andersonville. And you know I didn't contact my family then." At her nod, he continued. "Like I said I wrote letter after letter, but I destroyed each and every one. I came to the conclusion that my family had been right all along."

"I don't understand."

"Remember I told you that when I decided to join the army, I didn't tell anyone until the day before I was to leave, that's how selfish and unconcerned about their feelings I was. When my father found out, he was livid. He and I had a terrible argument, neither one of us able to, or willing, to see the other side. My father and I didn't part on the best of terms, he refused to see me off on the train. My brother berated me for joining that "stupid" war, my best friend thought I was crazy, and my mother and sister were afraid for me. But I left anyway without taking anyone's feelings into consideration, but my own."

Mykaela protested. "Surely you were old enough to decide how you wanted to live your own life? What were you back then 25, 26?"

"Almost 24, but even so, I never gave my parents the respect of at least discussing my decisions with them. Especially one so heart-wrenching for them. I was so full of myself, so full of my ideals of how I was going to change the world, how I was going to make a difference in the soldiers' lives." He shook his head. "All I did was patch them up so they could go back to the horrors of fighting or cut off their legs so they could go home crippled." He said this with such anguish that Mykaela felt tears well up.

"I can't believe it was all in vain; I remember the young boy you refused to leave behind. How fortunate for him to have had such a caring, compassionate doctor."

"And look where that got him?" He pointed out bitterly.

Legacy of Love

"If you had left him, he would have died thinking no one cared about him." She pointed out. He looked at her, then shook his head.

"You have a propensity to find the good in any situation, don't you," he commented ruefully. She didn't respond, silently encouraging him to go on with his story.

"Anyway, I fought with myself for the two and a half years I was in the penitentiary, going back and forth about whether or not to send a letter. I never did. However, when I was released, the first thing I did before I even took a real bath and change clothes was send my family a telegram."

He stopped here, staring intently into the fire, his memories crowding in. He didn't like thinking about what happened next, but he wasn't backing down from his decision to tell Mykaela everything. Sensing the climax to his story, she remained silent.

"I didn't have a lot of money at the time, obviously. Before I was incarcerated, I had instructed my lawyer to sell Blackjack and my equipment to pay his fees before I transferred to the prison. But he didn't do it. Instead, he took care of Blackjack and kept my equipment; he told me later that he knew I would be freed some day." Jax shook his head. "That lawyer had more ideals than I ever had, but I will always be grateful for his faith in me. Anyway, he gave me some cash to get me started which I only accepted because I was sure I'd be able to pay him back after I contacted my family. I didn't want to pay for a lengthy telegram because I still needed to buy a train ticket home for me and Blackjack and rent a hotel room for the night since the train west didn't leave until late the next day. I also had to buy some clothes, shaving supplies, that sort of thing. So, I kept the message simple: I just told my family that I was alive, had been in jail, and would be home in a few days and would explain everything then." He paused and absently rubbed at his forehead. "I sent the telegram through Denver rather than Boulder since I know a lot more people in Boulder; I didn't want my business known. I figured it would take a couple of days for someone to get the message to my home -- my family does most of its business in Prentisville which is the closest town to our ranch, but they don't have a telegraph office so I chose Denver. I was completely shocked when I received a telegram later that afternoon. It was from my father."

Jax sat forward, clasping his hands, staring into the fire.

"He had written only 4 words: 'Don't bother coming home.'"

Mykaela's heart went out to him as she heard the pain in his voice. "Oh Jax, I'm so sorry. But maybe he was just angry or hurt and lashed out without thinking."

"I actually thought that," he replied, looking over at her. "My father's temper is quicker than my own, and I know he can say or do things that he later realizes he didn't mean. So, I waited. I was sure he would send a retraction. Or have my mother do it."

A log fell into the grate; Jax secured it before speaking again. "I waited five days, but no telegram. I did, however, receive a letter from my brother. He was furious with me; he rebuked me over and over for the worry I'd caused our parents over the last 5 years, accused me of being so selfish and unfeeling that I hadn't even had the decency to let them know I was OK. And then to find out I had committed a crime and ended up in jail. He went on and on, and I didn't blame him one bit because everything he'd written was true."

Legacy of Love

"But it wasn't true," Mykaela insisted fiercely, leaning forward with hands gripping the arm rests of her rocking chair. "You are the *least* selfish person I know. You feel things more deeply than most, too much I suspect sometimes. And you are NOT a criminal! Plus he doesn't know the whole story, about Andersonville, about the things you've suffered these past few years. He shouldn't have written such a hateful letter." Mykaela was determined not to let anyone say anything against him; Jax was extremely moved by her support and had to swallow against the emotion clogging his throat before he could respond.

"Jerrod's perspective was a little different than your own, you have to admit," he felt compelled to point out. "I left home with a devil-may-care attitude, idealistic, hard-headed, stubborn-- a man who was dead set on following his path no matter what anyone else said. At the very least, I should have sat down with my parents and discussed with them what I intended to do, especially in regards to joining the army. Remember, I also went against my father's wishes and became a doctor. So, in his eyes, I'm sure he saw me as a disrespectful, foolish son who was too full of himself to even listen to his opinions and advice. And then, to top it off, I didn't contact them when I should have, I knowingly let them worry, let them think I was dead just because it was easier for me. No, Jerrod was right to condemn me in his letter. And he was right to agree with our father that I wasn't welcome home."

He stopped there to try and relieve some of his growing distress. He had been hurt by both his father and brother, but felt their set-downs were richly deserved. He didn't feel good enough to go home and try to repair his relationships, at least not now. It had only been a little over 6 months since his correspondence with them, but he saw no resolution in the near future, much as he ached to go home and see them. He missed them so much!

He had waited another 24 hours, but when no more messages had come his way from his father or even his mother, he spent the rest of his money on trail supplies and left that town. He'd needed time to be alone so he headed west to the mountains. He spent a month on the trail, in the foothills, living off the land. Being in commune with nature helped revive his spirit enough to at least try to find a job. He traveled to several small towns, found work as a wrangler on a ranch 50 miles away, but it was only temporary so he'd headed west again.

He glanced over at Mykaela who appeared to be seriously contemplating the flames. She had given him hope that he could be happy, that he could find a way through his inner turmoil. Deep inside, he secretly wished that she would love him the way he loved her, that they would marry, that he would be part of a new family although his 'old' one was never very far from his thoughts. Her voice broke into his reverie.

". . . . . tried to send another telegram or written them a letter?"

Understanding the jist of her question, he replied, "No, I-- think we all need some time. At least, they do for sure. I wandered around for several months, being smarter this time around, worked on a ranch over the summer, and wound up here."

"For which I'm very grateful," she told him softly, shyly.

Legacy of Love

"I am, too," he echoed, thinking it was nice to be wanted. Then they both lapsed into silence, each with his or her own thoughts.

Mykaela dozed off a little while later, her head lolling to the side. Jax debated about whether or not to carry her to her room, but decided against it. Instead, he spread an afghan over her and built up the fire to keep the room warm. Then he settled back into his chair, allowing his eyes to close. He was asleep within seconds.

The sounds of men's moaning and groaning were all around him, some crying out, some just crying. He started with the first man at the head of the row and worked his way down, going from one man to the other, offering what assistance he could. He never stayed too long, always needing to move on. But they kept reaching for him, grabbing onto his arm to hold him back, but he had to keep moving. He had to reach the end.

The row of men was never-ending, however. They stretched on and on in a seemingly unending line. He worked faster, skipping some of them, trying to ignore their cries of protests. He began running, dodging out of the way of reaching hands wanting desperately to pull him back.

Their arms became tree limbs as he stumbled along; the trees were alive and trying catch him. But he fought his way through; he had to reach the end of the path.

The forest grew darker and more forbidding; he was having trouble finding his way. He became fearful that he wouldn't reach his goal although he wasn't sure what that goal was. He just knew that if he didn't reach the end of the path, he would die. So he ran on, breath coming in gasps, heart pounding, but still he pressed on.

Finally, finally, in the distance, a break in the wall of trees, a small light peering through. As he reached it, he saw a huge cave looming just ahead. And standing in the entrance was his family; they were calling out to him to go back, waving him away. Confused, he slowed, trying to catch his breath. But he continued on. Their gestures became more and more frantic until suddenly his captors and guards from Andersonville raced past him with rifles raised high.

Shouting "NO," Jax darted after them, but he was too late -- the confederate soldiers fired into the cave mouth, his family didn't stand a chance. He threw himself in front of his family in a desperate attempt to save them although it was already too late.

"Jax, Jaxon, wake up, it's me!" a woman's voice penetrated the fog in his brain from the nightmare, and Jax woke up. Only to find that he was standing in front of his chair, trying to push Mykaela down into it. Quickly pulling her upright, his gaze swept over her.

"Did I hurt you?" he asked anxiously, looking for any damage he may have caused.

"No, of course not," she rebuked him gently, her hands gripping his arms.

He closed his eyes briefly. "Thank God." He struggled to get his breathing under control, to stop the trembling of his limbs, both an aftermath of his nightmare. He could feel the sweat across his brow.

"You look a little pale," Mykaela said. "Come and sit down at the table." He let her lead him to a chair and sank down into it, but when she went to move away, he caught hold of her hand.

"Mykaela," he began a lump in his throat. "I'm so, so sorry. I . . ."

"There's no need to be," she said firmly. "You just reacted to being suddenly awakened from your dream, a natural reaction."

Jax shook his head. "I could have hurt you."

"No, you couldn't have," she countered. "You could no more hurt me than one of the children." She placed her hand along his cheek and smiled down into his eyes. "You're the kindest, gentlest, most caring man I've ever known. I trust you completely."

With those heartfelt words, Jax placed his own hand behind her head and pulled her down gently. He couldn't help his next words which came straight from his bruised and battered heart.

"I love you, Mykaela Caldwell." He followed with a kiss that he put all of his heart and soul into. When she didn't resist, he put his other arm around her, stood up, pulling her to him while threading his hands through her thick, luxurious hair -- something he'd wanted to do for so long.

She willingly embraced him and boldly met him kiss for kiss. He deepened the kiss and realized that he'd never had a woman respond to him so openly and trustingly.

But all good things must come to an end, and reluctantly, he drew back slightly, effectively breaking off the kiss. Her bruise came into sharp focus, and he gently touched it with his finger, asking anxiously if he'd hurt her. Shaking her head, she opened her eyes.

"Did you mean it?" she asked, keeping her arms around him.

"If you're asking if I meant it when I told you I loved you, then yes, I absolutely meant it." He broke off, unsure and uneasy.

The smile she gave him was like the sun breaking through stormy clouds.

"I've been in love with you for quite some time now so I'm glad to hear you feel the same way," she said, letting her feelings shine in her eyes.

Grinning like an idiot, he swept her up and whirled her around and around. Laughing, she held on and burrowed her face into his neck, feeling a little embarrassed after her admission.

Setting her back on her feet, Jax touched his forehead to hers. "I'm not sure it will really sink in that you love me until later today, but I'm willing to take your word for it now."

"You'd better because I don't say that to just anybody."

"I should hope not," he agreed indignantly before giving her a feathery kiss on her bruised jaw line.

"Whas' goin' on?" asked a sleepy voice. Breaking apart, they saw Ryan shuffling from his room, rubbing his eyes; he didn't appear to have noticed anything out of the ordinary.

"We'll need to talk later," Jax whispered to Mykaela before greeting the boy. Neither of them had noticed that dawn was breaking. Jax ruffled Ryan's hair on his way to the door - - he may as well get the chores over with. His headache was just a dull ache now, and the nausea was gone.

Mykaela found it difficult to keep her mind on the morning tasks, but managed to get breakfast together. Jax came in, wolfed down a quick bite, gave Mykaela a wink, then headed to his room to get some much needed sleep.

After getting the kids off to school, Mykaela settled into her own bed, thinking she would have a hard time falling asleep since learning that Jax loved her. But she was wrong. Exhaustion overcame both of them, and they fell into a deep, nightmare free sleep.

CHAPTER 12

A mere 10 hours later found Mykaela busy cooking supper and helping Rachel with her spelling words. All the while, she kept an ear out for Jax's return; he had gotten up around noon and headed out. She had been awake and was enjoying being in bed in the middle of the day. But when she heard the outside door close (the one Jax used when he didn't want to bother anyone by leaving through the house), she got up and dressed, finishing in time to see him ride toward town.

She was helping Rachel copy a word when she heard boots on the front porch. Heart beating in anticipation, Mykaela automatically put a hand up to smooth errant strands back in place. She busied herself at the stove as Jax greeted the children.

Ryan still had questions about the "attempted robbery," and asked Jax if it was time to do the evening chores, hoping to get a chance to talk to Jax since his mother refused to answer any more of his questions.

"Yeah, let's go get them done," Jax replied, smiling down at the boy before meeting Mykaela's eyes. The look he gave her had her breathless in seconds, and she put a hand to her heart as if to slow its excited fluttering. *He's so handsome*, she thought to herself, feeling self-conscious. She'd seen the looks he'd received from some of the ladies at church ever since he started attending, nothing inappropriate, but definitely appreciative of a good-looking young man in their midst. But it was she he'd declared his love to, and if throughout the afternoon, she occasionally wondered if he really meant it, the love in his eyes and the endearing smile he now gave her chased all doubts away. Feeling light-hearted, she set Rachel to copy her words and set about finishing supper preparations.

The evening seemed to drag on more than usual, probably because she couldn't settle down to her usual tasks; she even tried to read the Bible while Jax played a game with the children, but she couldn't concentrate.

Finally, she put the kids to bed, listened to their prayers, and shut their door. Only to be swooped up in Jax's arms and kissed very thoroughly. Setting her on her feet, he kept his arms locked around her waist and leaned back a little.

"Hello, pretty lady," he said, smiling down at her. He ran a light finger across her bruised cheek. "How are you this evening?"

Mykaela blushed and ducked her head.

"Hello to you, too. And I am just fine," she replied softly, too embarrassed to look at him. She knew she wasn't all that pretty. She supposed she had a pleasant enough face, but her eyes and hair were an ordinary brown, nothing special. And she was too thin. And her nose was too long. And her mouth . . . Jax interrupted her silent mocking of herself by putting a finger under her chin and gently lifting her head up.

"I wish you could see how the firelight causes your eyes to sparkle," he told her softly. "There's a lake back home that shimmers in the moonlight after a rain shower. It's the most beautiful light I've ever seen." He paused for effect. "Until now."

"Thank you," she said, tightening her hold on him. He rested his forehead lightly on hers.

"I -- spoke to Reverend Brooks today," he told her, a little hesitantly.

She nodded.

"He and I agreed that my staying here isn't wise under the circumstances."

Mykaela knew the circumstances he meant were that they were unmarried, and now that they had declared their feelings for each other, it really wasn't appropriate. It probably never had been. Feeling suddenly discouraged, she stepped out of his embrace and headed to the fire, rubbing her arms as a pretext that she was cold. However, she needed some distance so she would know how to respond; she knew the right thing to say, and she knew what she really wanted to say. But before she could say anything, he was continuing, his voice coming from right behind her.

"Mykaela," he started, but when she wouldn't turn around, he put his hands on her shoulders and made her face him. "Mykaela, I love you with all my heart. It's -- hard to imagine my life without you and the kids in it. But when Spring comes, I still plan on leaving."

He stopped, but she wouldn't look at him. There was a lump in her throat, and she couldn't have talked even if she wanted to. Which she didn't. Not really. Ok, maybe she wanted to rant and rave that he couldn't leave her, to please not leave her, she didn't want to live without him in her life and . . . . .

"Wow, you're sure not making this easy for me," Jax said with a shaky laugh. Surprised, she finally looked at him and saw how edgy he seemed; she didn't think she'd ever seen such uncertainty in his eyes before.

"Jax, I .." she began, puzzled by his words and actions. He put a hand up to stop her.

"Let me finish or my nerves might fail me," he told her half-jokingly. Maybe less than half. "I want to leave because I have to find a more steady income and since Riverton doesn't need a doctor, I'll have to go somewhere that does. But I don't want to leave you, Mykaela, so I was hoping you would come with me. As my wife."

He watched her intently, anxiously, uncertainly. He believed she loved him, but that didn't automatically mean she wanted to remarry. Her first husband had been a first class jerk; she might not be so ready to dive back into a marriage.

"You want to marry me?" was her response, amazed wonder crossing her face.

"You bet I do!" he assured her sincerely. "I can honestly say that I have never been more sure of anything in my life including my decision to become a doctor. Nothing has ever felt so right, Mykaela. I love you so much, it would be my greatest honor if you agreed to marry me, to be my wife, to let me be a father to Ryan and Rachel."

Tears pooling in her eyes, Mykaela threw her arms around his neck.

"Jaxon Dumont, I would be honored to be your wife. And there isn't anyone who could be a better father than you," then she kissed him.

Cupping the sides of her face, he said with heartfelt sincerity, "Thank you for making me the happiest man in Colorado."

They spent an hour at the kitchen table making some immediate plans. In light of her recent attack, Jax didn't want to leave her and the kids alone at night. That gave him an excuse to suggest they marry sooner rather than later; she was all for it. They would talk to the Reverend tomorrow and see how soon they could get the wedding arranged.

"What about the children?" Jax brought up.

Dana-Sue Urso

"What about them?"

"Well, what if they're against us getting married?"

"They won't be," Mykaela was confident. "They *adore* you, Jax. They've never been so comfortable around a man before; you're their hero, and they'll be thrilled to have you as a father. Don't worry."

But later that night, lying in bed, Jax couldn't help but be worried. Not so much at the kids' reaction to the news, but more of his role as a father. He didn't know how to be one, and it scared him a little. He guessed he just treated them as he always had, yet there would be the added effect of his being the head of the household, another authority figure, even a disciplinarian if needed. He didn't want to fail.

He thought of his own father and knew right off that he would never reject his children the way his father had. Yet he couldn't really be angry, not anymore. He loved his father, he'd made some mistakes, and now he was paying for them by being apart from them when he wanted to be with them.

But now he had Mykaela; he'd told her the truth when he'd said he couldn't imagine his life without her. She had believed in him, had brought hope and joy back into his life; she had helped him to enjoy living like he once used to. He'd found the purpose he'd sought for so long. The thought of her being his for the next 40 or 50 years, God-willing, made his eyes burn as tears of humility threatened to spill over. Swiping at his face, he rolled over, trying to find a warm pocket in his chilly room. Soon, he would have his wife to cuddle with. With that enjoyable thought, he fell fast asleep.

Mykaela stood in front of the floor-length mirror, staring at her reflection. Even she had to admit, she'd never looked

Legacy of Love

better. The floor-sweeping silk dress adorned with tiny seed pearls, ribbons, and lace fit her trim body snugly; long sleeves ended in a point at each wrist, and her veil was festooned with long ribbons, more pearls, and artificial Baby's Breath. Misty Brooks had fixed her hair in a loose up-swirl with long tendrils draped dramatically over one shoulder. Holding tight to her bouquet of fake white roses trimmed with the Baby's Breath, Mykaela allowed herself to believe that she was really going to marry the man of her dreams today.

The last 10 days since Jax's marriage proposal had flown by. She had been kept unusually busy with her jobs, caring for her family, and sewing her wedding gown; Miss Hanks had given her the material as a wedding gift, a gesture that meant the world to Mykaela. The Ladie's Auxiliary had insisted on providing the wedding supper which would be held in the basement of the church; luckily, the large room had two fireplaces so the cold should be kept at bay as the temperature lately had consistently dipped well below freezing at night. Jax had insisted on supplying the needed wood since he didn't have to pay for the food.

Unbeknownst to Mykaela, Jax had made a trip to Pagoda Springs to buy her a wedding ring; he'd been saving as much of his salary as he could to buy her a winter cloak, but he'd also been saving the hides from his animal kills. He was able to not only buy the cloak, but also a pretty ring he hoped she would like. He also wanted to give her an engagement ring, but without being able to access his bank in Boulder, thanks to his father, he couldn't afford a diamond. But one day, he would.

The last problem he had to deal with was who to ask to stand up for him during the ceremony. It seemed only fitting that he ask Daniel Goodson since he had been the first person to believe in him and had worked so hard to prove his innocence. The young lawyer had readily agreed and had arrived yesterday.

The wedding ceremony was fairly short, but at the end, there were very few dry eyes. As Mykaela walked down the aisle, she had eyes only for the man at the end who awaited her.

Ryan proudly escorted his mother to the man whom he adored above all others; he also had the privilege of carrying a small pillow with the wedding ring. Rachel had gone ahead of them, feeling very important as she scattered rose petals along the aisle; she stopped beside Misty who was standing up with Mykaela. Opposite stood Jax and Mr. Goodson.

Jax and Mykaela faced each other, hands entwined, and recited their hand-written vows with all the love in their hearts. As they were pronounced 'man and wife,' applause broke out among the guests. Mykaela couldn't help comparing her first marriage to this one. She and Danny had been married by a Justice of the Peace with only his wife as a witness. There had been no special wedding supper; in fact, as soon as they were married, they left immediately on the stage for Riverton. Their wedding night had been postponed by two days. At the end of their journey was an empty cabin that was badly in need of cleaning & repairing (Danny had not been a diligent steward of his possessions) and the start of a miserable, lonely marriage of 7 years, her children the only bright spots.

But now, she was marrying a friend, a wonderful, responsible, hard-working man who made a point of telling her he loved her at least once a day since that fateful night of her attack. It didn't matter that they'd only known each other a little over two months; it felt like they'd known each other forever. He had been more of a father to Ryan and Rachel in the last couple of months than Danny had in 6 years. He made her feel safe and cared for. And she walked proudly beside him as he escorted her back down the aisle.

In the anteroom, he pulled her into his arms and kissed her; the one during the ceremony had been brief so as not to embarrass her in front of their friends and acquaintances. But now, there was no holding back. She eagerly returned his kiss until she heard a noise at the door.

Reluctantly breaking apart, Jax whispered, "Hold that thought until tonight," then grinned as she blushed.

The next couple of hours dragged by. Jax sat beside his wife, chatting to his guests although later he wouldn't remember a thing he'd said. He ate the supper, but didn't really taste anything. He smiled until he thought his lips would lock in place. And all the while he couldn't help but wish everyone would just go away so he could be alone with his wife.

Mykaela for her part seemed relaxed, enjoying herself. She made a point to talk to every person in the room, thanking them for coming and helping to make the day special for her and Jax. The kids ran around with their friends, energized and excited; they would be spending the night with said friends.

Finally, two and a half hours went by, and Jax decided that was long enough. Supper had been over for an hour, and now everyone was just mingling and talking. Jax worked his way through the crowd, being sure to say a few words here and there so as not to appear rude, eventually reaching his bride's side. Sliding an arm around her waist, he asked her if she was ready to leave.

"Of course," she replied, deliberately fluttering her eyelashes up at him, a coquettish look in her eyes. Swallowing hard, Jax made their excuses to the Williams', an older couple who ran the post office, and unobtrusively, tugged Mykaela toward the door.

But it was another 10 minutes before they were actually in the wagon heading out of town; Mykaela had to make sure the kids would be alright, giving last minute instructions. Their guests swarmed outside to throw rice at them as they ran for the wagon. From the wagon seat, Mykaela tossed her bouquet to the crowd, laughing along with the well-wishers when 66-year-old Miss Hanks caught it.

The newlyweds drove away amidst good-natured joking and laughing while bells, tin cans, and old shoes were dragged behind the wagon bed where the men and boys had tied them. Concerned that they would be "belled" during the night, Jax had spoken to the sheriff enlisting his help to assure that he and his new wife would be left alone. Jax nodded a thank you as Sheriff Hoskins gave him a thumbs up as they passed by.

A few minutes later, they pulled in front of the cabin. Jax told her to go on inside while he put up the horses. Mykaela walked into the dark, silent cabin; the coldness swirled around her as she hung up her wrap. The fire was low so she stoked it up, then went into the bedroom to do the same to the fireplace in there, but first took off her veil and placed it on the dresser before going back into the main room.

Feeling suddenly very nervous, she wasn't sure what to do next. Make coffee? Tea? Change into her nightclothes? She thought about the lacy nightgown Misty had given her as a wedding gift; it wasn't very practical for a cold winter's night, but it was extremely pretty. She wondered if Jax would think so, too.

Then he was there, stamping his feet as he hung up his coat.

"It's really getting cold," he observed as he warmed his hands by the fireplace.

"Do you want some coffee?" Mykaela asked, still nervous.

"Not really," he replied, then held out a hand to her. "All I want is you."

She walked over to him, placing her hand in his. She gazed up at him with wide trusting eyes.

"You are so beautiful," he told her softly, pulling her to him, then kissing her. She felt him reach up to her hair and start to pull the pins out, one by one. Soon, her hair was cascading down her back and around her shoulders. He wove his hands in it, then broke the kiss to bury his face in the mass. "Your hair smells like you -- rose; it's heady stuff."

She threaded her own hands in his hair, loving its thickness, its softness. He reined little kisses along her neck and shoulder, ear and cheek, before arriving once again at her mouth. But instead of kissing her, he bent his knees and lifted her up in his arms; she automatically grasped his shoulders. As he carried her into the bedroom, his gaze never left hers. She could see desire smoldering in their depths, giving them a life of their own.

Feeling shy, she buried her face in his neck until he lowered her to the bed, then sat down beside her. He placed his hand along her cheek and used the other one to push back a strand of hair from her face.

"What's wrong?" he asked quietly.

She shook her head. "Nothing. Really. I just . . . feel . . a little nervous, I guess. I know it's silly, I mean I've been married before, but I don't want to disappoint you and I . . . ."

He stopped her at this point by leaning over and giving her a quick kiss. Then, his face inches from hers, he said very clearly,

"You could never disappoint me, Mykaela. I mean that. And as for being nervous, well, I am too. But I also know how much I love you; I've been waiting for you -- for this night -- my whole life. But if you're not ready, if you want to wait, I'll understand." This last was difficult for him to get out; he wanted to make love to her, to make her his in every sense of the word. But his love for her was stronger than his desires and so he would wait. Even if it killed him.

He needn't have worried. She pulled him down to her and kissed him, showing him how much she didn't want to wait. And he happily obliged.

Much later, Mykaela lay entwined in her husband's arms, completely sated and satisfied in a way she'd never been with her first husband. Danny had been somewhat selfish and one-track minded. But Jax had been patient and giving, seeing to her needs in a way that made her feel thoroughly cherished. She fell asleep with a smile on her lips.

Jax could barely see her in the dim light of the dwindling fire in the small bedroom fireplace. But he could smell her -- that unique floral scent -- feel her so soft and warm, hear her breathing. He had never been with a woman who made him feel this coveted and satisfied. He knew instinctively that he would never tire of this woman. She was his soul mate, his other half, his *raison d'etre*. Even if he never reconciled with his family, he could be happy as long as he had her.

He was now responsible for three people, something that he took very seriously. A fierce wave of protectiveness came over him. He vowed to do his best to provide for them so that they would never have to worry about having a roof over their heads, whether they had enough food, that they would have proper clothes to wear.

These thoughts led him to think about his personal bank account back in Boulder. He had sent his army paychecks directly there, had spent very little of that money. Plus, he knew that the army continued to send his pay during the year he was "missing," until the war was over. That alone, was a tidy sum. But he also had money saved there from his years working for his father; he had never been a spendthrift, had always been careful with his finances; it was the one area in his life his father could never find fault with.

He had tried to access that account upon his release from prison and found it had been taken over by his father, presumably because he had been thought dead. And since his father had told him not to come home, Jax hadn't bothered to try and access the account again since he doubted his father would have released it back to his name.

Jax knew that he would have to try and mend the fences with his family, but his hurt and pride ran deep, a convenient excuse not to contact them. A voice in his head said that the real reason was that he was afraid of being rejected yet again. He knew his mother would never, could never, turn her back on him. But he didn't want to come between her and his father so he decided to wait; he planned on giving it a year before he contacted them again, to give himself, and them, time to heal.

So he had to make sure he could adequately provide for his new family. He had already sent out telegrams to various towns within a 100 mile radius to see if anyone had a need for a town doctor. So far, he'd received three responses, each of which he was considering.

Until then, he would continue to work at the feed store, and Mykaela would work her two jobs which he wasn't happy about, but it would only be for a few more months. Settling himself more comfortably, he fell asleep.

CHAPTER 13

The marriage of Jax and Mykaela didn't change the family's routine all that much. They still went about their jobs and chores, the kids still went off to school. In the evening, they all came together for supper, homework, a game if time permitted, then bed. The only difference Jax moved his few belongings into Mykaela's bedroom and closed off the loft area. Mykaela liked seeing his things in the bedroom and felt a little thrill whenever she thought of him throughout the day. He made her feel special, cared for, wanted in a way she'd never felt before. She found herself humming a lot while she went about her duties, her heart light as she thought about the wonderful man she now shared her name with.

At the end of the school day on a Friday, almost a week after the wedding, Ryan came racing into the house, breathless.

"Where's! Jax?" he asked, panting.

"My goodness, Ryan," Mykaela admonished. "Slow down and catch your breath."

She had just finished taking down the hotel wash from the clotheslines outside -- it had been a relatively mild day -- and was hurrying to get them folded; she'd gotten behind in her work that day, and supper would be late.

Taking a huge breath, Ryan tried again. "I have to give Jax something important."

"He's still at the store; he'll be home in an hour or so. Why don't you put it on his chair by the fire."

She saw him place a piece of paper on the chair, then turned as the door opened. Rachel came in, but a gust of wind

197

made it difficult for her to close the door. Mykaela helped push it shut, peering out the front window. Small sticks and dust swirled around near the ground.

"It looks like a storm might be on its way," she commented. The sky was full of gray clouds. They hadn't had a good snow since the blizzard, long overdue for this time of year. And sure enough, when Jax came in an hour and a half later, he brought in a swirl of wind and snow that blew down the length of the cabin including several pieces of Rachel's paper doll book that she was looking at.

Laughing, he struggled against the wind to shut the door. "It's snowing pretty good out there," he remarked as he took off his outer layers.

"It's not a blizzard is it?" asked Mykaela, looking anxiously out the back window.

"Not a chance. Just a good old fashioned Colorado snowstorm."

He greeted her soundly on the lips, his favorite part of the day. Coming home to her and the children filled him with such a sense of peace, contentment, and rightness that he woke up every morning wishing it was evening when he could be back home with them. Especially with his wife: his beautiful, loving, kind-hearted wife.

Giving her a wink full of promise for later that evening, he turned to greet the kids. And found Ryan looking up at him in anticipation.

"I put something on your chair," Ryan told him excitedly. 'It's from Mr. Wood, my teacher."

"Oh, OK. Let me wash up, then I'll look at it." Jax ruffled Ryan's hair and went to the wash basin by the sink; Mykaela preferred they use the bowl instead of "dirtying up her sink."

Legacy of Love

He was just glad that her well was deep enough to prevent freezing; so far this fall, there had been no trouble pumping water to the sink.

As he was drying his hands, a crash from the children's room had him and Mykaela racing to it. Inside, they found Rachel on the floor, struggling to sit up.

"I fell off the bed," she told them shakily, her cheeks wet with tears. Kneeling beside her, Jax asked if she hit her head.

"N-no, I hurt my arm," Rachel was holding her left arm close to her body. Very gently, Jax encircled her wrist. Mykaela held Rachel's head to her as they watched Jax examine her arm. Ryan stood in the doorway. After slowly turning it this way and that, and running his hand up and down the arm, he declared it unbroken.

"I'm fairly certain it's not dislocated either," he pronounced.

"It still hurts," reported Rachel, lower lip quivering.

"I know, sweeting," Jax said, running a knuckle down her cheek. "You have a little sprain, right here." He pointed to her wrist where a small amount of swelling could be seen. "I'll make a splint for it so that you won't have to move it for a few days. It should be much better by Monday."

Mykaela comforted her for a few more minutes before helping her to the kitchen table. The rest of the evening went by quickly. Jax spent most of it fashioning a soft splint to immobilize the joint so the sprain would heal faster; he made it out of a combination of wood, cotton batting, and swaths. It was bulky, but effective. Ice helped ease the pain somewhat and a cup of chamomile tea enabled the little girl to fall asleep without too much trouble.

Ryan was strangely quiet most of the evening, but it was attributed to the fact that his sister had been injured.

Later on while lying together in bed, Mykaela thanked Jax for what he'd done for Rachel.

"You don't have to thank me, Mykaela," he told her, embarrassed. "I'm just glad she didn't hit her head. When I saw her on the floor, I . . ." he broke off, uncertain how to express the fear he'd felt.

Mykaela reached up and kissed his cheek before settling her head on his shoulder. "I know. It's a helpless feeling. And one that will occur again, I'm sure."

"Wonderful," he remarked wryly. "Parenthood can be scary sometimes, can't it?"

"It can, yes, but it's all worth it. And kids are very resilient."

"When I think of some of the things that happened to me as a kid, some of the silly ways I got hurt, it's a wonder I didn't give my mother gray hairs."

Mykaela chuckled softly. "I'm sure your mother would agree that getting bumps and bruises are all part of childhood. As gray hairs are part of parenthood."

Jax nodded and turned towards her more comfortably, closing his eyes on a sigh. Mykaela laid her hand on Jax's chest. Watching him for a moment, she gathered her courage and remarked as casually as she could, "I'd like to meet your mother some day."

"MmmHmm," was his sleepy response.

"I was thinking . . . maybe if you wrote them that you had gotten married . . ." she broke off as his eyes popped open.

Brows drawn together, he replied, "I don't want to come between my parents."

"I don't understand."

"If I write my mother, she might feel compelled to choose between me and my father. He rejected me, told me not to come home, as did my brother, and I don't want her caught in the middle."

"But a lot of time has passed. Maybe your father regrets what he did."

"You don't know my father. Eric Dumont usually means everything he says and does. He's tough and forthright and never backs down. Except to my mother. Sometimes. But I don't want there to be any friction between them because of me." At her look of puzzlement, he went on. "My mother would want to make things right, but if my father is dead set against my coming home, then that would cause discord between them. I'll contact them at some point, maybe next summer. But now's not the time." He finished firmly before kissing the top of her head and closing his eyes again.

Mykaela nodded her understanding and closed her own eyes. But her mind was wide awake. She thought Jax was making a huge mistake by waiting so long. What if his family was trying to find him? Would they even know where to begin looking? Then again, what if they weren't looking? What if Jax was right, and his father didn't want him home? Jax knew his family better than she did, obviously. But she couldn't ignore the little voice inside of her that told her to do something to help Jax repair the rift in his family. And do it soon. The more she thought about it, she decided there really was only one thing she could do. With that decision made, she fell asleep.

Dana-Sue Urso

The next week brought about a change in Ryan that, by Friday, had both Mykaela and Jax completely perplexed. When he had first been told that his mother was marrying Jax, the boy had responded favorably. His face had lit up, and he'd asked if that meant Jax would live with them forever. When told yes, he'd grinned and hugged them both.

The week following the wedding, Ryan and Rachel began testing the waters by calling Jax 'Pa' sometimes, although Ryan still had a tendency to refer to him as 'Jax' when talking about him in the third person.

But by the second week, Ryan was back to calling him Jax all the time. However, that wasn't the most worrisome thing; his attitude began to change as well. As the week wore on, he became more sullen and withdrawn, not wanting to play games or have Jax help him with his homework. During the evening chores--a time when Ryan and Jax would talk about all sorts of things--Ryan now hurried through them silently, going back to the house as soon as he finished instead of lingering and hanging out with Jax like he used to do before the wedding.

Jax assumed he was having adjustment issues, but Mykaela wasn't so sure. She pointed out that their routine really hadn't changed all that much since they were married. They tried to figure out if he, Jax, had done something, but couldn't think of a thing. And whenever they asked Ryan what was wrong, he always said 'nothing' or he was 'just tired.' He spent most evenings in his room, playing with his wooden soldiers by himself. Even Mykaela couldn't get him to open up.

Legacy of Love

Rachel was quizzed about school, asked if there was anything wrong, but she had responded that she didn't think so.

On Friday night, things finally came to a head. Jax had come in from an unusually long day at the feed store.

"Boy, am I tired!" he admitted, as he washed up. "I can't believe how busy we were today; every farmer and rancher in the county must've needed feed. We actually ran out. Plus I had to make more deliveries than usual which is why I'm late by the way."

"That's OK; suppers just now ready."

As they ate, Mykaela could see the fatigue in Jax's eyes, the tiredness around his mouth; he had had a nightmare last night, after which he spent a good portion of the night in the main room sitting by the fire. She had found him there in the morning, wide awake. She had tried to convince him to go back to bed for awhile, but he refused saying he was needed at the store.

After supper, he practically had to drag Ryan to the barn to help with the chores. His attempts at conversation were met with short, one-word answers, grudgingly given so he gave up and climbed to the loft.

Ryan picked up the chicken feed bucket and filtered a handful through his fingers, allowing the seeds to fall on the ground outside the coop. Jax didn't say anything until Ryan did it a second time.

"Ryan, quit playing with the feed. It's for the chickens." He called down casually from where he was pitching down hay to the horses.

Ryan responded by scooping up a large handful and then lofting it in the general direction of the coop, but deliberately threw off his aim so that most of it landed outside the enclosure again.

"Ryan!" Jax said a bit more forcefully. "Feed is not free so stop wasting it. Scatter it *inside* the pen."

Ryan stuck his hand deep into the feed and mumbled something under his breath.

Jax paused, leaning on the pitchfork. Frowning, he looked down at Ryan. "What did you say?"

He was taken aback when Ryan looked up at him with bitterness in his eyes.

"I said you can't tell me what to do!" the boy cried out belligerently.

"I most certainly can and the sooner you accept that the better things will be between us," Jax's voice was low-pitched and firm.

"Things will *never* be better between us!" he shouted, angry tears forming in his eyes. With those words, he flung the bucket down and ran out of the door.

If he wasn't sure before, he was now. Something was dreadfully wrong. And it was getting worse, not better. It was time to confront the boy, try to get to the bottom of it. And he needed Mykaela's help. Quickly finishing the chores, he followed Ryan to the house.

Upon entering, he found Ryan standing in front of Mykaela with head bowed. Both hands were on his shoulders, and they both looked up as Jax came in. Jax didn't waste time.

Reaching out a hand to him, he said softly, "Ryan, I'm not sure exactly what's wrong between us, but I'd like to figure it out. Together."

Ryan knocked his hand away, yelling at him. "There's *nothing* wrong between us except I wish you'd never come here! I wish you'd never married my Ma! I'm *glad* you're not my real Pa!!"

With those hateful words, he ran into his bedroom and slammed the door shut. Mykaela and Jax stood there completely flabbergasted. Mykaela looked at Jax, her heart breaking over the pain she saw in his face.

"Jax, I'm sure he didn't mean it," Mykaela began confidently. "Whatever is bothering him is compelling him to say hurtful things. He loves you."

When he didn't look convinced, she laid her hand on his arm. "Trust me in this. Ryan has never been very good at expressing his more negative emotions; he usually keeps it all bottled up inside. The fact that he actually raised his voice to you means he does care, strange as that may sound. In years past, whenever he was upset over Daniel's brush offs, he just kept his feelings inside, never once letting on how he truly felt except to me in private." She tugged on his sleeve so he would quit staring bleakly at Ryan's bedroom door and look at her. "But since you came, he's been happier than I've ever seen him. *You* make him happy. I just need to find out what's wrong so that we can fix it."

Jax smiled ruefully. "You make it sound so simple." He rubbed a tired hand down his face and sighed. "It would be even easier of he just came right out and told me what was wrong."

"Maybe he's dis'pointed 'bout tonight," Rachel spoke up from her perch on the rug in front of the fireplace where she was playing with her rag doll.

The adults turned as one.

"What about tonight?" her mother asked.

"The project. It's t'night," she answered, looking at them with her head tilted to one side.

"Rachel, honey, we don't know what you're talking about," Jax pointed out, walking over and squatting down in front of her. "What project?"

"Mr. Wood sent home the paper 'bout it," she insisted.

Jax took a deep breath and asked very calmly, "Can you tell me what the paper said?"

Rachel heaved a huge dramatic sigh and rolled her eyes.

"It said all the boys are s'posed to build a birdhouse with their Pa's."

Mykaela was staring at Jax. "I remember now. Last Friday, Ryan came home all excited about something he had to show you; I think it was a piece of paper. I completely forgot about it what with Rachel's accident and all."

"But why didn't he show it to me?"

" 'Cuz you threw it in the fire,' " Rachel announced, looking up at him with an indignant frown.

Jax shook his head. "No, I didn't. I wouldn't have thrown away something from school."

"Then where is it?" demanded Rachel logically, still frowning.

Mykaela spoke up contritely. "I told Ryan to place the paper on your chair so you'd be sure to see it."

They both automatically looked at his chair as though it would magically appear. In one accord, they began searching the floor, Jax even lifting his chair, but no paper. However, upon lifting Mykaela's rocker, there it lay. It had been hidden from sight due to the large quilt Mykaela kept draped over the chair.

Legacy of Love

Picking up the paper, Jax quickly read over it; sure enough, it was an invitation to all the fathers and sons to meet at the school in one week to build birdhouses together; it was dated exactly one week ago. Which meant the event was tonight. In less than an hour.

"Poor Ryan," murmured Mykaela. "All this time . . ."

"He thought I'd thrown it away, that I didn't want to go with him," Jax finished for her, his voice heavy with regret. "I'll go talk to him, try to make it right."

Mykaela stayed him for a moment. "It'll be OK. It was just an unfortunate set of circumstances; he'll see that, I promise."

But Jax wasn't so sure. Ryan had been rebuffed by his real father most of his young life. If Mykaela was correct, the relationship he had with the boy prior to their marriage was the first stable male relationship he'd ever had. And now he must be feeling terribly hurt, thinking that the man he had slowly come to trust didn't want to spend time with him at a school event.

With a heavy heart, Jax went into the bedroom and sat down on the bed. Ryan was curled up into a ball, facing the wall, a quilt held tightly closed around his neck and shoulders.

"Ryan," Jax began tentatively, sitting on the edge of the bed. "I know why you've been so angry with me this week. And I don't blame you. You must have been hurt when I threw away the paper from school about the birdhouse project." He paused, but Ryan shrugged with apparent indifference; Jax knew better. "The thing is, I didn't throw it away."

"I saw you!" Ah, a muffled response. Good.

"You saw me throw something into the fire, but it wasn't the note from school. I have it right here." He shook it slightly so Ryan could hear the rustling of the paper.

A hand appeared as the boy slowly peeled back the blanket and turned his head, his eyes zeroing in on the paper in Jax's hand. Jax tilted it so Ryan could see what was written on it. "When I came home last Friday, the wind sent a blast of air into the cabin and must've blown the paper off my chair and onto the floor. Your mother and I just found it under her chair."

Ryan continued to turn over, staring at the paper. Jax went on. "I'd like nothing better than to go with you to the school tonight and build a birdhouse together."

Ryan's eyes filled with tears as he finally looked at Jax.

"B-but you're so tired. You-you said at supper you wanted to go to bed early." He sniffled and wiped his nose with his sleeve.

"I'm not all that tired, Ryan," Jax lied convincingly. "You mean more to me than getting to bed early." Which wasn't a lie.

"I do?" he asked in disbelief.

Jax laid a comforting hand on the side of Ryan's head. "Absolutely. I love you, Ryan, *very* much. And even though I'm not your real father, I consider you my son in every way that counts."

A tear slipped down Ryan's cheek right before he threw himself into Jax's arms.

"I'm s-sorry I said I w-wish you'd n-never come here," he sobbed into Jax's neck.

"It's OK, Ryan; I know you didn't mean it," Jax patted his back comfortingly, a lump lodge in his throat. Ryan hugged him even tighter. After several long moments, he leaned back, swiping at his eyes.

"I l-love you, too, J-Jax," Ryan hiccupped. "I wish you w-were my real P-Pa."

"We-e-e-ll, there might be a way, if you and your sister agree."

"How?" Ryan settled comfortably in Jax's arms, his arms still encircling the man's neck.

"I've been thinking maybe I could adopt you. Do you know what that means?"

Ryan frowned in concentration. "I--think so. Would I be your real son then?"

Jax nodded. "But you'd have to change your last name from Caldwell to Dumont."

"Oh." Then, "I think I'd like that 'cause then everyone'd know you were my Pa," Ryan said happily, then more solemnly, "Can I start calling you Pa again? But it's OK if you want to wait 'til the 'doption." He said somewhat anxiously.

Jax's heart went out to this tender boy.

"You're my son *now*, Ryan, so it seems only fitting that you call me Pa," Jax pulled him into another embrace, his throat tight with emotion. How he loved this child. "Now, how about we go build ourselves a birdhouse?"

"Yippee!!" cried Ryan in full agreement, hopping off the bed. Going out into the main room, he ran to his mother and hugged her. "Jax, I mean, Pa, 'xplained *every*thing. We're going to the school now."

Mykaela's eyes met her husband's whose were filled with warmth and affection as he looked at her son. Correction.

Their son. A few hurried minutes later, father and son were off to the school with tools and a lantern.

They returned a couple of hours later, Ryan proudly carrying his birdhouse. Mykaela praised it adequately, then sent him off to get ready for bed, extolling him to be quiet as his sister was asleep. Jax sat down in his kitchen chair with a tired sigh. He gratefully accepted the cup of coffee Mykaela handed him before sitting down next to him.

"You look worn out," she observed, pushing back a stray strand of hair from his forehead. Jax caught hold of her hand and kissed the palm.

"I am, but it's a good tired. Ryan looked so happy when we walked into that schoolroom -- and the way he looked at me as he introduced me to his teacher, well, all I can say is that being a father is the best feeling in the world. Next to being a husband, that is." He grinned at her.

"I can't argue with that," she leaned towards him, eager for a kiss, but they were interrupted by Ryan.

Padding to the kitchen in his pajamas, Ryan walked up to Jax.

"Thanks for taking me tonight," Ryan said shyly.

Jax put an arm around him. "You're welcome."

Ryan hugged him quickly, whispering in his ear, "I'm glad you married my Ma," then went back to his room with his mother to say his prayers and get tucked in, leaving behind a man with a heart full of gladness. If anyone would have told him upon his release from prison that before the year was out, he would end up married with two children, he would have thought they were crazy.

But now, he could only thank God that he had been led to this town because he could not imagine his life without them in it. He had been alone for so long and thought he was destined for a lonely life, but Mykaela and the kids were teaching him how much he needed them. And he liked knowing they needed him, too.

CHAPTER 14

Another snowstorm regaled Riverton one day during the last week of November that lasted two days. By the time it was done, a foot of snow lay on the ground. The kids were excited about Winter Break which would begin in about 4 weeks and herald the arrival of Christmas. Mykaela made a decision about this time that would have far-reaching consequences; although she didn't know it at the time, their lives would be changed forever.

She decided to go against Jax's wishes and contact his family. She debated who to write to, her mother-in-law or brother-in-law. But because she wanted to respect Jax's concern of causing a rift between his parents, she ended up writing a letter to Jerrod Dumont.

She kept it straight-forward and to the point:

November 26, 1868
Dear Mr. Jerrod Dumont,

Greetings! My name is Mykaela Dumont, and I am your sister-in-law; Jaxon and I were married last month in Riverton, Colorado. I have two children whom Jax is in the process of adopting. Our son, Ryan, is 8 years old, and our daughter Rachel is 6. Jax has told me of the falling-out with your family. While I can understand your anger and hurt over what you believe to be his *disregard of your feelings over the last few years, there are some important things you need to know. However, I am not at liberty to go into the details because it is a story for Jax to tell. Unfortunately, he is not ready to confront you as of yet; he agrees that you and your father were right to tell him not to come home. He believes he is being justly punished for his apparent lack of regard for your feelings although nothing could be further from the truth.*

To reiterate: I am not going to take time in a letter to tell you the reasons why Jax didn't contact you for so many years, but please believe me when I say that he had good reasons that made sense to him at the time. He never meant to hurt any of you, but thought he was protecting you. And himself. Jax has told me many stories of his life growing up in your family, and it is easy to see that he loves you all very much, would never intentionally hurt any of you.

I am asking that you and your father give him a chance to explain all he has gone through these last few years. He has endured unimaginable things, and he deserves the benefit of the doubt, to be heard and listened to by the people who are supposed to love and care about him.

Jax has no idea that I have contacted you. But I think it's time he knew, one way or another, where his family stands. So please, return this missive with a letter or telegram. If your family still wishes to have nothing to do with him, then you will not hear from me again. Send any correspondence in care of Reverend Brooks, Riverton, Colorado.

Thank you for your time,

Mykaela Dumont

Mykaela mailed it with trepidation because she didn't like going behind Jax's back, but after several heart-felt prayers, she felt it was the right thing to do. The postmaster wasn't sure how long it would take to arrive in Prentisville; snowstorms abounded throughout Colorado which caused delays of mail, train, and any other modes of traveling. So she waited, growing more anxious with each day that passed.

Life continued on with the little family becoming closer than ever. Jax spoke to a lawyer from Pagoda Springs who helped him with the paperwork he needed to adopt Ryan and Rachel. They had to be sent to Denver for filing, then sent back to be signed by a judge with the family present. It would take some time, but it would happen within the next couple of months.

Legacy of Love

As it turned out, Rachel was also glad about the adoption.

"Now, Timmy Sanders can't say we're not your kids anymore 'cuz we have a diff'rent last name than you do," she pointed out indignantly.

"Rachel, you know better than to listen to silly talk like that," Mykaela pointed out.

"He's just a stupid-head," the little girl declared with a toss of her head.

"Rachel Kathleen! You do not call people names."

"Well, he is," she was unrepentant as she crossed her arms stubbornly. "And he poked me when I stuck my tongue out at'im. So I kicked 'im, but Mr. Wood didn't see. Then he ran off crying."

"Who?" asked Jax innocently. "Mr. Wood?"

Rachel laughed. "No, silly, Timmy, the stupid-head."

"OK, Rachel, that's enough of the name-calling. Do you understand?" Mykaela spoke quietly, but forcefully.

The little girl remained standing with her arms crossed, lower lip jutted out. Jax had a sudden overwhelming urge to laugh as he imagined Timmy Sanders trying to win a battle with this fierce little girl. His eyes met Mykaela's who was frowning at him, telling him without words not to laugh. Swallowing hard and biting his tongue, he was able to maintain a stern façade. Just barely.

"Rachel, I asked you a question," Mykaela reminded her.

With a dramatic sigh, Rachel said defiantly, "O-**Kay**. But if he pokes me again, I'll punch'im."

Jax had to turn away at that point; he could *not* keep a straight face.

Behind him, he heard Mykaela tell Rachel to report Timmy to Mr. Wood if he poked her, that fighting was never the answer. In principle, he agreed, but he also knew from experience that sometimes you have to stand up for what's right. And if a boy was bothering his little girl, then she had every right to defend herself. *Especially if the boy was a stupid-head.* At that thought, a laugh escaped which he quickly turned into a cough. Raising children was never boring, that was for sure.

A few days later, about a week after Mykaela mailed her letter, she and Jax had their first real fight. Over the weekend, Mykaela had asked Jax to fix the ring in the trap door leading down to the root cellar; it had broken off, and she had trouble lifting the door without the entire ring to hold on to. He assured her he would get a new one from town and would have it repaired by Monday evening. She reminded him again Monday morning, and he again said he'd see to it, not to worry. By Wednesday, it still wasn't fixed. Nor had he re-chinked the wall surrounding the fireplace, a project he had taken upon himself, promising her he would have it done quickly, but hadn't begun yet. That was 2 weeks ago.

He had also come home late a few times with the excuse that they were unusually busy at the store, and he had long distance deliveries to make. Last Friday, she had been gathering his clothes to wash over the weekend and smelled liquor on one of his shirts. She didn't want to jump to conclusions so she hadn't said anything. Until tonight.

When he got home late again that Wednesday evening, she confronted him angrily. Looking back, she knew that she would never have come at him the way she did if her nerves weren't so raw from worrying about the letter she'd mailed to Jerrod Dumont. She'd been increasingly stressed all week.

Legacy of Love

"Hi, everybody," Jax greeted as he came in. "It looks like another storm is coming, should hit later tonight."

The children ran to give him a hug which was becoming a habit that he enjoyed quite a bit.

"I like the snow," Ryan said cheerily, smiling up at him.

"Me, too," chimed in his sister.

Jax ruffled both their heads. "We should be able to get a whole family of snowmen built this weekend."

"Yea!!" they both cried excitedly.

"Hey Ma, did'ya hear?" Ryan called out. "We're gonna build a snowman family."

"Well, I hope the chores get done first, and snow cleared away from the house to the barn," his mother said snappishly by way of a response, busy at the stove and refusing to turn around.

Jax went up to her and tried to encircle her waist with his arms. But she stepped out of his embrace, something she'd never done before. Frowning with concern, Jax asked her if something was wrong.

"Oh no, everything's fine," she replied on an overly bright tone.

"It doesn't sound like everything is fine." Jax reasonably pointed out.

"Well, maybe if you had to lift a 50 pound door by prying it up with a crowbar, you'd be cranky, too."

"Are you talking about the trapdoor? I thought you could still use the broken ring."

"Oh no, it broke into several pieces yesterday. Maybe if you actually went down to the root cellar once in awhile, you'd know that."

"Hold on a second, Mykaela. I hardly ever have a reason to go down there."

"You would if we had some meat to put down there, but since you haven't shot a deer in, oh, a long time, then I guess you wouldn't have a reason to go down." Mykaela couldn't seem to help sounding like a spoiled child.

Totally confused by her attitude, Jax tried again to reach for her, but she actually shoved him away and went to the sink to peel potatoes.

Very carefully, he said, "You know I go hunting when I can, but with the snowstorms and work around here, I haven't had a chance to go in awhile. I'll try to go this weekend."

"Fine," she replied primly.

"Mykaela, why do I get the feeling there's something more going on?"

She shrugged, peeling with a vengeance.

Becoming irritated by her attitude, Jax said, "Look. I can't read your mind so why don't you just tell me what I've done to make you so upset with me."

She slammed her hands down on the sink and turned towards him, her mouth set in an angry line. Ryan and Rachel watched them with wide eyes.

"It's not what you've done, it's what you haven't done."

"If you're talking about the meat, I've already explained."

"It's not just that," she snapped, pointing the paring knife at him for emphasis as she spoke. "You keep making promises you don't keep. Just like Danny used to do. You come home late, smelling of whiskey, just like he used to do. You let things fall apart around here, just like he used to do. I've already had one irresponsible husband; I don't want another one!" She was panting with exertion when she was done, her face flushed, emotions spinning out of control.

She knew the moment Jax's temper hit him; she could see it in his eyes as they darkened and narrowed, the set of his mouth, the tautness of his muscles. Her heart skipped a beat as she contemplated how angry he was likely to get. In her heart of hearts, she knew Jax was nothing like her first husband. But the set of circumstances over the last week or so were glaring reminders of Danny's irresponsibility. And the words she'd just flung at Jax were said as a way of relieving some of her stress. Unfortunately, she didn't bother to be more discerning, and now she was facing an angry man. A very angry and intimidating man.

Swallowing hard, she refused to back down as they stared at each other. During her marriage to Danny, whenever she showed weakness were the times he took the greatest advantage. He would yell in her face in a threatening manner. Sometimes, he would grab her by the arms, squeezing so tight she'd have red marks for days after. He shoved her several times, and twice he slapped her. It was the second slap that woke her up, and she began to fight back, albeit not literally. She told him in no uncertain terms that if he ever hit her again, she would leave. And she meant it. He never touched her again. Unfortunately, that was the final turning point in their marriage, and they were never able to fully reconcile. He died a year later.

Now, as she looked at Jax, she saw a different kind of anger. He just stood there, not saying anything, keeping a tight rein on his swirling emotions. When he clenched his fists in frustration, she automatically stepped back. She was sure he wouldn't hit her, but couldn't help the reflexive action. Jax didn't miss the movement which fueled his ire even more.

Very quietly, but all the more potent because of his tightly wound composure, he growled, "I'm going to the barn for awhile." And he turned on his heel and walked out the back door, carefully shutting it behind him.

Mykaela stared after him, the wind completely taken out of her sails. She had been prepared to do battle, to get into a good argument, to justify herself to him. Yet, he walked out. Without one word of reproach or defense. She didn't know what to think so she continued to peel the potatoes, trying to convince herself she had been justified in the things she said. Although, she did admit to herself that she could have been a little more tactful. OK, a lot more.

After a minute or two, Rachel asked, "Why did Pa go outside without a coat?"

"He . . . was in a hurry. He'll be alright."

"Is he mad?" This from Ryan.

Taking a deep breath, she replied, "A little, I guess. But don't worry, we'll work everything out."

This seemed to satisfy them as they didn't say anything more. By the time supper was ready, Jax still hadn't come in. Mykaela debated what to do. She needed to have this settled, but didn't want to do it in front of the children. So she set them to eating while she put on her wrap, grabbed up Jax's coat, and went to find him.

He was in Velvet's stall, vigorously brushing her. Mykaela stopped in the open doorway; he didn't look up. He had come to the barn to embrace its peacefulness in an effort to calm down. On the outside, back at the cabin, he had been in complete control, but on the inside, he had been fuming.

Legacy of Love

She had attacked him without cause or justification, but he supposed that misunderstandings would inevitably occur in a relationship such as a marriage. But it was her comparing him to her first husband that had made him furious. He felt his temper rising as she spoke and didn't want to get into a verbal battle with her because he knew that not only would she lose, but that he would say things he didn't mean, but would hurt none-the-less.

That's the way his temper worked. It actually took a lot for him to become as enraged as he was tonight. Growing up, he had been known for his slow-rising temper, his ability to maintain control in volatile situations. It was usually his father who could set him off more than anyone, and they had had their share of heated arguments. The misery of Andersonville and the chaos of prison had tested him in ways he wished he hadn't experienced, but through all those experiences, he had become a more patient and tolerant person. Which was why he was able to walk away from Mykaela without giving into his emotions; he also wanted time to settle down so he could talk to her calmly.

"We need to talk," she murmured.

He didn't say anything for a moment or two. He finished brushing the horse, then leaned his arms on her side, petting her neck. When he finally looked at his wife, he allowed her to see the anger still brimming beneath the surface.

"Mykaela," he began softly, yet compellingly. "I want you to come to me whenever you're angry or upset with me. I want you to be able to tell me anything that's bothering you; I promise to listen and fix it if I can. I don't want you to ever be afraid to talk to me -- about anything!" He paused here, waiting for her reaction. She nodded and opened her mouth to

Dana-Sue Urso

speak, but he interrupted her by holding up his hand and taking a step towards her. She could actually feel the intensity of his emotions and had to force herself not to step back like she did before.

He continued, his voice low and tight. "But one thing I will **not** tolerate is being compared to your worthless first husband. I am *not* Danny and despite what you obviously think, I am nothing like him. I keep my promises, I take my responsibilities very seriously, and I try to keep up with what needs done around here. I know I fall short sometimes and don't always follow through like I should, but I give you my word, I will always do my best to provide for you and the children. You will **never** have to worry about having a roof over your head or food on the table."

By this time, he was standing right in front of her, looking down into her eyes, but not touching her. If the truth were told, he was afraid to reach out for her, afraid that she'd draw away again like she'd done in the house. That more than anything had hurt him the most; the pain of her rejection had cut deep. So instead of trying to hold her, he accepted the coat she held out for him and put it on.

"You're right," Mykaela said contritely. "Comparing you to Danny was mean and completely unjustified. It's just that, . . ." She broke off, unwilling to get his anger stoked up again when it seemed like he was mellowing a little. But he prodded her on, assuring her he would listen.

"Well, you promised to have the ring in the trapdoor replaced by Monday evening and here it is two days later. And you've been promising to chink the walls for two weeks."

Jax nodded. "Anything else? Let's get it all out."

Legacy of Love

"You've been coming home late; I know you said you were working, but I . . . smelled whiskey on one of your shirts this weekend. You never told me you go to the saloon sometimes." She tried not to sound petulant, but couldn't help the slightly accusatory tone in her voice.

"I've only been to the saloon twice since I came to Riverton," he explained evenly, truthfully. "Once was before I met you, and once was right before our wedding when the sheriff asked me to go for a congratulatory drink. I don't have a drinking problem, Mykaela; I assure you. As for the liquor on my shirt, I ran into Duff Hodges on Saturday. Literally. He was walking out of the storeroom where he'd been sleeping off one of his drunken spells before going home, and he spilled his bottle of whiskey on my shirt -- I usually take off my coat when I'm working back there. I went home to change, but you were gone, over at Misty's I think, so I threw the shirt with the other dirty clothes and forgot all about it; I wasn't trying to hide anything."

"I believe you," she said, starting to feel guilty for how she'd attacked him. Suddenly cold, she wished she was in his arms, but was timid about initiating since he was still upset. So she crossed her arms instead and waited while he continued.

"As for the trapdoor, the blacksmith told me he wouldn't have the ring ready until today. I picked it up on my way home. I'm sorry that I forgot to tell you that I couldn't get it fixed when I said I would. And as for the chinking, the hardware store is out of the putty I need and won't have any until the next train which has been delayed because of the snowstorms up north."

Mykaela felt completely mortified. She'd let her emotions get the best of her, something she rarely did, and had hurt the one person who meant the most to her. When she thought over her actions and words from the past hour, she was ashamed. He had been falsely accused, and she was filled with remorse.

She tentatively wrapped her arms around his waist and laid her head on his chest. She felt a profound relief when his arms came around her; he rested his chin on the top of her head.

"I am so sorry for jumping all over you," she said sincerely. "I have no explanation except that my emotions are on overload for some reason." Now wasn't the time to bring up the letter. She leaned back to look up at him, gratified to see a warmth come into his eyes. "Jax, please believe me when I say that I truly don't think you're like Danny. You are stronger, more hard-working, more loving and caring, more protective and supportive than he ever was. I know I hurt you, and I can't say I'm sorry enough." Tears gathered in her eyes as he traced a finger tenderly down her cheek. And just like that, his anger melted completely away.

"I know. It's OK." He assured her with a gentle smile. "And I take some responsibility for the misunderstandings; I should have realized that when I promised to have the ring fixed by Monday, you would expect that to happen. A few days delay is no big deal to me, but it doesn't mean that I meant to break my word. I should have been more sensitive and will be more careful in what I say from now on."

"I need to not be so sensitive and trust you more."

"Why don't we agree that we both should work on our communication skills?" he suggested.

"Agreed!" She replied, then accepted his kiss. She was ready to continue for awhile, but Jax drew back, looking at her with a serious expression.

"Mykaela, I . . . we need to talk about something else," he said with what sounded like regret. With some trepidation, she nodded and waited for him to continue.

"Back at the house, right before I left for the barn, you . . . seemed . . afraid. Of me." It was almost a question, but he went on before she could respond. "From that reaction and from some of the things you've told me about your relationship with Danny, I know that he probably treated you roughly."

He stopped as she lowered her eyes for a moment. "He didn't abuse me or beat me if that's what you're thinking. Sometimes, when we argued, he would . . . get physical. You know, push me or grab me."

"Did he ever hit you?" Jaxon's gaze was very intense, his gray eyes smoky with emotion.

"Not really," she down-played it. "Just a couple of slaps. I told him I would leave him if he ever did it again. And he never did."

Jax closed his eyes as he struggled against the fury he felt within him at her words. It didn't matter if he slapped her twice in 10 years or beat her every day. The fact was, the man should be hung and quartered. Jax had been raised to respect women, not to take advantage of their being physically weaker, to always maintain control no matter what the provocation.

He explained this to her, ending with, "There is nothing you could ever say or do that would cause me to raise my hand to you. You don't ever have to be afraid of me." He felt so strongly about this that he was actually imploring her to believe him by gripping her shoulders, but he kept his hold in check and wasn't harming her in any way.

She smiled up at him reassuringly and laid a hand on his cheek. "I know. And I'm not. In the kitchen, I reacted out of instinct, not fear."

He touched her forehead with his, a favorite gesture of his, and grinned. "So is all forgiven?"

"Only if you forgive me first."

"Done," he kissed her again and would have kept on going, but Velvet had had enough of the humans invading her space and pushed Jax. Stumbling, he held onto Mykaela to prevent them from falling. Laughing, they closed up the barn and walked back to the cabin.

Jax spent the evening fixing the ring in the trapdoor.

A letter arrived at the beginning of the second week of December that brought an end to Mykaela's anxiety, only to fill her with a new form of apprehension. Reverend Brooks came to the house one afternoon while Jax was out hunting. Mykaela had spoken to him before she'd sent her letter, to get his advice; he didn't like her going behind Jax's back, but understood her desire not to have him hurt again. So he agreed to be the go-between, so to speak.

As he handed the letter to her, he wished her luck and assured her that God's plan would always win out, no matter what the letter said. Thanking him, she went inside to sit by the fire and just held the envelope in her hand. It was post-marked Prentisville, Colorado, Double D Ranch. The handwriting was bold and heavy so she was pretty sure it was from a man. With heart pounding, she opened it and quickly checked the signature, then read:

Legacy of Love

December 9, 1868

Dear Mykaela,

I'm not sure where to begin so I'll just jump right in. From your letter, I assume you know about the telegram and letter my father and I sent to Jaxon back in May. We deeply regret our actions and tried to rescind them; we each sent a telegram the day after I mailed off my letter, but we knew early on that Jax never received them. The telegraph lines were down in Topeka which meant that no telegrams could get through from Denver until they were repaired. So we traveled by train and stage to Missouri, but arrived too late; Jax had already left Jefferson City. No one in town knew which direction he had gone. We tried to track him, but it was impossible since he was traveling by horse -- that much we knew. He could have gone in any number of directions. So we went home, hoping he would be there, but no luck. So our father hired a detective from the Pinkerton Agency who has been trying since June to find him.

Your letter was a God-send! You were right when you said that some things need to be said face-to-face. My family and I have been out of our minds with worry over Jaxon, for a long time, it's time to make things right. Please tell him that he is greatly missed, and that we very much want him to come home!

My father and I hope to meet you soon, as well, so we can give you our personal thanks for reassuring us that Jaxon is safe and well. And also to welcome you to the Dumont family.

With fond regards, Jerrod Dumont

P.S. Tell Jax that Father telegrammed the bank in Riverton and authorized him to access his personal account from the Farmer's Bank in Boulder.

By the time she was finished reading the letter, tears were running down her cheeks. She had been right; Jax's family *did* want him to come home. Carefully folding the missive, she replaced it in the envelope then knelt in front of the fireplace to pray for Jax and his family. She prayed that Jax would receive the news with a glad heart and forgive her for going behind his back. She prayed that he would make plans to go home as soon as possible and not worry about her and the kids. She prayed very hard that hearts would be healed when he confronted his family; there was a lot of hurt and misunderstandings that would take time to mend. And most of all she prayed for Jax, that he could put this final chapter of his life to rest and find the peace that she knew he still lacked to some degree due to the rift with his family.

The rest of the day seemed to drag on and on. The kids were noisier than usual when they trooped in after school which just served to raise her anxiety level. Jax was late getting home; he came in with a dour expression stating that he was starting to believe that all the deer in the county had gone on vacation. He had a rabbit and a pheasant, but that was all. Mykaela assured him that was fine and set about dressing the hare; she'd roast the bird for tomorrow's supper.

Tonight's supper was simple, roasted rabbit with carrots and potatoes, but it could have been sawdust for all that Mykaela noticed. She wanted to show the letter to Jax when he first got home, but the kids demanded his attention, and he still had the animals to feed and bed down for the night. So she waited. And waited until she thought she'd go crazy with the anticipation. Finally, all work was done and the kids finally in bed. Jax sat down with a tired sigh, leaning back in his chair.

"It feels good to sit," he remarked, his eyes closed. "The fire feels good, too. It was really, really cold today especially with the wind."

Mykaela sat down in her rocker when Jax began talking. She pulled the letter out from her knitting basket where she had kept it safe. Jax's eyes were still closed so she leaned forward and said cautiously, her mouth dry, "I have something to tell you."

Eyes still shut, he said, "I'm listening."

"Well, I actually have something to show you," she amended, biting her lip nervously. He opened his eyes, brows knit together in question.

"You sound so serious. What is it?"

"It's . . . a letter I received today," she held it up, but the light was too dim for him to read what was written on the envelope.

"Bad news?" was his first response.

"Not exactly." She took the folded letter out and handed it to him. Taking it, he gave her a puzzled frown. "It's from your brother."

Watching him closely, she saw him hesitate, staring at the paper as though he wasn't too sure it wouldn't suddenly rise up and bite him. Then, very slowly, he unfolded it and began reading.

Jax read the words, but they didn't begin to penetrate until he read it a second time. And even then, he had trouble believing it. But there it was. In black and white: *Please tell him that he is greatly missed, and that we very much want him to come home!*

His hands started shaking as he held onto the paper he was starting to consider a lifeline. Swallowing hard against the lump in his throat, he sat forward, the letter clenched in his hand. He stared at it, his vision suddenly blurred. All these months, he'd been so wrong. He had allowed the hurt and bitterness he'd felt from the communiques he'd received in Jefferson City to direct his decisions instead of following his heart which was to confront his family head on. If he had, he wouldn't have endured months of loneliness and solitude.

But you also wouldn't have met Mykaela, an inner voice reminded him. And with sudden clarity, he realized that for the last year -- no, for the last five years, God had been guiding him to this exact time and place. He was reminded of a scripture that he'd read a long time ago, something about how God determined the exact places for His people to live. And felt the weight of the last years begin to drop away.

Jax looked over at his wife who was watching him with an expression of what looked like excited apprehension. The love she freely gave him easily made up for the years of pain, humiliation, suffering, and loneliness during his two incarcerations; he would gladly endure it all again if she would always be there in the end.

Needing to ease the ache in his chest with a bit of levity, he adopted a stern façade.

"You wrote to Jerrod."

"Yes," she admitted a bit forlornly.

"Even after I told you I wasn't ready."

She nodded. "I disagreed."

He stood up. "Oh really."

Crossing her arms, she also stood up and said stoically, "Yes, really."

He cupped her head and smiled, "Here's my personal thanks." And he peppered her face with butterfly kisses that caused her to melt in his arms. He scooped her up and sat with her in his chair, loving how she cuddled close.

"You're not mad?" she asked, looking at him from under her lashes.

"Oh, yes, I'm mad. Maybe you'd better make it up to me," he replied with a mock glare.

"Well, if you insist," and she began to plant her own little kisses all over his face and neck. After a few minutes of mutual play, he stood up and carried her into their bedroom to continue where they left off.

A little while later, Mykaela lay curled on Jax's chest, lethargically happy. Their love-making had been wonderful, as usual, yet there had been a raw intensity in Jax, an urgency and need that was new; she had found it thrilling.

"I didn't hurt you, did I?" he asked suddenly breaking into her thoughts. He was absently playing with her hair and staring up at the ceiling.

"Not at all," she assured him, curling her arm behind his neck. "You always have a way of making me feel cherished and cared for."

"Careful with the compliments. You wouldn't want my ego to get out of control, now would you?" he teased her.

"That would never happen," she reached up to kiss him on the side of the mouth.

Sighing, he continued more seriously, "I know what the letter said, but I'm still finding it hard to believe. I let my feelings override my judgment, **again,** and caused my family more worry and pain." His voice was heavy with painful regret.

"Well, the jury's still out on the time after Andersonville, but this time, the fault lies mostly with your father and brother." She responded indignantly.

He chuckled.

"You are definitely someone I need by my side to defend me."

"That's right!"

"And now you and I need to discuss where we go from here."

"You need to go home."

"But not without you and the kids." He pointed out.

Legacy of Love

"I'd . . . like to meet your family, but what about our jobs and the farm?"

Jax was quiet for a few moments. Then, "Mykaela, you know how we've talked about my finding a job as a doctor?" He waited for her nod of affirmation. "I've had a couple of offers, but I think I should hold off making any kind of decision until after I talk to my family."

"I agree. You should leave as soon as possible, and we can follow later."

Jax was silent for another moment. "I don't want to go without you, I've waited this long, I can wait another couple of weeks."

Mykaela leaned up on her arm so she could look directly at him. "Jaxon Dumont, you haven't seen your family in almost 5 years. You need to go now!"

"You and the kids *are* my family, Mykaela." He insisted. "I won't go without you."

She laid back down, troubled. She made an instant decision to speak to Mr. Wood in the morning and see how problematic it would be for the kids to miss the last two weeks of the term. Another thought occurred to her.

"What about the animals?"

"I'll take Blackjack, but I'll ask Mr. Billings to watch over the farm and feed the animals."

"I suppose we'll need to travel by stagecoach," Mykaela remarked.

"It's way too cold for that. We'll take the train as far as we can, then go by stage." Jax replied decisively.

"But that'll be expensive, what with four people and a horse. I guess we could use the money I've been saving," she thought aloud. "Maybe Mr. Jansen at the bank will understand

and give us an extension on the taxes. They're due at the end of the month." They had already talked about the taxes, before they were married as Mykaela wanted Jax to know just what was in store regarding the farm and its upkeep. He hadn't seemed all that concerned then.

"I don't want you worrying about that!" Jax pointed out, still unconcerned. "And anyway, it doesn't matter now. I want you to use your money to buy some material to make yourself some new clothes."

"That's all well and good, but that money is for the taxes. And I can get by with the clothes I have until we can save some more money. Oh, that reminds me. I don't think I can just up and take several week's vacation. A few days. Maybe. But that's all. Then there's your job at the feedstore. What ."

Jax stopped her diatribe by placing a hand gently over her mouth, then pushed himself up to lean back against the headboard, pulling her along with him.

"First of all, you don't have to worry about your job at the hotel because you're going to quit. Tomorrow. That goes for Miss Hanks as well."

"Jax, I can't quit! We talked about this; there are taxes due and . . . ."

"Mykaela," he interrupted her. "do you remember what Jerrod wrote at the end of the letter?"

"Something about your account in Boulder."

"That's right. Before I left for the War, I had quite a bit saved from my years working for my father. Plus I received a stipend while training at the hospital in Denver. I didn't have too many needs so I was able to save a good bit. Then I sent probably 90% of my Army salary home to be deposited into my account as well. I had no need to access it while in prison, and I found out last May that my father had halted all activity on the account so the money is still in there. That's what Jerrod meant; my father cleared it with the bank here so I can now access whatever funds I need."

"Oh," she wasn't sure what to say. How much could he really have? He worked as a ranch-hand on a small cattle farm, she was sure that doctors-in-training earned a mere pittance, and could the Army really afford to pay an adequate salary to their soldiers what with the war's expenses? "Quitting my jobs still seems a little premature."

"It really isn't. I -- haven't been, uh, totally forthcoming about my family," Jax admitted sheepishly.

Mykaela had a sudden sinking feeling in the pit of her stomach.

"My father's cattle ranch is small -- compared to most Colorado ranches. But the land he owns is the most fertile in the state with more ponds and fresh water springs than anyone else we know. There's a huge creek that is fed from the mountain and winds its way across our land. Our cattle is prime beef, sought after by most markets east *and* west of the Mississippi; in fact, my father supplied a large majority of the beef shipped East to the Union troops."

The sinking feeling was quickly turning into quicksand. And Jax wasn't finished.

"I earned the salary my father paid me during my teenage years; one thing he believed in absolutely was that there are no free rides even for his children. He taught us to work hard and earn our way which, believe me, I did. But not only that, when my grandfather died, my father -- being the only son -- inherited the ranch, lock, stock, and barrel. He left some money to my three aunts, but my father also had to partially buy them out so when I say that the ranch is a working ranch, it is. My grandfather also left "a little something" -- that's how he worded it in his will -- to his seven grandchildren, $1000 each."

Mykaela couldn't help her gasp of surprise. A little something? Was he kidding?

He explained further. "That money helped pay my way through medical school; I also had a job during that time to pay my room and board and other expenses. But I never touched my savings because I wanted to use it for my future, maybe open a clinic some day."

"I see," was all she said.

"Mykaela, I can assure you that I earned every penny in that account," he felt it was important that she understand that. "It's more than enough to support us for a long time while we decide what to do from here on out."

"Do you think you'll go back to working on your father's ranch?"

Jax shook his head. "Not full-time, that's for sure. Ranching has always been Jerrod's dream, not mine. Although, I have to admit, that working cattle isn't quite the drudgery I always thought it was. But I like being a doctor and find that I miss it more and more as time passes."

"And you're a good doctor, Jax; you care for people as naturally as you breathe," Mykaela praised him. "Maybe there'll be an opening near your home if that's where you want to live."

"You wouldn't mind moving that far?"

"As long as I'm with you, I don't care where we live."

Jax held her close, his love for her deeper than ever. "I don't know how I was lucky enough to find you, but I treasure everything about you. You're my life, Mykaela; I'd be lost without you."

They lay together for a few minutes, each with his own thoughts. Then, Mykaela stirred to ask him,

"Just how big is your father's ranch?"

"35,000 acres, but 15000 of it is wooded or unusable because it's close to the mountains and very rocky, no fertile land at all. He runs about 10,000 cattle, and we raise our own grain and hay."

Jax was right, that *was* small by Colorado standards, but not by hers. She had envisioned a small ranch of maybe 500-1000 acres with maybe 100 head. No doubt about it -- her husband's family was not poor!

Jax rubbed her arm and threaded his fingers through her silky hair.

"Tell me what you're thinking?" he asked.

"I'm thinking that I don't know you as well as I thought, and I'm not sure how to handle it."

"Sweetheart, I'm the same man who arrived at your doorstep three months ago, lost and alone, looking for a place to live. I'm the same man who fell in love with the prettiest, sweetest, kindest, most adorable woman this side of the Mississippi . . . and the other side, too." He tilted her chin up. "I'm the same man who was humbled by your trust and belief in him, and who thanks the good Lord above every single day for bringing you into my life. I can't wait to see my family, but, Mykaela, I tell you true, if I never saw them again, I could live the rest of my life content and happy. All because of you and the children."

The look he gave her was so tender and his words so loving that Mykaela struggled not to burst into tears.

Burying her head in his neck, she mumbled, "But you're rich."

Jax chuckled. "I'm not sure that's totally accurate, but we can rest easy for awhile, financially speaking." He paused for a moment, thinking how to broach what was on his mind. "Mykaela, after I was released from prison, I planned on going home and figuring out what I wanted to do with the rest of my life. I wasn't sure if I wanted to practice medicine; I just wanted to rest and sort out my priorities. Since being here, especially since meeting you, I feel more confident about continuing working as a doctor. In fact, what I'd really like to do is focus on surgery like I did before I joined the Army. And now that we'll be going to my home, I was thinking that maybe I could talk to the hospital in Denver and try to get on staff there."

He stopped again, watching her intently to see her reaction. She was frowning slightly, resting her hand on his chest.

"Are you saying that we should move to Denver?" she asked slowly.

"Not necessarily in the city itself -- it wouldn't be conducive to raising children in my opinion, but, yes, move somewhere close enough that I could commute easily. If I get on staff there. But if not, there are other options, even opening my own practice. Denver is certainly large enough to support multiple doctors. Maybe even Boulder. The point is, when we leave, I don't see any reason to come back."

There, he'd said it. They had discussed selling the farm and moving in the Spring, but he saw no reason to wait. Not now that he was in touch with his family. But he wasn't sure how Mykaela would feel.

Legacy of Love

"It will take time to pack . . . " she began. ". . . but if you go on and leave as soon as possible, the kids and I can follow you as soon as we can."

"Uh, uh," Jax shook his head firmly. "I'm not leaving you behind. We'll stay as long as it takes to pack and then go."

Mykaela turned concerned eyes to him. "But it's been so long. You and your family need to reconcile."

He kissed the top of her head, inhaling her unique lavender scent. "We will. But you are the most important thing in my life now; I'm not leaving without you beside me. My family will understand."

Mykaela snuggled close, unwilling to admit out loud that she was glad. After a few minutes of cuddling, Jax spoke again, his voice uncertain.

"Are you sure you're OK with leaving Riverton. I mean, you have a lot of friends here."

"So do you," she pointed out. "But we have to do what's best for our family. And being with your family is what's best, at least for now. You were right when you said there's no reason to come back here. Except maybe for a visit some day."

"Absolutely. We'll be sure to do that."

Satisfied, she settled down to sleep, but it was some time before Jax relaxed enough to follow suit. He couldn't quiet the excitement in his soul over finally seeing his family. There were so many unanswered questions, so many misunderstandings, yet, there was also hope. And hope was something that had been missing from his life for many years until he'd found it with Mykaela, and now again with Jerrod's letter. He eventually joined his wife in slumber, a smile on his lips.

Dana-Sue Urso

CHAPTER 15

In the end, the packing up and plans to leave went fairly smoothly. The kids were a little sad about leaving their friends, but this was tempered with the excitement of an adventure. Jax sent a telegram to his brother to tell him when they would be arriving in Boulder. He and Mykaela had decided that a week from Friday -- 11 days away -- would give them ample time to do what needed to be done.

Jax received a telegram from his brother confirming Jax's arrival time. He also received one from his mother; a pain, sharp and acute, pierced his heart as he read **Hurry home, darling. Love, Mother**. She had written him faithfully every week while he was stationed in Pennsylvania, a correspondence he had missed greatly over the years.

Jax met with the bank manager and affirmed he had access to his account in Boulder. He paid the taxes on the farm and then put it up for sale. The manager was frank with him, saying that it would probably take time to sell it, but Jax wasn't concerned. He gave the man his family's address and told him to contact him when he had a buyer.

He would work the rest of the week at the store and that would be it, something Mr. Billings understood and agreed to although he "hated to lose the best worker he'd ever had." The rest of his time was spent finding buyers for the cow and chickens as well as winterizing the cabin as it would sit empty through the long cold winter months.

Jax also wanted to sell Maestro and Velvet, but came up against Mykaela and the kids. They were attached to the animals and wanted to take them to Boulder; the expense of taking three horses wasn't cheap, but Jax felt guilty about dragging the kids away from the only home they'd ever known and agreed to take the horses. He could just picture the appalled look on his father's face when they arrived with the two huge horses in tow.

Mykaela was busy as well. She quit her job with the hotel as Jax requested, but was reluctant to follow through with his other request of buying material and make herself some new clothes. She had three perfectly good, serviceable dresses and one nicer dress for church; there was no reason to waste money. Jax had bought her a new warmer cloak as a wedding gift, and she had knitted herself mittens so there was nothing she really needed. However, at her husband's insistence, she did relent and buy one ready-made dress from Sam's that was very pretty and would do for their trip north.

Now the kids were another matter. She used her carefully saved money to buy material for two new outfits each for them, thus splitting her time between sewing and packing.

Jax had insisted that everything be ready to go the day before their departure. By then the cabin was completely bare except for the furniture and few dishes which would stay behind for the new owners. Their clothes, linens, and personal effects were packed carefully in two trunks; when Mykaela thought about it, she realized that for all the years she'd been an adult, she really didn't have that much to show for it, and neither did Jax. As she stood in the middle of the main room, she was filled with a strange melancholy.

Tears pricked her eyes. The most important things in her life had occurred while she lived in this cabin: the birth of her children, the death of her first husband, the marriage to her second husband. She was about to begin a new chapter in her life, one that she wasn't sure she was ready for.

She heard the door open behind her, but stayed where she was. Jax's arms wrapped around her in a comforting embrace.

"Having second thoughts?" he asked quietly, his warm breath brushing her ear.

"Second, and third, and fourth," she gave a short laugh.

Pressing his arms tight, she leaned back into his strong embrace, resting the back of her head on his chest. "I'm OK. It's always scary to make changes, but I know in my heart that we're doing the right thing. That this is the path God wants us on."

Jax nodded. "I believe it, too."

He turned her around and kissed her sweetly. "Our lives are just beginning, Mykaela. I'm excited to see what the future has in store for us and the children. We'll be OK as long as we have each other."

Smiling, Mykaela hugged him. "I know. And I'm ready to go."

"That's my girl!" Jax lifted her up and after taking one last look around, carried her out the door.

The Brooks had the family over for supper that night. Mykaela had been afraid that it was too much for the young mother to cook for six people, but Misty had assured her that she was feeling very well; she had made a full recovery. And Baby Christopher was growing like a weed.

Mykaela spent a good portion of the visit holding the sweet child in her arms. He cooed at her, making bubbles, and just being sweet. At one point, as she placed a little kiss on his forehead, Jax was watching her. A lump formed in his throat; they had talked a little about expanding their family, but now more than ever, he knew he wanted to see his wife as she was right now only with their child in her arms.

He and Reverend Brooks had a chat after supper, sitting in his office. Jax thanked him for the talks they had shared over the past few months.

"You really helped me get things straight in here," Jax said, pointing a finger at his chest over his heart. "Gave me some perspective."

"Well, sometimes all we need is a little nudge in the right direction. Like I said before, God led you here, to this town, at just the right time." He glanced through the doorway out into the main room where he could see Misty holding their son to her shoulder to burp him, both of them healthy and safe, thanks to the man sitting before him. "I will always thank God in my prayers for you, Jaxon Dumont, as well as keep you and your family in my daily prayers."

Jax was humbled. He, too, looked at Misty who was laughing at something Mykaela had said. Saving the reverend's wife and his baby had been something he had been trained to do, and he didn't think there was more to it than that. But he also knew that God had led him here not just for the Brooks and for Mykaela, but for his sanity.

And his wife was now talking earnestly to Misty, using her hands to emphasize a point. Then they both began laughing again, now sneaking covert glances at him and the young minister.

"You don't think they're talking about us, do you?" asked the reverend mildly.

"Probably. A cross we must bear, I suppose." Jax sighed dramatically.

Legacy of Love

The Dumonts left soon after, the women promising to write each other. Misty handed Mykaela a small package of notecards with a flower border as a going away gift. Mykaela was deeply touched and also saddened to be leaving behind such a dear friend.

They spent their last night in Riverton at the hotel, a rare treat for the kids. Ryan was excited not only because he was sharing a room with his Pa for the night, but that they would be eating breakfast in the dining room.

All of them had trouble settling down to sleep that night. Rachel, who was sharing the bed with her mother, kept wiggling around until Mykaela finally held her close and told her a bedtime story. When the little girl eventually dropped off, Mykaela lay awake. Her thoughts were topsy-turvy as she contemplated the new turn her life was taking. She had meant what she'd said to Jax about being content wherever he was, but that didn't stop her from feeling anxious. She was especially apprehensive about meeting his parents. She knew that despite Jax's words, he'd grown up wealthy. And she had not. This was at the crux of her anxiety: worrying over whether or not his parents would accept her. She didn't want to bother Jax with her concerns so she kept them to herself and prayed vigilantly that all would be well.

Ryan actually fell asleep fairly quickly, but only after asking Jax what seemed like a hundred questions about the Double D ranch. Jax was too excited to sleep and laid in bed contemplating his return home. He knew that going home would be easy and hard at the same time. Reuniting with his family was the easy part; explaining his actions over the last few years the hard part. He believed that the unexpected turn to his life was what God had in mind for him and his new family, but not knowing the immediate future made him nervous.

He'd had enough with living day-to-day . . . and he wasn't talking about financial security although that played a large part. Working things out with his family would take time, and he saw no other option but to live with his parents until the Spring when he could find them a place to live and build them a house, using the money from his account to buy the needed material and furnishings. He knew he could earn their keep by working on the ranch which was fine with him, but he knew it was a possibility that his father wouldn't want them to stay too long. If that was the case, then they would have to find lodging in Boulder or Denver at a rooming house or maybe an apartment, neither of which sat well with him.

Morning came quickly. And with it a rush to eat breakfast, gather the horses from the livery, and get to the depot. Jax was glad to see a clear sky without a single cloud; that boded a good trip. They would take the train west, then be forced to travel by stage for a day north. Then catch another train for the final leg.

Several of the townspeople were there to see them off. There had been a small reception for them after church last Sunday which Jax and Mykaela had been very encouraged by. But seeing them now, Jax felt a rush of affection for the kind people of this town; he'd gotten to know many of them during his time at the feed store. He really would miss them.

At long last, they said their final good byes and boarded the train. Ryan and Rachel sat across from each other so they could each have a window seat. They pressed their noses to the windows as the train began to move, waving frantically to anyone who was looking.

Legacy of Love

Mykaela also waved to the Brooks and Miss Hanks specifically. She would never forget them. Miss Hanks had also given her a going away gift; it was a sewing kit filled with brand new threads of all different colors, needles, a thimble, and scissors. Mykaela's eyes filled with tears as her friends and the town gradually faded from sight.

Settling back against the velvet cushion, she saw Jax looking at her, a tender smile on his lips.

"It's always hard leaving, I know," he said sympathetically.

"It's OK. I'll be fine. I can write, stay in touch," she tried to sound upbeat.

Jax admired her spirit. His love for her grew by leaps and bounds every day, and he knew without a shadow of a doubt that it always would.

The first half of their journey went smoothly. The kids were sufficiently entertained by the novelty of their first train ride. They spent equal amounts of time looking out the windows and asking lots of question about the things they were seeing. Mykaela was amazed yet again by Jax's patience. Hers had run out by the 20th question. But he continued to answer them, even the repeats, pointing out sights along the way such as a herd of buffalo on a hillside and what looked like Indian wigwams with fires burning in the distance.

They spent the night at another hotel and then climbed aboard the stage. This was a lot colder than traveling by train so they all snuggled up together, grateful for the heated bricks lining the floor. Thankfully, they made good time as it hadn't snowed in over two weeks. By suppertime, they were once again in another hotel in another town. But the next day would see them home.

This final train ride would be the longest. They boarded early and by lunchtime, had reached their first stop. They had to wait about an hour before continuing on, but Jax thought it would be best to remain on the train and eat their packed lunch provided by the hotel from the night before.

By the time the train started on its second leg, the children's energy began to wan. Three days of travel and sleeping in strange beds was taking its toll. First Rachel's eyelids started to droop; then she slowly leaned over and laid her head on Jax's arm. Within minutes, she was half lying on him, her legs curled on the seat beside her; she was asleep soon after. Ryan fought the urge for awhile, but soon caved in. He curled up beside his mother, resting his head on his arms.

Mykaela tenderly brushed hair off his face. "He's worn out."

"Too much excitement over the last few days."

"I know the feeling. I'm tired, too."

Jax yawned. "Me, too. I had trouble falling asleep last night."

"Thinking about your family?"

"Yeah. I can't wait to see them, but at the same time, it's a little daunting. I feel like I've been gone for twenty years instead of five."

"That's probably a natural feeling," She smiled encouragingly at him. "But I know everything will be alright."

Jax raised an eyebrow. "You sound so sure. Do you have some insight that I don't have?"

"Just the stories you've told me. It's obvious that you were close growing up; I can't imagine things not being OK."

Legacy of Love

"You haven't met my father yet," Jax was somewhat dramatically, only half kidding.

"Well, I'll meet him soon enough, and you'll see I'm right," she declared with a toss of her head.

"Now I see where Rachel gets her attitude from," he grinned at her, his arm tightening slightly around the little girl.

Gazing down at her, he grew more serious and said grimly, "And her looks. I have a feeling I'm going to be busy chasing the boys away in about 10 years."

Mykaela choked back a laugh at the dour expression on is face. "We could always keep her chained behind a locked door."

"Could we?" Jax looked up hopefully.

Mykaela laughed, but before she could respond, they were interrupted just then by one of the train's workers who arrived in the car to replenish the coal in the braziers at each end. Even so, the passengers had to keep their coats on to ward off the chill. Mykaela fixed her gaze out the window, watching the landscape speed by.

Snow covered most of the ground although no new snow had fallen in several weeks. She became mesmerized by the monotony and dozed off. Only to be jolted awake an hour later as the train slowed to head down a steep grade.

Jax's eyes were closed, but she couldn't tell if he was asleep although she suspected that he was; his features were relaxed and soft. She acknowledged, not for the first time, how handsome he really was. He hadn't taken the time for a haircut before they left, so now his bangs fell across his forehead. He had shaved that morning, but quickly and now she could just see the outline of his 5 o'clock shadow which always gave him that dark, rakish look, one that she used to be somewhat intimidated by, but now found very endearing.

His eyes snapped open just then, meeting hers. She boldly looked back.

"Is something wrong?" he frowned, sitting up straighter.

"No, just enjoying the view," she replied saucily. And was rewarded by a look of uncertainty, something that was rare for him. "You mentioned having to chase away the boys in a few years, but I'll bet you had your share of girls chasing after you."

She was thrilled at how uncomfortable he looked.

"Not that many, not really. A few, I guess" he managed to get out, not liking the conversation so far.

"I don't believe it," she poo-poohed, flapping her hand at him. "Not with your good looks and devilish smile."

Jax relaxed and smiled a bit cockily. "You think I'm good-looking?"

She smirked at him. "As if you didn't know."

"It's always nice to be told so by one's wife."

"Do you know that when I first saw you, I thought your eyes were hard and dangerous-looking."

"Really?" This was news to him. "I thought your eyes were the gentlest I'd ever seen."

"Really?" This was news to her.

He nodded. "Yep. I wasn't feeling all that great at the time. I was frustrated and tired. Lonely. And then you smiled at me. It warmed my heart."

Mykaela was humbled. She had been teasing him, but he had turned the tables and complimented her so beautifully.

"I realized very quickly how wrong I was," she admitted. "Your eyes aren't dangerous at all. They're gorgeous, warm and giving, the most tender eyes I've ever seen in a man." She suddenly leaned towards him, squinting slightly. "Are you blushing?"

He shrugged, clearly embarrassed. "Well, most men wouldn't want to be described as gorgeous, Mykaela."

She leaned back with a soft laugh. "I call them like I see them, husband-mine"

"Well, wife, I can tell you honestly that the only thing beautiful between you and me is you. And not just on the outside."

Now it was her turn to blush. "You do know how to turn a girl's head. Which leads us back to when you were a teenager . . . . "

"Oh no, we're not going there," he replied in horror. "Suffice it to say that there has never been anyone who even comes close to making me feel as I do about you."

"Good answer," Mykaela voiced her approval with a smile.

They continued to talk about this and that, until they were within an hour of Boulder. The kids had awakened an hour before, somewhat cranky and out of sorts. But Jax took them for a walk through some of the cars to stretch their legs and soon he was able to point out familiar landscapes as they neared Boulder.

As the train chugged into the station, Jax strained as hard as the children to look out the windows. The city proper came into view all of a sudden as the train squealed to a stop. People were standing on the platform, huddled in coats, but it was impossible to make out individual faces in the waning late afternoon sun.

Dana-Sue Urso

Jax led the way to the front of the car, the procession of passengers moving slowly. The children were wide-eyed as they looked out the windows at the booming town laid out before them; Boulder was 3 times the size of Riverton. Jax and Mykaela each clutched an overnight satchel. He had been afraid that their trunks wouldn't be able to get to the ranch until tomorrow. Rachel had her rag doll while Ryan's toy soldiers were safely ensconced in his mother's bag.

When it was his turn to disembark, Jax climbed down the steep steps then lifted each child down before assisting Mykaela, then turned and scanned the crowd of people. Mykaela saw the door of the depot open and watched a man walk out. He was wearing a wool coat without a scarf; his Stetson, boots, and gloves were black. Even in the dim light, Mykaela could see his resemblance to Jax. The same height and bearing, the same facial features, the same way he was also scanning the crowd.

Before Mykaela could say anything, the two men spotted each other. She was attuned to Jax's reaction and sensed his tension. After a long moment, the two men began walking toward each other, and when they were within a few feet of each other, Jax held out his hand.

"Jerrod, it's good to see you," an understatement to be sure, but Jax wasn't certain of his reception despite the letter his brother had written Mykaela. The countenance on his brother's face was hard to read.

Jerrod grasped his brother's hand and then pulled him into an embrace, something Jax wasn't prepared for from his usually staid and reserved older brother. As they stepped back from, Jerrod clasped Jax's shoulders firmly.

Legacy of Love

"Jaxon," Jerrod began. "all these years, we thought you were dead, and now seeing you, well, it's balm to my soul."

Jax felt emotion welling up in him at his brother's words. For so many months, he'd thought Jerrod despised him, but now, seeing the gladness in his eyes, he knew he'd been wrong.

"We have a lot to talk about, that's for sure, but it's best left for later. Let me introduce you to my family."

Mykaela found her hands grasped firmly in Jerrod's as he welcomed her to Boulder. He shook Ryan's hand, man-to-man, then kissed one of Rachel's hands and told her it was a pleasure to meet her. She giggled, ducking her eyes, holding tight to Mykaela, unsure of this handsome stranger, but enthralled by him as well.

The group walked into the depot office, Jerrod explaining that with all the snow on the ground, the best way to travel, other than horseback, was by bobsled. But his wasn't large enough for the whole Dumont family so it had been agreed that he would pick up the travelers while their mother and sister waited back at home.

"Father attended a business meeting in Mansfield and was supposed to be back yesterday. But the stagecoach line was blocked by an avalanche so he has to wait until Monday before the stages are running to Boulder again," Jerrod explained.

Jax felt relieved and disappointed at the news. Relief to not have to face his father quite yet, but disappointment because he missed him as much as anyone.

He and Jerrod arranged to have the horses stabled for the night to be picked up in the morning along with their trunks. Then they crowded into the 4 man bobsled. Jax rode with his brother in front while Mykaela and Ryan sat behind them with Rachel on her mother's lap. Blankets were tucked in all around with warm bricks at their feet.

It was a cold ride, but they were well protected from the worst of the wind. Mykaela snuggled with her children, content to listen to the conversation between the brothers without feeling the need to join in.

She learned a couple of interesting things. One was that Jerrod was engaged to be married. She already knew that Jerrod had been engaged once before to his high school sweetheart, but she had died a month before the wedding from a rabies bite. Jax had told her his brother had been devastated and thrown himself into the ranch, even attended an agricultural college for a couple of years.

Apparently, Jerrod's new fiancée was the school teacher in Prentisville. She had arrived two years ago and been courted by several of the men in the area. But it was Jerrod she fell in love with. They were to be married in May.

Jerrod also told Jax that their sister, Jenna, had been married for two years. To Jax's best friend Mick.

"You're kidding?" Jax was well and truly shocked. With good reason. Growing up, Jenna and Mick had never gotten along. He used to call her a pest, a green bean (she had been rather skinny as a child), and a nuisance. She would not be intimidated by someone whose picture was beside the word Neanderthal in the dictionary, as she told him on more than one occasion.

Jax always found their little spats highly amusing especially since Mick, who was usually pretty easy-going, could get riled up so effortlessly by a mere slip of a girl. Especially one who was 5 years his junior.

Legacy of Love

When he last saw his sister, she had been just 18. She had outgrown the name-calling, but deliberately ignored Mick whenever they were in the same room together. Jax remembered how frustrated Mick used to get by this, completely forgetting the fact that his most fervent wish had always been to not have to associate with Jenna in any way. And now they were married. It really was a strange world they lived in.

"Mick has been a great support to Jenna since you left," Jerrod explained. "They both grew up."

"Apparently," was Jax's only comment.

The ride took about an hour. Jax would check on the passengers in the back every so often, asking if they were OK to which Mykaela always replied, "We're fine." Which they were. But she was very glad when he called back that the house was just coming into view. She craned her neck to the side to get her first glimpse of her husband's childhood home.

CHAPTER 16

As the bobsled skimmed up the drive, the house grew ever larger. It was a one-story ranch style in an L-shape, but both sides were long. And wide. It was built out of some type of gray stone that looked as though it weathered well. The outer wall of a huge fireplace took up almost the whole end of the top of the L; smoke curled lazily above it. A wide covered verandah ran the length of the front of the house complete with wicker chairs and rockers, tables, and a hanging swing. It was a very large house.

Spreading out behind the house, Mykaela could see several paddocks, a stable, barn, and other outbuildings that were evidence of a working ranch. A patch of snow covered woods were seen in the distance with the Rockies arising as an intimidating yet beautiful backdrop.

As they all climbed down from the bobsled, two dogs ran up, barking, only to be shushed by Jerrod. The dogs were then all over the kids, tails wagging, tongues licking.

"They're our welcoming committee," Jerrod observed drily.

"I don't see Lucky around," Jax commented, referring to the family dog, a Collie.

"He was killed last year, I'm afraid," Jerrod told him. "I found Trudy two years ago." He pointed to the female Border collie who was trying to leap into Ryan's arms. "She'd been abandoned. She and Lucky became close, and after he died, we got Max to keep her company. Plus he's a heck of a cattle dog." Jerrod called the dogs and pointed to the barn; the animals reluctantly obeyed, but kept looking at the kids as if to say, "Come with us and play."

"Pa," Ryan tugged on Jax's arm as they walked up the steps to the porch. "Do you think we could get a dog some day."

"Count on it," he promised with a smile.

Jerrod held open the front door while Jax led the way inside. Taking a deep breath, he looked around the wide front hall. It hadn't changed all that much. Across from the front door was a hallway that led to the back of the house which housed the kitchen, dining room, the library, and his father's study. To the left was another hallway that led to the other side of the L and the bedrooms, bathroom, and back parlor. To the right of the door were two closed double doors. Behind them was the large main room.

The small group had entered the house rather quietly. Jax was trying to come to terms with the fact that he was finally back home. All sorts of feelings engulfed him as he looked around, not the least of which was a deep gladness. Mykaela was trying to assimilate it all, feeling a little intimidated by the grandeur of the house and property. The kids were simply in awe.

As everyone was hanging up their coats in a wardrobe to the left of the front door, the double doors of the main room suddenly flew open. A tall, elegant woman stood framed in the doorway, silhouetted by the light of a fire behind her. The first thing Mykaela noticed was how beautiful she was. Her honey brown hair was swept up into an attractive style, and she wore a modest gown of dark russet. A garnet necklace with matching earrings graced her neck and ears. The woman's dark eyes, sparkling with unshed tears, were fixed on Jax.

"Mother!" Jax managed to choke out before heading in her direction.

Constance Dumont hurried forward, meeting her son halfway. As he swept her into his arms, Mykaela heard her cry out, "Oh Jaxon!"

They held each other for several long moments; Mykaela found herself swiping the tears from her own eyes as she tried to imagine what Jax must be feeling. She had never known her own mother and felt that loss more keenly now than she had in years.

A small hand slipped into hers. Looking down she saw Rachel staring at Jax and his mother.

"Is that his Ma?" she whispered.

"Yes, she is."

"She's pwetty."

Mykaela nodded in agreement.

Jax pulled back slightly so he could look at his mother. Tears ran down her cheeks, his just as wet.

She framed his face with her hands, looking up at him with love in her eyes, and said shakily, "There were times these past few years when I wished more than anything to see you again, even when I thought you were ...." She broke off, unable to finish that particular thought. "And now here you are, my prayers answered." Her voice broke, and she gripped his shoulders to steady herself.

"There were times I wasn't so sure I'd ever make it home, Mother," Jax admitted in an emotion-filled voice of his own as he gazed in wonder down at the woman who'd given him birth. "I can't tell you how sorry I am that . . . "

Legacy of Love

Constance shushed him with a light finger over his lips and a quick shake of her head.

"Explanations can wait. There are others anxious to see you." She hugged him to her again just before a dynamo whirled into the hallway.

A young woman leaped into Jax's arms, almost knocking over Constance. Laughing and crying at the same time, she squeezed him hard, sputtering between how much she had missed him and how dare he let them think he was dead. Jax lifted her up and gave her a bear hug.

As he set her back on her feet, he remarked, "It's good to see you, too, Brat. And just look at you." He stepped back and eyed her up and down.

His little sister had grown into a very attractive young woman, looking more like their mother than she ever had. The same light brown hair, the same pert nose, and high cheekbones. But Jenna's mouth was all her own and was now smiling up at him with a mischievous tilt to one side -- her trademark.

He went on. "You're all grown up. And if I'm not mistaken, soon to be a mother?" He had felt the slight tell-tale bulge of her waist and abdomen when he'd picked her up.

"That's right. In about 5 months. And all I can say is that I'm glad my daughter will have two uncles to spoil her."

"Don't you mean *our* son?" A deep voice behind her said. Jax looked over her shoulder to see his best friend, now his brother-in-law, standing there, grinning at them.

Stepping around his sister, Jax held out a hand to him. "Congratulations, Mick!"

"Thanks, Jax. It sure is good to see you alive and well." Mick firmly grasped Jax's hand with both of his.

Dana-Sue Urso

"It's good to see you, too," he glanced at his sister who was arm and arm with their mother. "So you married the Pest. What happened? D'you lose a bet?"

That earned him a swift punch in the arm by the woman in question; he wasn't totally pretending when he winced and rubbed at the spot. His sister was stronger than she looked.

"We-ell," Mick threw an arm around his wife's shoulders. "She scared off most of her beaus over the years, and let's face it, she wasn't gettin' any younger. Somebody had to take her off your parents' hands so I figured I'd make the sacrifice for the good of all mankind."

He sighed loudly and placed a hand over his heart right before Jenna elbowed him in the stomach. Laughing, he caught her up in his arms and planted a hard kiss on her lips. As Jax watched the two of them, he wondered if he and Mykaela displayed the same besotted look whenever they were together.

With that thought, he turned to find her and the kids standing by the front door, looking a little lost. He felt a stab of guilt. He had been so caught up with reuniting with his family that he had almost forgotten about his other one.

Going to her, he gently drew her forward, Rachel clinging to her skirts, Ryan holding his sister's hand.

Reaching his other hand to Constance, Jax introduced them. "Mother, I'd like you to meet my wife, Mykaela."

Mykaela smiled shyly, trying not to let her nervousness show. "I'm pleased to meet you, Mrs. Dumont."

"Oh, my dear," cried the older woman. "The pleasure is all mine, I assure you." She placed her hands on Mykaela's shoulders and kissed her on the cheek. Smiling warmly into her eyes, she continued, " Welcome to the family, Mykaela."

Legacy of Love

Mykaela felt her eyes sting at the kindness she saw in her mother-in-law's eyes that were so like Jax's. "Thank you."

Jax then introduced the children who stared at Constance with wide eyes. She knelt down and told them how glad she was to meet them.

"My, what a pretty girl you are," she told Rachel. "You look just like your mother."

This pleased Rachel, and she squeezed her mother's hand tight, grinning up at her with her tooth-gapped smile. Constance went on, "And look at what a fine young man you are, Ryan. It's so nice to meet you."

"Same to you, Maam," he mumbled back, embarrassed, but pleased.

The rest of the family pressed forward to meet them, then Constance ushered everyone into the main room where it was warm and comfortable. The first thing that Mykaela noticed was the massive fireplace. The stonework was intricate and lovely while the mantel held an array of bric-a-brac and a framed photograph of what appeared to be the Dumont family although they were older than they were in the photo Jax carried. She counted 10 stockings hanging down.

The first thing the children noticed was the massive Christmas tree that was holding court between two huge bay windows over looking the front lawn. Garland and candles and ornaments adorned the tree; several wrapped gifts rested below. As if by an unseen hand, Ryan and Rachel were drawn over to stand in front of it, mesmerized. The tree stood almost as tall as the 8 foot ceiling; they had never seen one so large nor with so many presents under it.

Constance came to stand behind them.

"It's big, isn't it?" she asked.

"It sure is!" cried Ryan enthusiastically, forgetting his shyness for a moment.

"And so bootiful," whispered Rachel in wonder; then she glanced at the gifts. "Did Santa alweady come?"

"No, these are the gifts I give my family," Constance answered, placing a gentle hand on the little girl's shoulder. "But don't worry; Santa will be here in just a few days."

Ryan turned to her. "Really?"

She smiled reassuringly. "Really."

"Wow!" he turned to look at the tree again.

"D'you think Santa'll know we're here? Cuz we didn't write to him to tell him we were coming," Rachel pointed out, looking at Constance with a serious, unwavering gaze.

"Well, from what I know about Santa, he's real smart," she reassured the little girl. "I have a feeling that he not only knows you're here, but that he has something special in mind for you this year." And gave the child a reassuring wink.

The animated look on her children's faces brought Mykaela to tears. Conflicting emotions waged within her. On the one hand, she had no doubt that Jax would do everything he could to ensure the children had the best Christmas they'd ever had. On the other hand, she had a lot of guilt over the sadly lacking holidays they'd had in the past.

The other adults watched the tableau from the main seating area near the fireplace. Jenna stood next to Mykaela and remarked, "Your children are so precious, Mykaela. How I envy you."

"Me?"

"You've been a mother for what 7, 8 years?" Jenna placed her hands on her abdomen. "I can't wait to be a mother."

Legacy of Love

Mykaela smiled knowingly. "There's no other feeling like it. I'm very happy for you."

Jenna grinned and gave her new sister-in-law a side-arm hug. "Thanks."

Again, Mykaela was overcome momentarily by the affection and tenderness of Jax's family. Both women seemed to accept her, no questions asked. Jerrod had treated her respectfully, and Mick had greeted her with what seemed a sincere attitude. The only person left was the patriarch of this family. She mentally crossed her fingers.

A loud cry was heard at a doorway across the room from the tree. A small stout woman in an apron came into the room, crying, followed by a man wearing jeans and boots. Both looked to be in their 50's and both headed for Jaxon.

Mykaela watched the three greet each other with the same warmth and affection she had noted about the Dumonts. She soon learned that the couple were Annie and Miles O'Connor. Although she was the housekeeper, and he was the foreman, they were treated like family. They had been with the Dumonts for 20 years and lived in a house on the property a couple of miles away. Mykaela later learned that they had not been blessed with children, but were like surrogate parents to Jax and his siblings.

After another round of introductions, Annie brought out tea and coffee, milk for the children as well as a platter of sandwiches and cookies. The next couple of hours was spent sitting around the fire, eating and talking, the family catching Jax up on the events around the ranch and Boulder since he'd been gone. By unspoken agreement, no one brought up the last five years of Jax's life. It was as if they were all waiting for the right time.

The rest of the day was spent in peaceful relaxation although there was always an invisible energy in the air, as if everyone was holding their breath. Constance was a thoughtful hostess and gently insisted that Jax and Mykaela take the kids to their rooms so everyone could rest before supper. Mykaela was grateful for her foresight as she and the children took a short nap, something she never did but couldn't resist today. Jax spent the rest of the afternoon outdoors with his brother, greeting old acquaintances who still worked on the ranch as well as meeting the new ones.

By the time everyone met for supper, Mykaela was well-rested, and Jax was buzzing with excitement at being home. They were all getting seated at the long dining room table when Jenna, who was sitting across from Jax and Mykaela and was in the middle of telling them about her wedding, suddenly broke off and stared at something over their heads. All conversation came to a halt as Jax slowly turned around.

Standing in the doorway stood his father. Mykaela noticed right off how much like his sons Eric Dumont looked. He had a commanding presence and an air of authority that was almost tangible. His eyes, though lighter than Jax's, were much like his younger son's, shrewd and intelligent. This man was nobody's fool.

Time seemed to stand still as Jax and his father stared at each other. It was Constance who broke the spell. Getting up from her place at one end of the long table, she went to her husband.

"I'm so glad you made it home sooner than you expected," she said, enclosing his arm with her hands, smiling up at him. He smiled tenderly at her, giving her quick kiss on the cheek.

Legacy of Love

"I rented a horse and rode straight through," he explained, before looking at Jax again, an enigmatic expression on his face.

By now, Jax was on his feet, but remained standing by his chair. He had trouble identifying what he was feeling at that moment. Gladness, anxiety, bitterness, relief, uncertainty -- they were all wrapped together and settled into a knot in the middle of his chest which hurt every time he breathed.

Swallowing hard, Jax said, "Hello, Father."

"Hello, Jaxon," Eric replied, took a hesitant step forward, then stopped. Jax frowned. Was that doubt he saw in his father's eyes? *Surely not.* His father never lacked confidence about anything. And yet, he could swear that the expression on his sire's face was one of uncertainty and trepidation. *Could it be that his father was as nervous as he was?*

Constance was watching him with a look of desperation on her own face. And then Jax understood. His father was a proud man, too proud at times. With their past history, Eric Dumont was uncertain of his reception by his youngest son. Constance knew that both men were full of the Dumont pride, but she was silently asking Jax to make the first move.

Jax closed the gap between them, holding out his hand as he'd done with Jerrod. A look of what could only be described as relief came over Eric Dumont's face, and he gripped his son's hand firmly.

"Welcome home, Son," he greeted warmly.

They stood eye to eye, and Mykaela knew that in about 20 years, her husband would age as well as the elder Dumont, something she would look forward to as Eric Dumont was a very good-looking man with not an ounce of fat on his trim frame and only a few shots of silver in his full head of black hair.

"It's good to be home," Jax responded sincerely.

Eric nodded and then turned to greet the rest of his family. When introduced to Mykaela, he told her his son couldn't have chosen a lovelier wife. He greeted the children in a friendly manner, then settled into his seat at the head of the table.

Conversation was light at first, again no one brought up what was really on everyone's minds. Mykaela was glad because talking about Jax's past in front of the children wasn't proper.

Halfway through the supper, Jerrod and his father started to discuss a cougar problem they were having out in the "north pasture." Rachel, who up until now had not said a word, feeling overwhelmed by all the people, suddenly piped up,
"My Pa shot one; he was a bad kitty 'cuz he tried to eat me!" she ended the sentence indignantly, arms crossed.

Mykaela and Jax tried not to laugh at her piqued expression, but the rest of the Dumonts just stared at her in horror as they imagined this sweet child being attacked by a mountain lion.

"What happened?" asked Jenna, eyes wide.

Jax quickly explained, completely down-playing his part in the entire event. But Ryan spoke up next.

"Pa saved her. I saw the whole thing. You shoulda seen it. That cougar was humongous and . . ."

"Ryan, I've already explained. And he wasn't that big. Actually kind of scrawny," Jax interrupted him.

"My goodness, Rachel, you must have been so scared. I'm so glad you weren't hurt," Constance remarked. She knew how dangerous cougars could be when aroused or hungry. But having them roam ranches near mountains every so often was part of ranch life which was why boys were taught early on how to shoot.

"That bad kitty scwatched Pa and . . ." It was her turn to be interrupted.

"Rachel, everything turned out fine. Why don't you finish eating?" Jax prodded gently.

It was clear to all that Jax was uncomfortable with praise so they respected this and nothing more was said. But Constance couldn't help a little stab of fear that ran through her as she thought about how close Jax had to be to the cat to get scratched. She made a decision to ask Mykaela about it in private.

An hour later found the family once again ensconced in the main room with lamps lit as well as the candles on the Christmas tree. Ryan and Rachel stared at it in fascination, the twinkling of the candlelight mesmerizing. That effect on top of the meal and the tiring last few days was enough to make them drowsy before much more time passed. Jax and Mykaela herded them to the room they shared (which was Jax's old room and held two twin beds), helped them change into their pajamas, and tucked them into bed. It wasn't long before they were fast asleep.

As the adults tiptoed out, Mykaela commented that she'd never known Ryan to go to sleep so quickly.

"I think I envy him," remarked Jax as they headed back down the hall. Mykaela put her arm around him.

"Your family has been so nice and welcoming," she pointed out. "I really like them. Even your father although he doesn't say much."

"He rarely does. He's one of those people who say what needs to be said then moves on."

"That can be a good thing."

"Usually. Unless you want to know what he's thinking and then it's like pulling teeth."

"Like father, like son," Mykaela said airily, grinning.

"Oh yeah," he caught her up and nuzzled her. "Guess what I'm thinking now." He growled playfully. Laughing, she circled his neck and leaned into him. As they eventually broke apart, he asked with a hopeful gleam in his eyes, "How about if we just sneak away to our own room and don't come out until tomorrow? Or the next day?"

"I wish," she said wistfully. 'But putting off the inevitable will just make it that much harder."

He sighed. "I know although it's going to be hard enough as it is. My stomach is all twisted up in knots."

She linked hands as they continued down the hall. "I'll be right beside you.
And besides, your family loves you."

"You really believe it's that simple, don't you?" He stopped her outside the double doors.

"Why shouldn't it be? I mean, I never had a family like yours. And I never missed that as much as I do right now. You're very lucky, Jax, and I'm lucky to have you."

Humbled, he gazed into her eyes with an urgent intensity and said almost breathlessly, "I am absolutely convinced that my life would still be full of loneliness and heartache if I hadn't met you. You are what makes my life complete, Mykaela; don't ever forget that."

Legacy of Love

He was so serious that she had no choice but to believe it. Together, they opened the door and headed into what Jax thought of as the Inquisition.

Several long hours later, Jaxon and Mykaela lay in bed resting in each other's arms. Mykaela had fallen asleep, but Jax's thoughts kept him wide awake. The evening hadn't been the painful experience he had expected. In fact, in telling his story, he felt the last of the guilt and burden slipping away, leaving his heart lighter than ever.

Of course the fact that his family was so understanding helped quite a bit. They had expressed their horror and dismay over his imprisonments although he'd kept most of the dreadful details to himself. They expressed their acceptance of the decisions he'd made even though it had hurt them. And forgiveness was easily given. On both sides.

But the most wondrous thing of the night occurred after everyone had finally talked themselves out and gone off to their separate rooms to get some much needed sleep. Eric had asked Jax to accompany him to the library. With some trepidation, Jax followed his father inside. The elder Dumont proceeded to open his wall safe and remove a sheet of paper from it, then handed it to his son.

It was a bank draft, dated 9 months ago, around the time he'd sent the ill-fated telegram. $1000 had been deposited into his personal account. Frowning in puzzlement, Jax looked at his father questioningly.

"That's your inheritance from your grandfather," Eric told him.

"But I already received that," Jax protested.

Eric nodded. "Yes, but you used it to pay for medical school, did you not?"

"Ye-es, but that's what I wanted to do with it. No one forced me."

"I know, but I stubbornly refused to pay for your education like I did for your brother and sister. And that wasn't fair."

"It's OK, I. . . ."

But Eric wouldn't let him continue. Holding up his hand in a familiar manner of getting his family's attention, Eric waved Jax into one of the leather bound chairs in front of his desk while he sat in the other.

"Jaxon," Eric said softly. "what I have to say to you is a long time coming. And should have been said many years ago." He stopped and took a deep breath. "When you made the decision to go to medical school regardless of what I wanted for you, I admit I was angry. Not because of the choice you made, but because it wasn't **my** choice. My pride wouldn't let me be there for your graduation, and I've regretted it ever since."

Jax stayed silent, instinctively knowing it was important for his father to have his say.

"Being a doctor is a noble profession, and I know how respected you were at Denver Hospital from my friends on the Board there. Then you joined the War, and again I let my anger at your choice override my good sense; I was afraid for you, but didn't know how to tell you. I couldn't bring myself to come to the train station that day, once again, a decision I've regretted." The Dumont patriarch took a deep breath and stood to stand by the mantle, bracing his hand on it. "I read every letter you wrote to your mother, treasured each one just as she did. When they stopped coming and then with no word from you for so long, my only thought was that you had been killed, had died believing that I was angry and disappointed in you; that nearly drove me crazy because both couldn't have been further from the truth."

Jax was stunned. His father admitting to these feelings, wrong choices, just wasn't like him. For the first time, Jax was beginning to truly understand just how deeply his father loved him.

"I watched your mother struggle not to give in to despair; she kept hoping you were alive. My own heart was breaking, and I didn't know how to help her. Then, suddenly, your telegram arrived out of the blue." Eric shook his head as he stared into the fire; one could have heard a pin drop in that room. "My relief was profound, I want you to believe that. But when I thought you were in prison all these years and that's why we hadn't heard from you, well, I let my temper get the best of me. Again!" He turned to look at his son, his eyes suspiciously bright. "Jaxon, you asked for forgiveness, but it is I who ask for yours. You see, I believe that had we parted on better terms, you wouldn't have felt like you couldn't contact us right away. And I take full responsibility for not telling you how I really felt all those years ago. I'm very proud of you, Son. Proud of the man you were back then and even more so now."

"Father, I . . . thank you. For your understanding. And I really am deeply sorry for the pain I've caused you." Jax stood up and went to where his father stood.

Eric shook his head, placing a reassuring hand over Jax's upper arm.

Dana-Sue Urso

"Water under the bridge. Like your mother said, the fact that you are home, alive and well . . .," he shook his head. ". . . nothing is more important than that. Now, take the money and use it to build a home for your family or start your own practice or whatever you want. With my blessing."

They embraced, and Jax parted from his father with his soul lightened and a new understanding of the man who'd sired him.

Now, as he lay beside his wife, his heart was so full, he thought it might burst. The future couldn't have looked more bright or promising. With the money his father had given him, he could start to build the kind of life he knew Mykaela deserved. And he knew just where to start. Besides the money, each Dumont sibling had inherited a tract of land to use at any time for any reason. His was a 100 acres of fertile grassland surrounded by forest and located about 10 miles from his parents' house, towards Denver rather than Boulder; Prentisville was only a 30 minute wagon ride which was important because that's where the kids would go to school. A deep running creek ran through the middle of the woods as well as a pond sitting smack dab in the center of the fields.

He would build a house near the main road of the ranch and erect fences around the perimeter of his property. He didn't want to ranch, but he did want to raise horses. However, this would be a side job as he definitely wanted to get back into medicine, to work as a surgeon.

With those exciting thoughts filling his head, Jax found his elusive slumber.

CHAPTER 17

The days leading up to Christmas were full and busy. Jax and Mykaela made several trips to town on gift buying expeditions; Jax insisted on making this a special Christmas for everyone. The children were entertained by their new grandparents who doted on them. And Constance ran around helter-skelter with preparations for her annual Christmas party; she had not held one in the four years since Jax's "disappearance," but now she was ready to go all out especially since she was combining it with a wedding celebration/welcome home party.

The big event was held the day before Christmas Eve. Mykaela and the children found themselves surrounded by aunts, uncles, and cousins of all shapes, sizes, and ages. Dumonts as well as some relatives from Constance's side and many friends filled the house from top to bottom; several would stay over until after Christmas Day.

Although she was a bit overwhelmed at times, Mykaela found herself enjoying the party immensely. She got to know many of the Dumont relatives and found herself becoming fast friends with Jenna and Lara, Jerrod's fiancée. The night ran long and then Christmas Eve arrived, bringing with it cleaning up after the party and preparing for the next day. She and her new family were kept busy, but she found herself enjoying it as she got to know them all the better.

The hour before supper on Christmas Eve found her settling into an overstuffed easy chair by the fire in the main room; the relatives who were staying through Christmas were either resting, outdoors, or in town. Her own children, along with several second cousins, were outside with some of the men building forts in order to have a massive snowball fight. Thus Mykaela managed to find a few minutes by herself to recharge..

Constance came into the room and threw herself down into a matching chair opposite. Smiling at her daughter-in-law, she remarked

"The Dumont family is easier to take in small doses. I'm afraid you were thrown right in the middle."

Mykaela smiled ruefully. "They are a lot to take in all at once, but mainly because I'm not used to such a large family. It was just me and my father for most of my childhood, then just me and the children after my first husband died. I've lived a rather quiet, non-exciting life I'm afraid."

"There's nothing wrong with that. And once everyone gets used to the fact that Jaxon is home, safe and sound, your lives will settle down once again as well."

They both stared into the flames for a moment, each with her own thoughts. Then Constance spoke up again,

"Jaxon isn't the same man he was when he left here 5 years ago." Her voice was pensive, soft.

Mykaela looked at her with understanding. "He. .hasn't had an easy life since the war, that's for sure," she remarked cautiously.

Her mother-in-law shook her head. "No, he hasn't. When I think of that Confederate prison camp," she broke off with a shudder. "The thought of him having to endure the horrors . . " again she stopped for a moment, eyes closed. "We may have been far removed from the realities of that war, but we got newspapers. They were filled with information about those camps, the atrocities that occurred there. That experience is what changed him, I'm sure."

"Changed in what way?" Mykaela asked.

Constance smiled, a far away look in her eyes. "Jerrod was always my serious child. He would think through every angle before making decisions, he wore the mantle of responsibility from a young age, not because we demanded it of him, but because that's the way he wanted it. He knew he would end up running this ranch one day, and he was careful never to veer from that path. Jenna was always trying to keep up with her older brothers; she was a tomboy through and through which frustrated Jerrod to no end." She chuckled. "He used to lecture me on the proper way a young lady should behave, but then he'd turn right around and defend her whenever she got into trouble, which was more often than not." Her expression sobered, eyes narrowing slightly. "She actually matured and settled a bit when we thought Jaxon had been killed." A wistful smile. "Jaxon was my free-spirit. He could find the bright side to any situation, was always so light-hearted and care-free, mischievous and irrepressible sometimes. Eric tried so hard to get him to accept the responsibilities of a rancher, but that wasn't where his life was headed, something Jaxon knew at a young age. He and Jerrod worked hard on the ranch, but if they herded a group of cows down off the range, and they scattered for some reason, Jerrod would have a fit whereas Jax would laugh and start hooting and hollering just to get them more riled up. He had such an easy-going manner, could find humor in almost every situation; hardly ever became angry or upset."

She leaned toward the fire to poke at it for a moment. Mykaela stayed quiet, sensing her mother-in-law wasn't quite finished.

"I've been watching him this past week," she continued as she sat back once more. "There's a gravity to his eyes that never used to be there. He's much more grounded, less animated, and he doesn't laugh as much. I guess after what he's been through, that's to be expected."

"When I met Jax, he actually frightened me at first," Mykaela admitted. Constance's eyes widened in surprise. "He never smiled, he wore dark clothes, and he was so serious. It's hard to believe he's the same person that you've been describing. And yet, I can see glimpses of that younger man."

"Really?"

"Definitely. Since coming here, he's been a lot more relaxed and at ease. I've never seen him smile so much. Hopefully, as time goes by, he'll return to that young man you knew."

"You've been good for him, Mykaela," Constance told her sincerely. "I can see how much he loves you when he looks at you."

Mykaela swallowed against the lump that rose in her throat at the other woman's words.

"I think you've been his anchor. He told me how lost and alone he'd been for so long, and that you and the children filled the painful, empty void in his heart. Thank you for that."

"It's Jax who's made our lives complete, I can assure you. The children adore him -- he's been more of a father to them than their biological one ever was; he adopted them right before we came here, something that has made all of us very

Legacy of Love

happy. I am truly sorry that he took the long road home, so to speak, but I thank God every day that he was led to me first."

Constance leaned over and grasped her hand. "I, too, thank God for such a beautiful daughter-in-law and for such wonderful grandchildren."

Just then, the doors burst open and in tumbled seven snow covered children, all hurrying to the fireplace to warm up. Jax led the adults in, going right up to his wife. He had seen the tender moment she was sharing with his mother, and although he wondered what brought it on, he was glad they liked each other.

Sitting down on the arm of Mykaela's chair, he bent his head for a quick kiss. She laughed, a bit embarrassed, and pushed ineffectively at his chest. With twinkling eyes, he allowed himself to be pushed away, but only after securing her hand comfortably in his.

He regaled the ladies with the tale of his victory during the snowball fight, embellishing it for effect, then his cousins and the kids joined, telling what really happened. As Mykaela listened, she felt the love for him swell within her to the point that when he caught her eye, he suddenly stopped talking, overcome by what he saw in her eyes. The others never noticed, not even when he lifted her hand and planted a small lingering kiss in her palm. She cupped his cheek tenderly, then smiled a seductive smile when he mouthed the word 'later.'

But it wasn't until the next night that they actually found themselves able to spend some time together. Christmas Day was drawing to a close. The children, who had been on a whirlwind for several days, actually went to bed a little early without any protests, not even from Ryan. He and his sister had never had such a wondrous Christmas or an extended

277

family to spend it with. They were on the go from dawn until way after dusk, exhausted enough to go right to bed after supper.

The adults sat around together for awhile, talking and enjoying each other's company. Mykaela had gotten to know Jared's fiancée over the last week and really liked her. They were fast becoming good friends, something Mykaela didn't take for granted seeing as she hadn't had many close girlfriends before. She was coming to love the Dumont family and was loved in return. Eric still intimidated her a little, but he was extremely kind to her, and he and Constance went out of their way to make her feel at home.

The adults didn't linger too long. Most were planning on leaving early the next morning so wanted to get a good night's sleep. Jax's immediate family were the last to bed, each reluctant to part just yet after such a joyous week. But Jax and Mykaela soon found themselves alone together for the first time in several days. Jax had been up much of the previous night putting together sleds, a carousal horse, and a dollhouse. Even with Jerrod's help, it took quite awhile.

The night before that had been the party where he'd stayed up most of that night chatting with old friends and family; Mykaela had been fast asleep both times he'd finally made it to bed.

As he prepared for bed now, Jax was surprised that he still felt somewhat energized. Even Mykaela noticed.

"I don't know, I guess with all the excitement, I'm still feeling full of energy," he said by way of explanation. "It was so good to see everyone; it felt like I'd never left." He paused, sobered. "Almost."

Mykaela wrapped her arms around him from behind.

Legacy of Love

"It was good for everyone to see you, too," she pointed out. He turned in her arms and held her while she spoke. "It was obvious to me how much your family loves you, loves each other, your extended family included. They missed you as much as you missed them."

He nodded. "I am grateful to have such a caring family. But, if I had to give th

She punched his arm lightly.

"No you wouldn't. You care about them too much."

"I care about *you* that much," he pointed out emphatically; he gazed down at her, his gray eyes full of intensity. "You are the one who brightens my day, you are the one I count on to be there in thick and thin, you are the one I love the most. Mykaela, my homecoming wouldn't be as wonderful as it has been if you weren't here with me." He gripped her upper arms, something he had a habit of doing when he was emphasizing an important point. "You fulfill me in ways I never knew I needed, gave my life meaning and purpose. I can't even begin to imagine my life without you or the kids in it. I am well aware that I would never have met you if the events of my life hadn't occurred exactly as they did; if I had to relive all the ugliness and cruelty to have you, then I would gladly do it all over again."

Mykaela gently laid her fingers over his mouth and shook her head. "Don't say that. No one should ever have to endure what you went through, for any reason," she whispered fervently, eyes full of unshed tears.

He affectionately kissed her fingers. "If you are the end result, then it was all worth it." And with that, he covered her mouth with his and kissed her with all the love and passion in his heart. She clung to him, giving back with all her soul, before pulling back slightly to look into his eyes.

"I told your mother today that I thanked God for bringing you into my life. But I don't think I've ever thanked you. You are everything I've ever wanted in a husband; your strength and courage and compassion fill me with a peace and security that I've never known before. Being with you feels so right that I'm only sorry we didn't meet years ago. I've never felt so safe and so fulfilled as I do with you." A lone tear rolled down her cheek. "If it took all you went through to lead you to me, then I also thank God for watching over you."

Jax caught the errant teardrop on his finger and smiled the most tender smile she'd ever seen. "Our love is truly a gift that we can share with our children, then pass it on to future generations, many I hope they will be."

And with those words, he lifted his precious wife into his arms and carried her to the bed where they proceeded to express their love in the way that God intended a man and his wife should.

EPILOGUE
5 years later

Mykaela rocked gently on the back porch, watching the children playing beneath a mighty oak. Rachel was showing Sara how to make chains out of yellow dandelions; Seth was building a fort out of sticks and leaves. Mykaela was so proud of her oldest daughter who was now going on 12; she was patient with the younger children, so nurturing and loving that Mykaela knew she'd make a wonderful mother some day.

Today was the twins' third birthday. The rest of the family would be arriving soon to help celebrate. Mykaela and Sophie, their couldn't-do-without-her housekeeper, had fixed up the tables that were sitting on the back lawn, festooned with ribbons and balloons. Sophie was putting final touches on the food while she sat out here keeping an eye on her children. And on Ryan's dog, Copper, who kept eyeing the tables, tongue lolling.

Looking at the little bundle in her arms, Mykaela's heart swelled with love. The newest addition to the family had put in an appearance a month earlier with a little help from her father. Susanna Leigh was contentedly nursing at the moment completely unaware of the upcoming festivities.

Mykaela traced a finger lightly down her nose and cheek, marveling at how soft her skin was. The baby looked right at her with smoky bluish-gray eyes; Mykaela had no doubt that they would end up the exact same color as her father's.

Mykaela's gaze roamed past the oak tree to settle on the paddock just beyond. Ryan sat on the top rail avidly watching Jax put a young filly through her paces. Jax and the horse were fluid and light on their feet; her husband truly had a way with horses. He bred them in his spare time which was why he only had five broodmares at the moment, but he was also becoming known for breeding only top quality foals. He had a reputation as honorable as his father's, an accomplishment which meant the world to him.

He primarily worked as a leading surgeon at Denver Hospital. If his reputation as a horse breeder was excellent, then his reputation as a doctor was superb. He was a top-notch surgeon who only improved on his skills as the years went by, much sought after by the surrounding community, the city of Denver itself, as well as outside the region.

Mykaela thought back over the last few years, good years as they established themselves into the community. They lived on the Dumont property, on the piece of land that Jax had inherited. She and Jax would be celebrating their 6th anniversary later this year, and she couldn't have been happier. They had had their ups and downs, of course, but she was grateful to God that the happy times far outnumbered the not-so-happy ones.

She looked off to her left trying to focus in on a young willow tree growing on top of a small rise, a thicket of forest just behind. The beautiful tree stood watch over a tiny grave, a delicate stone cross in place. And although she couldn't see the engraved words, Mykaela knew them by heart: *Rebecca Mae Dumont; Born November 2, 1869; Died November 2, 1869; Precious and Treasured Daughter & Sister.* Rebecca had been her first child with Jax, born three months too soon. Jax had done everything he could to prevent the birth from happening so quickly, but God had had other plans.

Legacy of Love

As their tiny child died in their arms minutes after her inevitable birth, Mykaela and Jax comforted themselves with the knowledge that she would dwell forever with their Father above. And that someday, they would be reunited.

A year later, God blessed them with the births of Seth and Sara. And now, there was Susanna Leigh. Mykaela's heart was full to bursting; before she'd met Jax, she never dared to dream that she and her children could have a life so rich and full. Under Jax's patient guidance and unwavering consistency, not to mention his unfailing love, 13 year old Ryan was growing up to become a respectful, trustworthy, and compassionate young man. Rachel adored her father and fervently treasured the times when he would single her out for a special father-daughter bonding time; the trust and love she felt towards the man who adopted her was truly a wonder to behold.

Mykaela noticed that Jax was finishing for the day. He took off the horse's lead rope and let her loose in the paddock before he and Ryan headed towards the house.

Seth saw the two most important males in his life coming his way and ran up to them. He grabbed onto Jax's hand and tugged him along, excitedly telling him to "Come see my fo-wat."

Mykaela finished feeding the baby and laid her down in her mosquito-netting covered bassinet, watching as Jax dutifully knelt down to admire the sagging fort. Rachel plopped a crown of dandelions on his head which sent Sara into a fit of giggles. She herself then looped a crown over one of his ears, pealing with laughter. Mykaela watched in amusement as he swung the toddler up into his arms, high in the air then pulled her down for a sloppy kiss on her cheek, her favorite kind. He then leaned down to hug Rachel to him, kiss her on the top of the head, and thanked her for the crown which, he assured her, made him feel like a king. Pleased, Rachel hugged him tight, then sat back down with Sara on her lap to finish making crowns for the entire family. Seth begged Ryan, whom he was absolutely devoted to, to play with him; pretending reluctance, Ryan sat beside him, secretly pleased at the adoration his little brother showered on him even though he could be a pest sometimes.

Jax watched them for a minute, then looked over at the porch to see where his wife was. His playful smile turned more seductive as he saw her saunter down the steps. He was still amazed at how quickly her lithe figure came back to her after each pregnancy. His desire for her had yet to wan, sure it never would. Her eyes boldly met his, and she allowed a cheeky grin to come out as though she knew where his thoughts were heading; they still had two weeks to go before intimacy would be safe for her. Unfortunately for him.

As they came abreast of each other, Jax reached out and tenderly cupped her cheek. He would *never* tire of this woman. His prediction from years ago was coming true: his love for her grew stronger with each day that passed and even after more than five years, had not lessened in any way. She was his savior, his biggest fan, his one true love. It was because of her that he reunited with his family, that forgiveness abounded; it was because of her that he had a family of his own, children who loved and respected him, and a wife who looked at him as though he were her hero. Which of course, he wasn't. But it felt kind of nice to believe it once in awhile.

Legacy of Love

Mykaela still marveled at the love shining in his eyes, those beautiful eyes that were haunted no longer. In them, she usually saw peace and contentment. The pains of the past were buried in a place not to be forgotten, but also never to fill him with gut-wrenching despair ever again. He still had the rare nightmare, but she was always there for him to hold onto.

"Hello, Wife," he greeted her, putting his forehead against hers.

"Hello, Husband," she reached up to gently kiss him. "Your daughter has quite an appetite, I'll have you know."

"Does she?" he responded by kissing her back, more firmly.

"She has your eyes," Mykaela pressed her lips to his a bit longer this time.

"Does she?" he gave her a lingering kiss, then drew back slightly, his eyes suddenly grave, gripping her upper arms firmly. "I want you to know I will always love you, Mykaela. *Always*." He looked so serious that Mykaela grew concerned.

Tilting her head, she clasped her hands behind his neck and said softly, "What is it, Jax? What's worrying you?

Taking a deep breath, he said, "Nothing really. I just . . . . sometimes I wonder how long this can last. How long will God allow us … **me** … to be so happy? For so long, I thought I'd never be happy again, would never see my family again, but now that everything is working out in our lives, I keep waiting for the other shoe to drop. Even now, after all our years together."

Mykaela wasn't surprised at this revelation of his. Every now and again, he would express doubts that he deserved the life he had, that something would come along to snatch it all away. His wounds ran deep and although they were now scars, they would never be completely gone. And so the doubts would surface every so often.

"There are no promises of good times or happiness in this life we lead," she said quietly, looking to the distant grave of their daughter. "But we have to make the most of what we have, the time we have together." She looked up at him with a fierce determination. "No matter how long God gives us together, I will treasure each and every moment with you. You are the reason I get out of bed in the morning, you are the one I always want by my side, you are the one I love with every fiber of my being!"

Jax believed her as he could see first-hand the love sparkling at him in her eyes, truly awed and humbled by it. Behind him, the children were laughing as Ryan led them in a game of Ring-around-the Rosie, Copper barking and prancing around as he tried to join in. Their arms entwined, Jax and Mykaela watched their children, their hearts full of a parent's love.

"You are my light, my way back from the darkness I was in for so long," Jax said softly. "They," nodding toward the children. "... are our legacy, now and for our future descendants. Thanks to you."

"Thanks to both of us," Mykaela corrected gently, laying her head back against his chest. And she was absolutely right.

Their deep and abiding love for each other endured through the good times -- and sometimes not so good -- for over 60 years. Until the day when Mykaela and Jax were taking their daily walk together in their extensive flower garden; they ambled along slowly, he using a cane now for balance, she holding onto his other arm for support. Mykaela

Legacy of Love

was unable to walk far so they usually rested on a bench before heading back. On this particular spring day, she suddenly collapsed in her husband's arms, suffering an acute heart seizure. He held her close as her tender, caring heart gave out, words of love on her lips.

Jax lived through the next months in a fog of pain and loneliness, unlike any he'd ever known. He continued to live alone in the pretty little cottage he had built many years ago for him and his cherished wife to live quietly in retirement.

Ryan and his wife lived in the main house (with their oldest son's family), working the horse ranch, keeping a close eye on them as they grew inevitably older, assisting them when the need occasionally arose. But now, Ryan didn't know how to help his father; his heartache and grief was just too deep.

Six months later, Jax passed away peacefully in his sleep. The official diagnosis for his cause of death was "heart failure," but his children all agreed that he had died of a broken heart.

On a small rise, close to the cottage, a mature willow tree stood guard over the tiny grave of an infant girl. Her parents were laid to rest next to her, sharing a common headstone. Besides the birth and death dates, these words were eternally engraved: *Jaxon and Mykaela Dumont; Precious and Beloved Parents, Together Forever.*

Their 5 children, 17 grandchildren, 43 great-grandchildren, and even their 9 young great-great-grandchildren could all attest to the fact that Jax and Mykaela had indeed left their descendants their most treasured gift: a Legacy of Love!

Lightning Source UK Ltd.
Milton Keynes UK
UKOW07f1452141214

243121UK00012B/132/P

9 781631 222467